CHICAGO
BOOGIE WOOGIE

CHICAGO
BOOGIE WOOGIE

GREGORY C. RANDALL

Printed in the United States of America

Windsor Hill Publishing, Inc.
Walnut Creek, California 94596

ISBN: 978-1-7365013-0-6

*This story is dedicated to
my grandmothers,
Eva Struble and Beatrice Smith*

1

By early September 1933, over 14.5 million visitors from around the world had passed through the gates of Chicago's Century of Progress World's Fair. They came to see the wonders of the future, for the wholesome entertainment, to celebrate the ending of Prohibition, to gape at moving pictures with sound, and most especially witness the almost magical advances in the automobile, aviation, and the newfangled world of technology. Notwithstanding this bright future along the shore of Lake Michigan, the most popular and provocative draw on the fair's midway was the fan dancer, Sally Rand. While the public images promoted were ones of proper science, technology, and culture, the underlying lure—especially on warm summer evenings—consisted of the peep shows, topless dancers, and a bawdy edginess the police and the politicians tolerated for one simple reason: money. Money that spilled out of the fairgrounds and into the city's coffers. The fact that businessmen of a less reputable ilk also filled their pockets was merely winked at. Between Prohibition's still illegal liquor and the mob's prostitution and gambling halls, the dark underbelly of Chicago literally made money hand over fist.

Chicago was really many cities: the Irish in Bridgeport,

the Italians along Taylor Street and in Little Italy, and the Jews on Maxwell Street all lived in what could be generously called "neighborhoods." Mostly they were blocks of marginal housing and dense squalor. Two miles almost due south of the fairgrounds, between West 27th Street and Garfield Boulevard, was the Negro community. Here in the black South Side of Chicago, dozens of bars, clubs, and speaks straddled the city's most important north–south traffic spine, State Street. At one end, sixteen blocks north of the Chicago River and the Loop, State Street served the plush neighborhoods where Jimmy Dorsey played and the likes of Bing Crosby sang. But in 1933, in amongst the overcrowded tenements of the South Side Black Belt, the real voices and sounds of Chicago filled the streets and alleys. Itinerant musicians, in from New York and up from New Orleans, played at the Royal Gardens, the Vendome, the Deluxe Café, the Pekin Theater, and dozens of other joints and honky-tonks. These blowers, ivory ticklers, and strummers from the real Black Belt of Louisiana, Mississippi, and the Deep South rolled into town at the Illinois Central Railroad station at 12th Street and State. Self-taught musicians and Depression refugees, they came for work, for money, and to play their kind of music. Singers and musicians like Bessie Smith, Jelly Roll Morton, and Tony Jackson. Erskine Tate's orchestra featured Louis Armstrong and Fats Waller on the organ; King Oliver played at the Royal Gardens; and Glover Compton and Earl "Fatha" Hines lit up the street. Nightly, State Street was congested with the sweet, syncopated melodies squeezed from the lives of these jazz, ragtime, and boogie-woogie-playing musicians. On warm nights especially, the sidewalks were crowded with well-dressed black folks taking the "stroll" down State Street.

At the half-empty lot at the corner 46th and State, Tony Alfano parked his titanic black Packard in the spot the young man pointed to. He handed the boy a five-dollar bill. "Watch it careful, Lionel. I want it here when I come back," he said.

"Detective Alfano, sir, it sure as hell will be here. Ain't it always?" the gangly black kid said, his soft, rolling New Orleans accent sharpened by the harder and sharper-edged Chicago banter.

"Just reminding you, that's all. Who's where tonight?"

"Couple of the Hines gang are playing the fair tonight, but they will be back at one o'clock—I's think at the Grand. The Savoy's got that sax player . . ."

"Lester Young."

"Right, and there's a rumor about someone im-po-tant at the Vendome."

"Too big. I want a small place, tight, sweet sounds."

"So's you in the mood?" The kid snapped his fingers and tapped out a cadence on the sidewalk. "Got it. You remember old Deacon Smith?"

"Sure, D-Smith, sax man, played with Armstrong; he's not that old."

Lionel snapped his fingers again. "In my book, he's one of the old ones. The Deacon's got a new place, intimate, tight like you like. A few blocks that way. And next door, I hear there's an upstairs where's you can get warm and cozy."

"You're too young for that, Lionel."

Lionel snapped his fingers yet again and grinned at Tony. "Maybe yes, maybe not. The Deacon's got a new piano player and a hot-looking singer from Jackson, Mississippi. I'd go there, Mr. Alfano; I's hear they good, damn good."

"What's Deacon's place called?" Alfano asked.

"D's Café Delite. He's likewise got a cook he brought up from New Orleans. Finally, some good grits on this street, and when the shrimps is fresh, hot damn."

Detective Anthony Alfano tugged at the hem of his crisply

pressed dark grey suit jacket, snugged up his red silk tie, and adjusted the Colt in his shoulder holster. He was tall, snappishly thin. The pinstripes in his suit added the illusion of an inch or two to his height. His face was narrow, with a hard, long jaw, thin mouth, and a fashionably crisp William Powell mustache. The mustache enhanced a sharp, slightly hooked nose (with a perceptible kink on its ridge due to being broken a few times) that anchored his face like a spike driven between his dark grey eyes. Hidden under his grey fedora was a thick head of black hair that was evolving to grey at the temples. If grey were a meal, Tony Alfano was a serious grey serving. After setting the brim of his hat, he lit a cigarette and strolled north up the west side of State Street. This night the sidewalks were full; the weather, for a Friday night in mid-September, was warm and dry.

The tradition of the "stroll" had been brought up from New Orleans. And it was a Negro thing. The tenements and apartments were hot, and now late in the evening, people would do anything to get out of their sweltering apartments. It was a time to socialize, to see and to be seen—and who didn't like to show off? But midsummer, when tenements became like ovens, the sidewalks were the escape.

At 43rd and State, Alfano dropped a dollar in the case set out by a kid plucking a guitar.

"Thanks, mister," was the reply.

Deacon Smith was a tenor sax player and had been a fixture on State Street for more than twenty years. He was a strait-laced Bible man, his wife sang in the Baptist church, and he could still tease the reed of his saxophone so as to pull your heart out of your chest and put tears on your cheeks. The deacon was a good man in a profession that had ruined musicians before they were forty; Deacon was nearing fifty. With late-night hours, too much time on your hands, too much liquor and drugs, and the offered enticements of the flesh, it was hard to grow old in the entertainment profession. Alfano knew it was the same for cops: too much of too much. Chicago could and would offer temptations to both the body and the soul.

"I'll be damned," Deacon said when Alfano walked into the café. "Anthony Alfano."

"Lionel said you just opened," Alfano said, looking around. "Nice, very nice. This used to be a ladies' shop, didn't it, Deacon?"

"Indeed, Tony. Good memory," Smith said.

"And I've seen that bar," Alfano said as he studied the crowded length of bright mahogany with polished nickel inlays.

"Salvaged it from the Acme Club. It sat there gathering dust all these past twenty years of Prohibition. I've wanted it someday for my place. It was the right price, free to just haul it away."

Eight men and their dates sat at the long bar; almost in unison, they turned and looked at Alfano. Two of the men the detective knew right away, petty stuff, but still possible trouble. He returned the impassive stares as the men sized him up and then slowly turned back to the bar. They watched Alfano in the back-bar mirror as he crossed the narrow room to the small table near the stage that Deacon pointed to.

"Don't pay them no mind. What do you want to drink? Wait, I know. Still drinking Canadian?" Deacon asked.

"You remembered," Alfano answered as he sat.

"I'll see what I can find." Smith winked and walked back behind the bar.

Alfano was the only white customer in the bar. He'd been hanging around the Chicago jazz scene since he was twenty years old, when he saw his first black review with Jelly Roll Morton at the Pekin Theatre. During the Great War, the Chicago scene, as it was called, had changed. The musical exodus from New Orleans to the North could be blamed on the navy. As the gaudier and more prurient places were shut down, one by one, by the navy, all to protect American soldiers, the entertainers moved north. Chicago was more than willing to provide venues for these black performers. These southern migrants were more than saxophone and trumpet players; they brought a culture new and fresh to a staid old city.

Prohibition was to formally end in four months, on December 31, 1933. Alfano recognized that it was the greatest political and moral failure that had ever seized America's collective conscience. Institutional crime took control of every vice, innocents died in the subsequent shootouts and bombings, bribed politicians grew rich, and the criminals richer. Alfano couldn't count the number of times he'd been approached to look the other way; he never did. He was both loved and hated, especially when he had to arrest one of his own.

The whiskey arrived, an unopened bottle of Canadian Club, and Alfano began to methodically, sip by sip, empty the bottle.

A small stage was built into the back corner of the room; two spotlights lit the area just large enough for an upright piano, a drum kit, and maybe three or four musicians. This evening, as the lights came up, two people sat at the piano. A striking black woman sat on the end of the piano's bench seat so that she faced a microphone; next to her sat a black piano player—neither could be eighteen. The piano player began to play a variation of "St. Louis Blues" that Alfano had never heard. It was full boogie-woogie, a beat that bounced and echoed, a new sound to jazz. As the boy played, the girl tapped his right thigh to the beat. When the player turned to the audience, Alfano saw the dark glasses and the look of ecstasy on the boy's face—he was blind.

When the song finished, Deacon took the stage. "Ladies and gents, these two youngins just arrived from Jackson, Mississippi. Give a Chicago welcome to Lucius and Desdemona

Black." A smattering of applause followed the announcement. Deacon walked off the stage as Desdemona began a sexy version of Don Redman's "Two Time Man." Her rendition of the song made the patrons at the bar turn and listen.

For the next thirty minutes, the duo progressively pulled the patrons to their side, each song teased and titillated. Forty blocks north, they would have been arrested for the lyrics. The bar crowd, now salted with even a few more white faces, listened appreciatively. A few couples got up and danced.

At the end of the set, Deacon led the musicians to Tony's table.

"I want to introduce you to a good friend," Deacon said.

"The chair's in front of you, Lucius," Desdemona said as she pulled it out. "And who be that, D?" She sat.

"Detective Tony Alfano. He's with the Chicago police."

Desdemona immediately stood. She took Lucius's hand and tried to pull him up.

"Desi, when a man comes into your house, you should be civil," Lucius said, resisting her tug. "A pleasure to meet you, Detective." Lucius reached out across the table. Alfano met his hand halfway.

"The pleasure's mine, Lucius. I've heard Jelly Roll, Grover Compton, and I even saw Tony Jackson at the Pekin. I think you were in that band, Deacon."

"Yes, I was. You always got a good memory."

"Son, you are as good as them—I especially liked your interpretation of 'Midnight Special.' A ballad with a broken heart, a lot different than the old cowboy song. When did you come up?" Alfano said, looking at Desdemona.

"About three weeks ago—saved every penny, took the Illinois Central north. Our parents is dead. Nothing left there in that town these days; all dry as dust," Desdemona said as she settled back into her chair. "So, Detective, you like Negra jazz?"

"Ever since jazz rolled into Chicago. A cop's got to have something to break the boredom. Besides, I was getting tired of Italian opera."

Lucius chuckled when he heard the remark. "In this town, from what I hear, I doubt any cop is bored."

It was Alfano's turn to laugh.

"I lost my sight when I was twelve—measles," Lucius told him. "Momma taught me to play, and she'd drag every piano player coming through Jackson into the house to teach me for a meal. Same for Desi. We learned from the best. I got good even back then. Being blind made me focus."

"Love your voice, Desdemona," Alfano said. "Bessie Smith, right?"

"Yes, sir. I love that woman." She crossed the first two fingers of her right hand. "Gospel and jazz are like this," she added, smiling at Alfano. "I listen to her records."

"She does put her own sweet spin to it," Lucius said.

"Can't do better. She broke my heart when I heard her," Alfano said.

"You've seen her?"

"One time. She was in town, at the Vendome."

"I'd kill to see her," Lucius said with a big smile.

"That isn't funny," Desdemona said.

"You should see my side of it," he answered.

The yelling started at the far end of the mahogany bar, near the entrance. Two men were in a shoving match. The din made it impossible to make out what they were saying. The ladies sitting with them, as if knowing where this was going, got up and maneuvered through the crowd and out the door. Alfano grabbed Desdemona and pulled her to the floor as the man on the left reached under his suit coat and pulled out a silver-plated Colt.

"Stay down!" Alfano yelled. He pulled Lucius down next to his sister.

The silver pistol flashed beneath the overhead lights. Alfano first thought: *Big gun, little man.* The other man was quicker. A blade glinted; the man with the knife struck like a snake. Everyone heard the pistol crack, then dove to the floor. The two men, in a death dance, stumbled together. The man, still holding the knife and a now .45 slug in his chest, stepped back and fell, pulling the man with the gun and the blade embedded in his chest to the floor with him. Yelling mingled with the noise of overturning tables as customers shoved back their chairs and ran out of the bar. In moments there remained only the two bartenders, the Blacks from Jackson, Deacon Smith, Tony Alfano, and two bodies sprawled on the linoleum floor.

For the next two hours, Alfano answered questions from the police and his fellow detectives from the 19th District. Not one patron, customer, or girlfriend remained in D's Café Delite. The obvious evidence and the story were easy; yet no one knew the reason for the winless argument. Alfano recognized one of the men, Tiny T. Darnell, a two-bit marijuana and dope dealer from the neighborhood. Darnell was the man with the six-inch, black-handled stiletto stuck in his heart. Alfano didn't know the other guy, the man with a Colt .45 slug in the same general area. Both were unknown to Deacon and the bartenders.

The two detectives from the 19th talked to Alfano. This was their case, he told them. He was just curious about the men. Go ahead, said the detectives.

Alfano went through the dead men's pockets. In Darnell's pockets he found a roll of money, maybe a grand in twenties and fifties, an extra magazine for his pistol, and two tickets to the fair for that day. No other identification. In the unknown's pockets, he found two hundred in twenties, another knife, a torn movie ticket stub, and a punched train ticket. The ticket was from New Orleans two days earlier. Whatever it was that set all this off might have started in Louisiana and come north. The guys from the 19th would follow it up.

"Well, damn," Deacon said, looking at the dark pool on the floor. "That's why I put down a tile floor. But shit, Tony, I thought it would be at least a month before my place was baptized."

2

Monday morning, Alfano walked into the Racine Street station. His head throbbed from the rest of the bottle of Canadian, and the backup Deacon had given him. The twin Canadians had helped him through the rest of his quiet weekend. Sergeant McDunnah sat at the front desk.

"Good morning, Detective," McDunnah said. "Cavanagh said you were at the double homicide on State Street Friday night."

Cavanagh was the weekend desk sergeant.

"More like Saturday morning. Word does get around," Alfano answered, as he looked at the notes that McDunnah handed him. "Somebody already bitching about jurisdiction?"

"Surprisingly, no. They found out who the dead men were."

"I knew one: Tiny T. Darnell, dope dealer. T.T. to his few friends."

"The other was a known contract killer from New Orleans, one Tobias Delaplaine," McDunnah said, looking at his notes. "New Orleans PD said the word on the street was that Darnell had backed out of a deal in the Big Easy. Delaplaine was sent here to set the deal right."

"I'd say it didn't work out for either of them. Maybe us and New Orleans are now two ahead in the game. Anything else?"

"It's Monday. You want the top of the pile?"

"What else is there?" Alfano said, looking at the short stack of papers on McDunnah's desk.

"Last night, Palmer House. The chief wants you there. A body was discovered about four this morning. Patrolmen on scene; detectives on their way—they are waiting for you."

"Coffee first."

McDunnah swiveled his chair around and grabbed a mug off the credenza behind him. He held it up for Alfano.

"Still hot?"

"Just poured. And, the next one is a note from the mayor's office. He wants to see you at nine thirty, something about a priority assignment."

"Shit. We know all about these priority assignments."

Alfano and the mayor had a relationship like a mongoose and a snake. Plain and simple, Alfano did not like Mayor Edward Kelly. The "snake" had been handed the mayor's job after his predecessor, Anton Cermak, was shot trying to defend the newly elected Franklin D. Roosevelt during an assassination attempt in Miami seven months earlier. The thwarted assassination attempt stunk to high heaven and led to a rigged mayoral selection. Thanks to whoever was pulling the strings of the Illinois state assembly, the former sanitary chief of Chicago now headed the second largest city in America.

On the other hand, the new mayor liked Alfano, mostly because during the last six months Alfano had, more than once, pulled his nuts out of a political fire. Alfano wanted nothing to do with the man and his political fixer, Patrick Nash, but short of quitting, he had no alternative.

"Nine thirty? Did he say why?" Alfano said, grimacing at the coffee.

"He didn't say," McDunnah said. "Just be there."

"Great." Alfano looked through the rest of the messages, then threw them in the can next to McDunnah's desk. "The

Palmer isn't in our jurisdiction."

"All I know is you are wanted at the scene. Be careful about the toes of the other detectives."

"From where? Downtown?"

"Somewhere around the police chief and city hall."

"Damn."

Alfano had become Mayor Kelly's go-to guy. A role that did not please Alfano. Often, it led to his stepping on the toes of other detectives, departments, and chiefs. And his being Italian, in the largest Irish police force outside of Dublin, Ireland, didn't help either.

The Palmer House was the swankiest and most pricey hotel in the city. Alfano parked his Packard at the curb in front of the Monroe Street entry.

"Checking in, Detective?" the doorman said with a smile. He opened the car door.

"No, Henry. But I believe you have a dead woman inside?"

"Such is the rumor, Detective," Henry said as he turned his head away.

"Where?"

The doorman stepped back. "Top floor . . . sir, top floor."

"Leave the car here. I'll be back shortly."

"Yes, Detective."

Alfano quickly walked through the spacious lobby. Its ornate ceiling, gold trim, and painted doodads dominated the impressive room. Guests sat in comfortable chairs, eating breakfast and having their coffee. Alfano's stomach growled; a dowager overheard the rumble and tsk-tsked at the sound. Tony smiled at her and continued to the bank of elevators. A patrolman stood at the open door of one—next to him, an elevator operator.

Alfano flashed his star to the patrolman. "Which floor?"

"Twenty-fourth, northwest corner, top floor," the patrolman answered.

"Shall we?" Alfano asked and pointed to the open elevator and the attendant. As the door closed, he turned to the operator. "What time did you come on?"

"I work the six-to-six shift. So, I've been here two hours and twenty-five minutes," the operator answered, looking at his watch.

"When did the police arrive?"

"Don't know. They were here when I came on."

"The other operator, where's he?"

"I assume at home. Al's been on this car almost as long as me; he likes the all-night. Me, I want to be home with my wife and kids. Al's a loner."

When the door opened, the operator pointed to the left. "That way, Detective. Can't miss it, maybe a dozen cops still there. I've heard it's quite a mess."

"And how did you hear that?"

"People—people talk. I stand here in the corner and just listen. More entertaining than the radio." He pulled the doors closed.

When Alfano approached the room in the corner of the northwest wing, people milled about in the hallway; half were in uniform. Hotel guests wrapped in robes cluttered the doorways of several nearby rooms. A black woman in a maid's uniform stood flat against the hallway wall, a patrolman next to her. Explosions of light and the pops of flashbulbs burst from the open door at the end of the hallway. Another patrolman stood just outside the doorway. Alfano held up his star.

"Don't know you," the patrolman said. "Stay here."

"Not my problem. I'm going in." Alfano pushed his way past the objecting uniform. Inside was chaos. He looked around the room and was blinded by another flashbulb.

"Out!" Alfano yelled. "Everybody out! Everybody except you, Flynn. I want everybody else out, now."

The crowd of four policemen, two photographers, two men in suits, and a man in a formal suit jacket filled the one, surprisingly large room. Alfano stood to the side of the door as the assembly filed its way out.

"You, in the monkey suit, wait," Alfano said to the formally dressed gentleman. He turned to the man he called Flynn. "What's going on here, Detective? You know better than this."

"What the hell are you doing here, Alfano?" Flynn said. "This ain't your party. You stay to your side of the river."

"I can assure you, Flynn, I would like to. The chief told me to be here. I do what I'm told. So, if you have a beef, talk to the chief." He looked around the room, his eyes quickly passing over the bed to the floor. He looked at the guy in the tuxedo. "You the hotel manager?"

"Yes, sir, Claude Dubonnet."

"Well, Mr. Dubonnet, who's room is this?" Alfano asked.

Flynn started to say something. Alfano put his hand up. "Quiet."

"It is one of four rooms that were booked by the Sierra Films Production Company," Dubonnet told Alfano. "One is next door, with the pass-through door, and the other two are down the hallway."

"Who is Sierra Films?" Alfano asked, looking back to the floor.

"I believe they make moving pictures. May I ask who you are?" Dubonnet asked. He was trying not to look at the floor.

"Detective Tony Alfano. I'm working with Detective Flynn on this case."

Again, Flynn started to say something. Alfano shut him off with a look.

"You can go stand in the hallway like a good little boy, Mr. Dubonnet; I'll get back to you," Alfano said.

As Alfano turned away from Flynn and the manager, he took in the full scene. Four windows, curtains drawn, lined two walls of the corner room. A large leather couch, two matching chairs, a coffee table, a mahogany desk, filled half the room. Two bedside tables with ornate lamps flanked the outsized and unmade bed. All the wooden edges of the furniture were painted beige with gold trim; the only unnatural light in the room came from a lamp on the desk and the two bedside lamps. The lamps cast a harsh light on the body that lay on the floor. The overhead chandelier was not on.

"Turn that light on, Flynn," Alfano said, pointing to the ceiling.

The woman was beautiful and nude. Which was probably why the police, and God only knew how many others, had been in and out of the room since its discovery. The corpse was white, not just Caucasian white, but almost as white as the area rug she was sprawled on. Her hair was white as well.

"When was she found?" Alfano asked Flynn.

"The maid found her at four thirty this morning," Flynn said.

"That's strange. Maids don't do rooms till later in the morning or when asked. So, why was she here?"

"She's down the hall. You can ask her."

"I'm asking you, Detective. What did she say?"

"She said she was sent up here by the housekeeping manager. There was a request for towels. She was told to put them in the bathroom."

"By who?" Alfano said, looking at the woman.

"The assumption was by whoever was in the room. They used the phone," Flynn said.

"Your assumption or the maid's?"

Flynn paused. "My assumption."

"Find out for sure. First, ask her to come in here."

Flynn walked out and returned with the maid.

"Yes, sir?" she said.

"Can you please bring me a clean sheet?"

"Yes, sir." The maid left.

Flynn watched her leave. "She said the door was locked when she knocked. She used her passkey when no one answered. She immediately saw the body, quickly left the room, and called the manager."

"Him?" Alfano said, looking toward the hallway where Dubonnet waited in his formal coat.

"No, the night manager. Mr. Dubonnet came on at seven."

"Did you interview the night manager?"

"No, Bob and I arrived at seven fifteen. We will later," Flynn said.

"And where's Detective Bobby Gloan?"

"He went to get coffee."

"So, for the last two hours and forty-five minutes, people have been coming and going from this room. Good God, Flynn, did you charge fucking admission?"

Flynn ignored the question. "I still don't know why you are here, Alfano. This is my crime scene."

The maid came to the door, a folded white sheet in her hands. Alfano took the sheet from her and stepped back to where the body lay. "Grab the corners, Flynn."

Flynn obeyed, and they covered the naked body.

"What you need to know is irrelevant, and this so-called crime scene is more like a train wreck," Alfano told Flynn, not bothering to hide his intense irritation. "Stand over there and make sure no one else comes into the room. I want a list of everyone who's been in here since the body was discovered—and I mean everyone—and I'll check it with the elevator operator. When the coroner arrives, he is the only person I want you to let in—and you and your partner can cool your heels out in the hall. Until then, say nothing to anyone." Flynn looked pissed but tramped out.

Alfano walked slowly around the room, looking at the desk, the wastebasket, the chairs, and the two bedside tables.

An ashtray with a crushed cigarette sat on the left-side table, no jewelry or other personal effects. An electric clock sat on the right-side table; it was stopped at 3:33 AM. Alfano looked behind the side table and saw that the clock was unplugged. On the carpet, next to the plug, lay a watch. Using a pen to poke through the metal and leather clasp, Alfano picked up the watch and placed it on the table.

He crossed the room. On the coffee table, a bottle of champagne sat in a bucket. The ice was melted. There were two glasses. Alfano knelt and looked closely. One glass had visible fingerprints; the other was empty and clean. Why was obvious: either not used or wiped clean—he was going with wiped clean; even room service would leave fingerprints. He did a cursory check of the bottle, not expecting any fingerprints; he was right.

He went back to the sheet on the floor and carefully raised one corner. The woman's face was turned toward the left bedside table. Besides being ghostly white, the body was a bizarre display of death. Knotted around the neck was a brilliant red scarf. Oriental images of dragons and flowers decorated the cloth. From two holes between her breasts, blood had run down her chest and soaked the white rug. The stain was about two feet round. The bullet holes were clean, crisp, a splatter of grey and black surrounding the wounds. Her left arm draped forward; bruises, like a dark bracelet, wrapped her wrist. No jewelry on the fingers. No shadow that would have hinted at a ring was visible on the white skin. A richly colored kaftan-like robe wrapped her left arm and shoulder; however, most of it was bunched up under her body. Further up the left arm, in the fold, the fossa, between the upper and lower arm, were a series of red dots, pin pricks—needle punctures based on Alfano's experience. The right arm was twisted and hidden under the body. A small tattoo decorated the left buttock. It was a simple heart shape.

Alfano replaced the sheet, walked around to the opposite side of the body, raised the sheet on the other side.

"Detective," Flynn began.

"I told you to keep quiet. Stay that way," Alfano answered without looking.

Her eyes were open; they were green, emerald green, once bright, now a bit hazed, fully dilated. Dried tear tracks left their course on her right cheek. Other than red lipstick, he saw no makeup. From the corner of her mouth, a line of spittle had dribbled down her right jaw and dried. She was exceptionally pretty and hauntingly familiar.

Alfano looked under her right side at portions of her body not hidden by the kaftan. An obscene dark grey shadowed the areas of her body that lay against the white rug. Alfano assumed she had died in this position; the coroner would confirm this. He touched her left arm; it was cold. With one finger, he tried to raise her arm. It was somewhat stiff and wouldn't move.

"Rigor, I assume?" a voice said over Alfano's shoulder. It wasn't Flynn's.

"Yes, Doc. Almost full rigor—dead at least four, maybe five hours," Alfano said.

"Or more," Doc Abrahamson, the coroner, answered. "Pretty," he added as he peeked over Alfano's shoulder.

"Yeah. She doesn't seem to have been moved after being shot. Her fall was violent—see the bruises on the left wrist?" Alfano turned to Flynn. "Did anyone touch or move the body?"

"Not since I got here," Flynn said. "I asked the maid the same question. She said she knew better than to touch the dead, 'evil thing.' Besides, this wasn't the first body she found. This floor has a history."

"The hotel's only been reopened for eight years," Alfano said.

"Seems the rich like the high floors and suicide," Flynn

said. "I've been here twice during the last five years."

"Damn fools. Why do they have to get the police involved?" Alfano stepped back and let the coroner take his place. "Bizarre?"

"Very. I'll know the cause of death after the autopsy."

"The two slugs to the chest might be contributing causes, but you are the coroner, Dr. Abrahamson." Alfano walked around the body to face Flynn. "I found this watch on the floor behind the table. I'm taking it with me."

"You think I'd steal it?" Flynn said.

"Of course not. You and your partner are like fresh winter snow, virginal."

"What do you mean by that?"

"That snow covers up all the shit underneath," Alfano said.

"You are one serious Guinea asshole, Alfano."

"That's Detective Alfano to you, you Mick bastard."

"Stop it, you two. Keep it in the house," Dr. Abrahamson said. "I'll let both of you know what I find."

3

Alfano paced back and forth across the tile and carpet of the outer office of the mayor of Chicago. He had been five minutes early and, while waiting, smoked two cigarettes. The young woman behind the receptionist's desk was new.

"What's your name?" Alfano asked, coming to an abrupt stop in his travels.

"I know all about your reputation, Detective Alfano. I've been well informed."

"And I know so little about you, Miss . . ."

"Alcott, Sarah Jean."

"Well, Miss Alcott, where do you come from?"

"Duluth."

"Minnesota? Gets cold there."

"No, Nebraska. And it gets even colder there."

"Never heard of it."

"No one has. When I left on the train for Chicago, only two people remained—my ma and pa."

"Small-town girl."

"No, actually a no-town girl."

The box, covered with switches and dials, on Sarah Alcott's desk buzzed.

"He will see you now, Detective."

"Will I see *you* later?" Alfano answered as he crushed his third cigarette and set his hat.

"I really hope so."

"Even with my reputation?"

"Every soul can be saved," Sarah Alcott replied. "I'll pray for you."

"Many have tried," Alfano said.

The mayor's door was pulled open from the inside as Alfano reached for the handle. A lanky Irishman with a thick mustache walked briskly out, looked at Alfano, nodded, and went out the office door. Alfano's brain began working on where he had seen the man's face.

The aromas of lavender, cheap cologne, and cigars slammed into Alfano's nose as he closed the door behind him. Mayor Edward Kelly stood leaning his butt against the front of his desk, a cigar in his hand. A narrow-faced older Irishman sat in a chair near the window: Patrick Nash.

Nash was thirteen years Kelly's senior and had, over the last five years, built and then maneuvered his political machine into one of the toughest, well-run, and successfully corrupt city halls in the United States. Through a series of bizarre incidents, Detective Alfano had become Kelly's go-to guy—Alfano wished that Kelly and Nash would just go to hell. A man and woman sat on the sofa and another man sat on one of the other chairs.

"Detective Alfano, thanks for coming," the mayor said. "Big things going on, big things. I want to introduce you to some special people. You may know two of them from the movies. They are big stars. And I'm their biggest fan."

Alfano knew exactly who two of the three were the moment he walked into the room; he, too, was a big fan.

The mayor gestured toward the man in the chair. "This gentleman is Hines Melnik. He is the famous director of westerns and cop movies."

The man stood and walked to Alfano. He was about five feet five inches tall; round was the first word that came to mind: round face, round body, round eyes, round glasses, just everyday round. Alfano shook his round hand.

"Mr. Melnik owns Sierra Films; he is from Hollywood. This is, of course, actress and film star Maxime Durant, and leading man Adam Roberts."

"Sierra Films?" Alfano looked at Melnik.

"Yes, Hollywood," Melnik answered.

"Yes, I heard, interesting. Miss Durant and Mr. Roberts, a pleasure. I've enjoyed your movies." Alfano shook their hands.

"Adam, the man has seen your pictures," Durant said. "Amazing, even here in Hicksville."

"Detective, just ignore her," Roberts said.

"We are more progressive here in Hicksville than you think, Mr. Roberts," Alfano said. "I especially liked your gunslinger in the western *The Man on the Black Horse*. I've never seen anyone shoot like that."

"Special effects and editing help. I have a great team," Melnik injected. "I've done five pictures with these two wonderful actors. They starred together in two of them."

"Yes, *Maggie Mae* and that ghost film, *Angels and Stars*," Alfano said.

"See, there are sophisticated hicks. He's seen your pictures, too, Hines," Durant added.

"And you are an idiot," Roberts said.

Alfano studied the two; he was developing a new appreciation for the acting profession, one that was not what he believed ten minutes earlier. These two reminded him of a bickering married couple, the kind the police visit.

"Tony, Mr. Melnik is shooting a new picture that features Chicago as the background," the mayor said.

"A gangster film?" Alfano asked. "There's already been too

many of those about Chicago. There's *The Public Enemy*, *Scarface*, even *Little Caesar*—none of those helped our image."

"Let me worry about our image," Nash said from his chair.

The mayor brushed off Nash with a wave of his cigar. "Never enough publicity, that's what I say. And now especially with the fair."

"Don't worry, Detective," Melnik said. "This picture is from the cop's point of view, no glorifying the bad guys. I want to show how the police deal with scum; how they face evil and vanquish it. Adam is a detective, not unlike you, Detective Alfano—experienced, tough, no nonsense. He gets right into the grille of the bad guys, shows them who's boss. Mayor Kelly has high praise for you."

Alfano looked at the mayor and watched a smile break on the face of His Honor. *Now what?* he thought.

"Thanks, Hines. Yes, Tony is a one of my best," Kelly said. "He's an excellent detective, always gets the bad guy, and I consider him to be a friend. He's my go-to guy."

I am so screwed, Alfano thought. He looked at Maxime Durant. The coy smile on her lips was directed at him. His first thought was of a high-class hooker, not one of Hollywood's highest-grossing female actresses. Yes, he was screwed.

"Tony, may I call you that?" Melnik said. Then, not waiting for an answer, "I am looking for authenticity. I want the real face of a streetwise detective. I want Adam to look and be the part."

"And how am I going to help him do that?" Alfano said.

"Tony," the mayor said, interrupting Melnik, "for the next few days, I want you to take Mr. Roberts with you on your investigations, show him the ropes, have him learn from you."

"You have got to be kidding me," Alfano said. "No way. I work alone, you know that. That's why I'm effective."

"That's what I'm looking for," Melnik said excitedly. "I want the Continental Op, or the Sam Spade type."

"Those guys were private dicks, not professional police officers—and they are fiction," Alfano said. "Here the bad guys really kill people, dump their bodies in the lake, shoot up bars, run brothels, even pander women. It's not a nice place out there." He pointed to the window.

"I love this guy," Melnik said. "Did you see that, Adam? The passion, the vibe, the intensity. That's what I want."

"I got it, Chief, no problem," Roberts answered.

"You are all idiots," Durant said. She stuck a cigarette in the end of a long gold holder and waited. Eventually, after a couple of beats, Roberts lit her cigarette.

"Tony, do I have to make this a direct order?" Kelly said. "I was hoping that you would get on board and help us out here. Hines has a great idea for the film. He'll send a crew here to shoot local scenes and set the mood of the city." The mayor was practically gushing. "Hines says this will be the most authentic cop movie ever made. Some of the filming—well, most of it—will be in Los Angeles. We talked about doing the work local here, but he has his crews already in place in California."

Alfano stared at them in turn. Screwed didn't begin to cover it.

"Mr. Melnik, what is the name of your production company again?" he asked.

"Why do you ask?"

"It was a simple question, nothing more."

"Sierra Films Productions. We are located in Los Angeles."

"Yeah, you said Hollywood."

"Interchangeable."

"Did you book four rooms at the Palmer House?"

"Why are you asking these questions, Detective?" Kelly said.

"An ongoing investigation, sir." Alfano looked at Melnik. "Did you?"

"My people did. We are staying there," Melnik said. "We

spent last night in Evanston—it's on our publicity tour. Came straight back here this morning, haven't been back to the hotel. You said an ongoing investigation?"

"A dead woman was found on the twenty-fourth floor in one of the rooms you booked. Preliminary findings suggest she was murdered."

Durant's response was a quick and loud inhale. Roberts turned pasty white. Melnik said, "Do you know who she is?"

"There has been no identification made. She was nude, on the floor, and most probably shot. The crime scene was a bit muddled."

"Muddled, Detective?" Nash interjected.

"Yes, muddled. Contradictory signs, confusion, staged—muddled." Alfano looked at the movie director. "Do you know a woman with bleached white hair, cut short, green eyes, pale complexion? She has a tattoo of a heart on her upper left thigh."

"How did you know that?" the mayor asked, obviously not remembering what Alfano had just said.

"My God," Roberts said. "That's Kitty."

"Who's Kitty?" Alfano said.

"Kitty Hill. She has worked at Sierra for the past five or six years, bit parts, reasonably good. I was grooming her for big things. But her real job was working as executive assistant to me," Melnik said.

"Yeah, your very personal big things," Durant said.

"You shut the fuck up. She was found last night, Detective?" Melnik said.

"Actually, early this morning," Alfano said. He looked at the three Californians and had a thought. "Mayor, I'll take on Mr. Roberts, show him the ropes as you asked. After a couple of days, he will be so bored he'll want the role of the gangster and not the cop."

"When do we start?" Roberts said.

"Right now. I'm parked out front," Alfano said. "I'm at the beginning of this investigation, so you can watch how it unfolds. Ask any questions you like; I'll answer what I can. That work for you, Mayor?"

"Damn, that's why I like you, Tony. You grab on and take off."

"Adam," Melnik said, "remember that we have that appearance tonight at the fair. It's at seven o'clock. The press and your fans will be there. Do not be late."

"I'll make sure he gets there," Alfano said.

"Detective, just make sure you don't need backup," Durant said, blowing a cloud of cigarette smoke into the air. "He really can't shoot a gun. He'd pee in his pants if he had to shoot a real one."

"Stuff it, you bitch," Roberts answered.

"Ooh, sticks and stones."

Alfano looked at Roberts. "Let's go, Hollywood."

Alfano turned and walked out of the mayor's office with an overly eager Roberts on his heels. As he started down the stairs, the face from earlier, walking out of the mayor's office, got a name: Spats Lanigan.

4

After making a few phone calls at the phone bank off the lobby of the Palmer House, Alfano went outside to wait for Roberts. He lit a cigarette. The leading man had asked for a few minutes to clean up and change clothes. He brought his overnight bag with him from the mayor's office. Alfano gave him fifteen minutes.

During the eight-block drive from city hall, Alfano learned that Adam Roberts was twenty-nine years old and born in Fresno, California. His father had been a fig and walnut grower before the crash. Roberts was now paying their rent; at some point he planned on buying their farm and giving it back to them. His mother was a homemaker. He had a younger brother still working the farm. Roberts graduated from UCLA in 1924, was on the football team, did some acting in school plays, and was spotted by Melnik during a game with USC. The movie director tested him for the role of third cowboy on a two-reel silent western. Roberts stood out and had made ten films during the past four years, all with Melnik. Roberts was hardly the reticent, deep-thinking character he played in the movies. Alfano was pretty sure Roberts would drive him nuts during the next few days.

The central bronze doors of the hotel swung open, and

Adam Roberts walked out. To Alfano's shock, the man had changed into a suit and tie that almost matched what he was wearing. This included the grey fedora. Two women standing outside waiting for a cab instantly recognized the actor; within seconds they were holding out pens and papers for him to autograph. Soon three more acolytes converged.

"Roberts," Alfano yelled. "We are late. We need to go, now."

"Yes, Detective, one minute," Roberts answered.

"No, now—or I'm gone."

Roberts broke away, smiling and shaking hands. One woman tried to kiss him; he gently pushed her back. Alfano believed the expression on her face was orgasmic.

Two blocks later, Alfano asked, "Is it like that all the time?"

"No, more when we are on the road promoting; there's a bit of expectation involved. Those ladies had been waiting since early morning for me to show up."

"Do Durant or Melnik get that kind of attention?"

"No. Sometimes, someone waves a photo of Maxime in one of her more indelicate costumes and asks for an autograph. I hate to think why—lot of weird people out there—but you know that being a cop. So, where are we off to?"

"The coroner and the morgue."

It was like a door had slammed shut. For the next ten minutes, as they drove through traffic, Roberts didn't say a word. He just looked out the window.

Alfano parked in the alley behind a nondescript brick building. A sign tacked to the wall read: *Police Only*.

"This way," Alfano said as he went to a steel rear door. A button was secured to the right frame. When he pushed the black button, they could hear the buzzer sound through the door. A minute passed, and then the door opened.

"Hi, Doc," Alfano said to the man standing in the open door. "This is Adam Roberts. He's my ride-along today, at the mayor's request."

"Aren't you lucky," Doc Abrahamson said, looking at Roberts.

"Yeah, I guess," Roberts said.

Alfano followed the coroner into the hallway that led into the guts of the morgue. Alfano couldn't help the smile on his face, a mildly sadistic smile. He could hear Roberts breathing shallowly. The door slammed behind them, and the doc threw the dead bolt.

"Why are we here?" Roberts said.

"Adam, as I've said, last night a woman was murdered in the Palmer House Hotel, your hotel. In fact, she was found two doors down from the room that you were assigned by Sierra Films. We do not know who specifically was staying in the corner room; maybe you can help me there. We also did not know who she was until Hines Melnik gave me the name, Kitty Hill. My people have been doing some checks on her identity." He looked at the coroner. "I believe that it has been confirmed?"

"Yes, confirmed," Doc Abrahamson replied. "And, as requested, I placed the young lady at the front of the line. I finished the autopsy fifteen minutes ago."

They walked down another hallway. The smells of chemicals and putrefaction hung in the air. Roberts reacted with a gagged cough. Gurneys were spaced along the cool hallway; white sheets covered all of them.

"And these are?" Roberts asked meekly.

"The unlucky dead," Doc Abrahamson said. "All types and kinds. The weekend was busy here in Chicago, couple of shootings and a knifing. I'm told you are aware of two of these unfortunates, Detective?"

"Yes. However, I wouldn't use the word 'unfortunates,'" Alfano said.

Abrahamson nodded toward one of the gurneys. "That one's a drowning. There's some that appear to be drug overdoses, and a few yet to be determined. My job is to determine the cause of death, maybe the manner, and collect evidence. Not all the dead are here due to malicious activities, or murder. But the manner of their death must be determined. I am the last voice many of these people have."

Roberts staggered and bumped his hip against a gurney. A woman's hand dropped out from under the sheet, a wedding ring still on her finger. Roberts stepped back and bent over, dry-heaving.

"There's a can over there, if you have to vomit," Abrahamson told him. "Try not to. I've got enough to deal with today."

"My case?" Alfano said, watching Roberts.

"Still on the slab. Follow me, and I'll tell you what I know and what I don't. But I'll tell you up front, someone is trying to be funny—and I don't like funny."

The detective and his sickly sidekick followed Abrahamson through a set of swinging double doors into a room that was significantly cooler than the rest of the hallways. One wall was a bank of refrigerator doors, each about two-by-two feet. Four marble tables were aligned in the room's center. Various metal tools, stacks of towels, and other barbaric-looking pieces of equipment sat on shelves. To the uninformed, such as Adam Roberts, the room would appear to be a medieval torture chamber. A naked woman lay on the second table from the right; a towel draped across her midriff allowed the corpse some dignity.

"That's Kitty," Roberts blurted between dry heaves. "My God, what have you done to her?"

"Adam, this is an autopsied corpse. Dr. Abrahamson has investigated the body thoroughly to determine the cause of death. His work has led to many convictions of killers and has, occasionally, even surprised me with his results and findings."

"Thank you, Detective Alfano. Are you okay, Mr. Roberts?" the coroner asked.

Roberts's California tan had become as white as the corpse. "Yes, I guess I am. Good God, she didn't deserve this."

"No one does, son," the doc said.

"Is this definitely Kitty Hill?" Alfano asked.

"Yes," Roberts whispered.

"What did you find out?" Alfano said, going to stand next to the coroner at one long side of the exam table.

"This will be more detailed in my report, but here goes. As I said, someone was trying to be funny, not ha-ha funny but screw-you funny. First, the scarf around her neck was not used to strangle her. She was already dead when that happened. As you can see, there are some abrasions but little bruising; the blood had been stilled. There are two bullet wounds to the chest, there and there, large caliber. One of the bullets is in the envelope on the counter—looks to be about a .32. I was surprised to find it; normally they both would have pierced the body. The other did go through the body; I've told Detective Flynn. She was shot at close range. There is gunpowder stippling around both entry points—almost point blank. One bullet would have been enough. Between the two, her heart was shredded. I'm guessing that the load in the bullet might have been compromised, less force."

Roberts turned and quickly walked to a sink and vomited.

Both Abrahamson and Alfano waited for the actor to recover. The doc looked at Alfano, a question on his face.

"Please continue," Alfano said as he watched Roberts. "And you, why don't you go sit in the coroner's office. I'll be right there."

Roberts left the autopsy room.

"There is some old needle scarring on the arm, nothing new. I would suggest that she was or possibly is a heroin addict, but I need to perform additional lab tests to confirm this. Whoever did this is a sick bastard. It was as if they wanted to toy with us, and I don't like to be played with."

"And the cause of death?"

"The two gunshots, though as I said, one would have been enough. I also found wine, most probably champagne, in her stomach, at least three glasses full."

"A shot to the heart. Possibly something significant there?" Alfano asked.

There was a crash from down the hall as Roberts fell against an empty gurney and then dropped to the floor outside the office. Alfano and Abrahamson walked out and stood there for a moment looking down at the actor.

"I'll get the smelling salts," the doc said.

5

The glare of the late-afternoon sun shone through the front windshield of the Packard; Roberts sat in the passenger's seat, his breathing labored and heavy.

"One more time," Alfano said as he held a glass vial under the actor's nose. "I've still got a busy afternoon, and I have to get you back to the hotel. You need to be at the fair in three hours, and I do not want Mr. Melnik upset with me."

Roberts took a deep breath and coughed a few times. "Been a lot of years since someone stuck smelling salts under my nose—it was the Cal game. Got my bell rung. Ten minutes of that shit, and I was back in. It was the fourth quarter, scored twice. It's something you never forget. Smells can bring that all back."

"You ready to go?" Alfano asked.

"I was out before Doctor Abrahamson told us how she died."

"The gunshots. While sometimes obvious, the cause of death still needs his signature."

"You saw her there? When she was in the room?"

"Yes, just before we met in the mayor's office."

"This was a fucking test, wasn't it? You wanted to see how I'd react when I saw Kitty. You are a cruel bastard."

Roberts held out his hand for the vial. Alfano passed it to him, and he held it under his nose and inhaled.

"I do not like to see women murdered," Alfano said. "I don't like to see anyone murdered, but this killing was calculated and if you want cruel, this is it. The murderer planned this out; a gun was brought to the room, she knew the killer, she let him in, there was no forced entry. Then she had a scarf tied around her neck after she was killed."

"What scarf? I didn't see a scarf."

"The doc removed it. There was one wrapped around her neck." Alfano took back the smelling salts. "From your reaction, I'm not sure you have the stones to do this."

"Sure about what?" Roberts said. "Whether I'm the killer? Last night I was in Evanston at the Varsity Theatre until almost midnight. I signed autographs and talked with fans. I took an early train back into Chicago. Right now, I haven't had a full night's sleep in three days."

"That why the bennies? Something to keep you awake?" Alfano said.

"How the hell did you find those?"

"When you fainted, I checked your pockets."

"I have a prescription," Roberts said.

"I don't care. Was Melnik on the train?"

"Not that I remember. He and Maxime left early, around eight o'clock after the movie was over. Probably took the limo. I hung around."

"Did you get lucky?"

"What the hell are you talking about?"

"Just a guy question, big boy. A good-looking stud like you, girls three deep looking for a signature. Maybe some were there to count coup."

"Count coup?"

Alfano shrugged. "There are women who collect things. Screwing a guy, especially a celebrity, puts a notch in their garter belt—so to speak."

The color quickly returned to Roberts's face.

"I suppose you don't have a name to go with those rosy cheeks?"

"Fuck you, Detective."

"Let's be clear. I'm fairly confident you didn't kill Kitty Hill, and after a call to the theatre in Evanston, your story has been confirmed. In fact, the woman my sergeant spoke with offered this little tidbit. She said to make sure I tell you: thanks for the magical evening."

"I'd slug you if I could," Roberts said.

"Now, there's the actor I admire."

Alfano pulled the car up to the curb in front of the Palmer House. Without waiting for Henry, the doorman, Roberts climbed out and disappeared through the bronze doors.

An hour later, Alfano walked down the midway of the Century of Progress World's Fair. The midway titillated and tempted those who traveled a thousand miles to see both the exotic future and the tempting fan dances of Sally Rand. A ticket to the fair was an escape from the dreariness of the Depression. The midway bisected the fair; along its flanks were concessions manned by American Indians, a roller coaster, and an overhead sky ride. There was a Living Freak Show with dwarfs, Siamese twins, fat ladies, tattooed men, and other sorts of weird humans, all on display for a nickel. There was even a woman who could swallow her own nose; Sergeant McDunnah was an unbeliever until Alfano showed him.

Alfano hated the fair. On opening day, three months earlier, he'd saved both the fair and the mayor from being blown to bits by a mad woman and a bomber. That same day, his heart was blown to pieces when that same woman died right in front of him: she'd put a bullet through her own heart. Almost every strange thing that man could imagine could be found somewhere on the midway or in the hundreds of pavilions and halls spread along the Chicago lakefront.

He liked Sally Rand; she was a true entrepreneur. She'd found a way through her stylish fan dances to both titillate and enrage. Well before the fair, she had commanded a following at the Paramount Club on Rush Street. Alfano had seen her dance there twice. She'd spit in the eye of the city, and a couple of gangsters, and survived. This publicity probably saved her career and even her life. She had her followers and imitators. The fair leadership, while publicly distancing themselves from the midway's gaudy displays of nudity, certainly enjoyed the money rolling in through the fareboxes. When you got a piece of the action, morality was bent to fit the crime. And if it weren't for the city's tacit disregard of liquor laws and sexual displays, the fair would likely be a bust.

It wasn't Alfano's place to object to the changes happening in the world. He had enough problems with the daily grind of gangs, thuggery, theft, and murder. He knew the city officials and the vice industry were linked more than financially; it was a rot that affected everyone. He'd sadly accepted the reality that if it didn't kill the customer, it was probably acceptable. He hated himself for that. He felt like a priest who hated sin and what it did to people, and all he could do was manage the perverse outcomes. He could not offer forgiveness; all he could do was separate the worst offenders from society. He also hated to be taken as a fool, and the death of Kitty Hill was exactly that. *Here, Detective, is my work. I have put before you my crime, my art, my solution to my problem. I dare you to find me.*

This evening, as he walked the crowded midway with its noxious sounds, barkers, and entertainments, he hated humanity more than usual. Fuck them all.

The movie industry didn't miss a beat at the fair. Alfano had read that Mary Pickford, the famous and now retired actress, had stopped at the fair just a few weeks earlier and met with her fans in the Hall of Religion.

Hines Melnik and Sierra Films was showing *Guns and Saddles* at the Lagoon Theater tonight, which was why Melnik, Durant, and Roberts were there. The last time Alfano had been at the theater was to watch a boxing match; anything you could sell a ticket to was fair game.

He sat in the last row, high enough to look out over the North Lagoon directly behind the theater. The dark expanse of Lake Michigan cut broadly across the horizon. Lights from the tour boats coasted through the night.

Alfano wanted to walk away from the movie. It was a mishmash of *Cimarron* and *The Big Stampede*, lots of black hats and cattle running over the Oklahoma territory. While the story was awful in Alfano's opinion, he admitted that Maxime Durant looked fetching in the low-cut checker shirt that she took from Roberts after he was staked out on the prairie by ruthless Indians. She saved his life. Later, after he returned the favor and saved her, she held him in her arms as he died from a gunshot wound in front of a white-steepled church.

As the credits rolled on the screen, Hines Melnik walked to the center of the stage to a microphone.

"Thank you for coming to my movie," Melnik told the crowd. "We hope you enjoyed it. With me are the famous actors Maxime Durant and Adam Roberts. They are thrilled that you took the time from your holiday here at the fair to join us. We will be signing posters and autographs over at the Hollywood Pavilion. We look forward to seeing you there."

The smattering of applause was muffled by the sounds of the restarted fountain jets in the lagoon. The impressive waterworks, towering a hundred feet above the surrounding pavilions, were unleased several times a day.

Alfano stood in the back and watched the crowd push out to the midway. Many were turning to cross the Science Bridge that led to the Hollywood Pavilion. As he lit a cigarette, he caught Durant looking at him. She was smiling. It was like the smile a spider would make as it crossed its web to the stuck quarry. She nudged Roberts and whispered in his ear; he looked up at Alfano and gave him a salute from the brim of his Alfano-like fedora.

He'd told Roberts to be ready at nine o'clock the next morning. He'd pick him up out front of the hotel. He wanted to show the actor the Racine Street station, then the jail, and if there was time, the courts building. He watched as the trio left the stage and headed toward the pavilion. He turned and went the other way; he was bone tired.

6

The next morning, cold rain filled the street gutters; Alfano was glad the activities he'd planned with Roberts were indoors. The drive across the city from his apartment to the Racine Street station was both wet and slow. His intent was to review Doc Abrahamson's report and refresh his memory of the crime scene. The last thing he wanted to do was run into Melnik or Durant, so he did not go back to the room where Kitty Hill had been found. His theatricals the day before with Roberts might prove fruitful now that the man had a chance to marinate over what he'd seen on the marble slab. Dead bodies did that to you, Alfano knew from experience. He had an hour and a half before he was due to meet Roberts at the Palmer House.

"Good morning, Sergeant," Alfano said to McDunnah as he shook the rain off his slicker.

"And the top of the morning to you, Detective," Sergeant McDunnah said. "I brought in some muffins that the wife made—much better for you than the donuts."

"Thank her, will you? Did she make the coffee?"

"No, I'm the criminal."

"Then I'll have a cup. I want to talk to you, my desk."

The always-efficient sergeant had already set up the murder board, as they both had been calling the corkboard set up near Alfano's desk. It was about four feet by eight feet, nice oak frame, thick cork surface. Four casters were mounted on the lower frame, allowing it to be rolled around. On the ledge was a box of thumbtacks to post pictures and notes. An identical backup murder board stood against the wall behind the primary board. McDunnah had one of his Irish friends make the two boards, which had become an integral part of their crime solving.

A few photographs were tacked to the board: one of the deceased lying on the floor, one of the interior of the hotel room. Another photo, the pretty face of Kitty Hill that appeared to be a promotional photo, was posted alongside. A long strip of paper was secured above the photos; McDunnah had already noted the murder time and date on the left-hand end of the timeline strip. A square of paper displayed fingerprints; the name *Kitty Hill* was written along the bottom margin.

McDunnah placed a cup of coffee on the desk and offered Alfano a muffin on a napkin. Alfano smelled orange.

"How did she know? This is perfect for a day like this—I love your wife," Alfano said.

"She does know how to take care of you. She tells me you are her favorite cop. Pisses me off."

"You must treat her better, Sergeant. Look what she did for you when you were laid up after the shooting. She put up with you for weeks. She is a saint."

A few months earlier, McDunnah had been wounded during a shootout where he took down a gangland killer and his men. Alfano knew that today's weather was playing havoc with his leg.

"No argument. Just keep it between us," McDunnah said.

"Mum's the word. What else do we have?"

"The coroner has confirmed the gunshots. The body was

posed after death. The recovered bullet in the body was confirmed as a .32 caliber, probably from a Colt or similar revolver. Flynn found pieces of the second buried in the headboard, went clean through the body. Flynn is sending the bullets to the crime lab on East Superior. The scarf was made in Japan. It will be difficult to track down. I'll make sure it's sent with the bullets; maybe the lab can find something. The champagne was from the Palmer House. It had been delivered to the room at ten thirty. A woman was in the room when the boy dropped it off. He remembers she gave him a five."

"Was the woman Hill?" Alfano asked.

"From the boy's description, yes. He said she was the whitest white woman he'd ever seen."

"Is this Flynn's work?" Alfano asked.

"Yes, he must be trying to get on your good side. He's copying everything to us. You must have scared the bejesus out of him."

"He has an attitude problem. Anything else?"

"The watch you left is a beauty," McDunnah said. "Why didn't you want Flynn to deal with it?"

"I wanted this kept close. What did you find out from Jules?"

He meant Jules Semitof, the sergeant's go-to jeweler on State Street.

"It is something special—a Cartier Tank Basculante, Swiss made. The face rotates within an armature that places the crystal face against a protective interior surface—all gold, of course."

"Of course."

"According to Jules, it is a favorite watch of rich active men, polo players, fox hunters, golfers, and even tennis players."

"Right, for when you need to know the time when hitting a little white ball while riding a thoroughbred horse. I get it."

"And it isn't cheap—in fact, very expensive. When I showed it to him, he whistled."

"Interesting."

"And he got all excited. He likes when I stop by."

"I'll tell Moira; that will get you in trouble. And the punch line?"

"The watch was bought during the last year. It's only been out in this model since Christmas. The inside of the band is engraved with the name of a Los Angeles jeweler: Laykin et Cie. The engraving on the back of the watch, the face when the crystal face is closed, is the logo of the Will Rogers Polo Club in Santa Monica, California."

"How the hell does he know that?"

"Will Rogers brought his West Coast polo team here to Chicago this summer for a match against the East team. Jules is a big polo fan and recognized the logo."

"Of course he does. Fascinating. You know the strangest people. You didn't try to call this Los Angeles jeweler to find out who bought it, did you?"

"Time differences—it is six o'clock in the morning in Los Angeles. I assume they open at ten West Coast time. I was going to call at noon."

"Excellent. Keep what you find to yourself for now. Not everything is a two-way street."

"Got it. Any ideas?"

"A few, but too early to say." Alfano nodded at the architectural sketch McDunnah had left on his desk. "Where did you get the hotel floor plan?"

"I called Holabird & Root, the architects; they ran over a copy of the layout for the twenty-fourth floor."

"You are a wonder, and the muffin is even better."

"I'll tell Moira."

One hour and thirty minutes later, Alfano stood next to the Packard in front of the Palmer House.

"You are beginning to scare away the customers, Detective," Henry said. He stood just outside the bronze doors. "That looks like a goomba limo, hardly a police car. It has *gangster* written all over it."

"Do we have an attitude problem, Henry Bucci?" Alfano said, walking up to the man. The doorman stood his ground.

"No, sir, just stating a fact. This is the third or fourth time you've parked here since the . . . unfortunate death of the woman on the twenty-fourth; everyone is talking about it."

"And what do they know about it, Bucci?"

"This is a hotel, Detective. The staff watches, listens, talks, loves rumors; they even try to make a dollar or two."

"And who'd pay you?"

"Well, let's just say the free press likes to grease the wheels of those who ride the highway of truth."

"*Tribune* or *Daily News*? Neither of them wants the truth, but they pay well for salacious rumors. You know that and I know that, especially when it comes to celebrities. Besides, you and I go back a few years. What's been going on?"

Henry glanced around; he and Alfano were the only ones near the doors. "My memory ain't what it used to be this early in the morning," Henry said.

"Your memory was never good, Henry. And, if I remember, it is always thirsty. Would a cup of coffee help?"

"A large cup might."

Alfano slipped the man a five-dollar bill. "Better?"

"Could use some sugar."

"Later."

Henry looked mildly disappointed, but his memory came back. "Both papers are sniffing around—big deal when an actress is murdered," he told Alfano. "The story in this morning's paper—mostly the truth, as I was told by those that read it.

You should read it. Seems that actress was from around here."

"Now you are an investigator?"

"Nope, just the guy up front." As if to illustrate, Henry went to the curb and helped a couple out of a cab. He turned back to Alfano. "Who you waiting for? That guy from yesterday, Melnik, and the rest of his armada?"

"The word is entourage, Henry. More particularly, Adam Roberts."

"Well, good luck with that."

"Why?"

"This morning, just after I came on at six, Roberts, that classy actress dame, and Melnik came down with a bellman. They wanted a taxi; I loaded their luggage, and they left."

Stunned, Alfano said, "Do you know where they went?"

"Melnik told the driver Chicago Municipal Airport; they had a seven-thirty flight."

Alfano looked at his watch: 9:32 AM. "Shit. Anything else?"

"Melnik was a lousy tipper. Roberts said, 'Tell Detective Alfano I'm sorry.' Then he slipped me a twenty."

"You know Melnik? He been here before?"

"Nope. Till now, I just seen his movies—go to them a lot. But he went in and out a dozen times while his *armada* was here. As I said, bad tipper."

"Watch the car, Henry. I'll be right back."

Alfano walked into the lobby of the Palmer House, went to the front desk and talked with the hotel manager, Claude Dubonnet. He then went to the bank of pay phones in the vestibule off the main lobby and placed a call to McDunnah.

"Find out which plane left from Chicago Municipal at seven thirty this morning. Find out who was on the plane and where it was headed. I'll be there in ten minutes. And get Flynn there, too. And get the morning *Tribune*—they got something on Hill." He hung up before McDunnah could answer.

As promised, ten minutes later, Alfano pushed his way

through the station doors and went straight to his desk. Mc-Dunnah followed. In their wake was Detective Flynn.

"Flynn, here's where I am in this mess," Alfano said, and then told both men what had happened.

"Guess they didn't want your help all that much," Flynn said, obviously trying to get a jab in.

"Why didn't you know they were leaving this morning, Flynn? I'm holding you responsible for this screwup. Did you tell them they couldn't leave town? Did you call the airport to try and stop them?"

"Until McDunnah called, I didn't know they had left. Besides, by that time they were ten thousand feet in the air."

"Where were they going, Sergeant?" Alfano said, turning to McDunnah.

"The woman at American Airlines said they had tickets to Los Angeles."

"Damn. Is there any way to intercept them?"

"Sure, they stop maybe five or six times between here and there. All you have to do is find a local sheriff willing to piss off an airport manager. If they are on schedule, they have already left St. Louis for Oklahoma City, then on to Dallas before heading west."

"Face it, Detective, they are gone," Flynn said. "You should drop all this."

Alfano took a step toward Flynn, pointed at the man with his index finger. "Don't you ever tell me what to do."

"Look, sure you're pissed off, I get it. Even you know they were not involved in Hill's death. They were all elsewhere."

"That's not been confirmed. We're still waiting on the last of the interviews from Evanston."

"I got the answers this morning," Flynn said.

"Why didn't you say something?" Alfano said.

"Really, the way you busted in here?" Flynn answered. "Their itineraries for the night in question were verified. According to the theater manager, Melnik and Durant left in a limo at eleven o'clock Sunday evening. They had drinks in the Palmer House bar when they got back to the hotel. The bartender remembers them both; it was just the two of them. The night elevator operator took them to the floor around three in the morning. That was at least three hours after Hill died, according to Abrahamson."

"Obviously neither of them entered Hill's room," Alfano said.

"If they did, no one saw them. They sure as hell didn't say anything. I assume they went straight to their rooms. Melnik was staying in the room next to Hill's corner room."

"And Roberts?"

"I pressed the woman on the phone about Roberts. She finally admitted to being with Roberts after the show until about five the next morning. She drove him to the train station for the six o'clock train."

"Why the hell didn't they come out of their rooms during all the chaos of us being there?"

"Because, according to the elevator operator, Melnik and Durant got back on his elevator about four that morning and went to the lobby. The doorman said they took a cab; he didn't know where."

"It wasn't Henry Bucci, the doorman we talked to, was it?"

"No. It was the night doorman, a black guy."

"So, Melnik and Durant went somewhere around four o'clock Monday morning, then met Roberts after he arrived," Alfano said. "I saw them at the mayor's office just before ten. The mayor had me cool my heels in his lobby for almost thirty minutes, during which our three suspects were having a conversation with the mayor, Nash, and Spats Lanigan. That's when His Honor stuck me with Roberts."

"Stuck you?" Flynn said. "Lanigan was there?"

"The sergeant will fill you in. When are they expected in

Los Angeles?"

"According to the schedule and the woman at the airport," McDunnah said, "they will arrive shortly after midnight West Coast time. That's almost twelve hours from now. That assumes they don't get stuck somewhere due to weather."

"The wonders of the modern world. Shit," Alfano said.

7

Melnik, Durant, and Roberts emerged from the mid-door of the American Airlines Ford Trimotor and walked across the apron of the Union Air Terminal in Burbank. Their luggage followed them; it was stacked on a cart pushed by a stevedore. They were three hours late for their scheduled 12:15 AM Wednesday morning arrival time. If any of the three had bothered to look up, they would have observed that the stars were obscured by the marine layer extending in from the Pacific Ocean; the air mass was lowering. If they had been delayed any longer that evening as their plane crossed the mountains, they would have had to land in San Bernardino, sixty miles east, and finish the flight in daylight. The weather in Texas—a hellish thunderstorm with high winds around the Dallas airport—had delayed their takeoff. As they flew through the late-evening heat rising from the desert west of Tucson, the plane had made gut-wrenching climbs and drops. Not many of the passengers made it without some form of stomach problem; Durant had vomited twice, Roberts once. Only Melnik, who'd flown a lot over the past year, survived unscathed. All three were exhausted as they climbed into the hired limousine.

"I swear, Melnik, next time I'm taking the train," Roberts said as their car began its trek.

"We had to get back."

His companions exchanged weary looks but said nothing.

"We need to get this production going," Melnik said. "Three days on the train might as well be three weeks. The camera equipment is available. If I didn't commit, it would be four months until we could get those cameras and all the gear."

"Why the hell don't you buy your own equipment?" Durant said as she lit a cigarette. "You make enough fucking money."

"Tax reasons and expenses." Melnik poured himself a drink from the crystal carafe secured to the back of the driver's seat. "You two already cost me a fortune, and I don't want the cameras to sit around gathering dust when we are out of production. We lease them when we need them, and right now, and for the next sixty days, they are mine. We start shooting *State Street Killers* on Monday."

"The script sucks. It's all wrong," Roberts said. "And how the hell are we going to get organized in a week? Kitty handled all that shit. You couldn't organize a birthday party."

"I borrowed a guy from RKO," Melnik said. "He helped put together *King Kong* with Schoedsack and Cooper. Wished to hell I'd done that picture; RKO is making a fortune. Last year they came to me for a loan, they were that close to sinking. I lent them ten grand; it kept them afloat. In six months, they've made half a million off the fucking ape."

Schoedsack and Cooper owed him, Melnik told them. During the Texas stop, he had placed a call to his guy at RKO, who arranged for Schoedsack's assistant to temporarily take over for Kitty. "His name is Jorge Jones, J.J. to most of us who know the kid," Melnik said.

"I've worked with him. He's an idiot," Durant said.

"My guess, he turned you down when you wanted to fuck him," Roberts said.

"You are such a sweetie. Screw you."

"Stop it. I don't want your catfighting for the next month," Melnik said. "Keep it up, and I'll get replacements—for both of you."

"I have a contract, H.M.," Durant said.

"I'll pay you half, like the contract says, and dump your pretty ass in the street—and still make money. So, quit being my second-biggest problem, and shut the fuck up."

That ended further conversation. Melnik stared out at the early morning gloom as they drove through the mountains on Cahuenga Boulevard to Sunset Boulevard. Durant glowered at the back of his head until she grew bored. The small party in the limo remained silent as the driver navigated the familiar, lofty streets of Beverly Hills and wound up North Crescent Drive to Melnik's mansion. After Melnik opened the gate, he climbed back in and the driver pulled into the circular drop-off.

"Either of you want a drink before going home?" Melnik asked. The driver removed his suitcase from the trunk.

"I'm beat," Durant said. "Besides, the sun will be up in half an hour."

"Me, too—we start Monday?" Roberts said.

"Eight o'clock. Be there at the studio," Melnik said. "I want to go over the script. If it's as fucked as you think, Roberts, we'll make it right. I feel real good about this project." Melnik got out of the limo.

Durant gave a shrug that might have indicated agreement. She and Roberts watched Melnik follow the driver to the front door.

The Sierra Films studio was in a warehouse complex on Santa Monica Boulevard that Melnik had rented two years earlier. Before Prohibition, it had housed a brewery and then sat empty for ten years. The owner, a Jew from Melnik's old neighborhood off Fairfax Avenue, was a friend of the movie director's father. Melnik made him an offer, and the owner was thrilled—especially at the prospect of a moving picture studio as a tenant. Melnik also had an option to buy the place; time would tell if he could pull that off. He had ten thousand dollars to lend a fellow producer, but not a hundred thousand to buy the five acres and all the buildings, yet.

Melnik stood just outside his front door and watched the limousine drive down the hill. Its taillights disappeared as it followed the curving street back to Sunset Boulevard. Roberts had rented a house somewhere nearer Santa Monica Boulevard. Durant had a three-room suite with a sunset view at the Beverly Wilshire Hotel—Melnik had never been invited to their residences.

He'd given the maids and butler the week off as he traveled. They would be back at noon today. He dropped his bag in the foyer of the Italianate house that had become opportunistically available a year earlier. He'd snapped it up after the unfortunate death by narcotic overdose of a mildly successful silent film actor.

Melnik poured himself a bourbon and took it out to the terrace that overlooked the pool. The view beyond was the glow of the rising sun over the high-rises of downtown Los Angeles ten miles away. He stripped off his clothes and stood at the edge of the pool, took a deep breath, and jumped in.

Roberts walked through the front door of his rented twelve-room Julia Morgan wannabe mansion in the flatter neighborhood of Beverly Hills. His taste had shifted from the dust-covered furniture and fly-ridden ranch of his youth spent in Fresno to this collection of Arts and Crafts frou-frou. He'd sworn never to go back to that valley life; his taste was now for cognac and champagne, not tequila and beer. He also knew that his other needs could be met in Los Angeles, needs that in the small community of Fresno County might bring embarrassment to his family. He loved them—but when they found out, he left. Not as much to avoid his own exposure as to reduce theirs.

"You're early," a man's voice said from the top of the wooden stairs in the spacious entry. "Thank you for the call. I'd have met you at the airport . . ."

"Unnecessary. H.M. gave us a ride. I need something to eat, then sleep. We start production Monday. I've got three days to myself."

"To ourselves," the lanky man said, correcting Roberts. He crossed the tile floor in his bare feet. He was nude. "I'll make you some eggs. There's still some bacon."

"Excellent, I'm famished."

The man took Robert's hand. "Where's your watch?"

"I can't find it, Wells," Roberts said. "I looked everywhere. It still might be in my bags. If not, I'll file a claim."

"I gave you that watch. You loved that watch."

"I know—you gave it to me; that's the worst part. I'll keep looking for it. If not, I'll replace it. And, young man, put some clothes on. I want nothing singed or splattered; I've a special three days planned," Roberts said as they headed toward the kitchen.

The lobby of the Beverly Wilshire Hotel was empty aside from a maid dusting the furniture and a man in formal attire stationed at the front desk. He nodded to Maxime Durant as she crossed the spacious room, then put up his hand, gesturing for her to stop.

"Good morning, Cecil," she said. "Mail?"

"Of course, ma'am. One moment." He disappeared into a cubicle behind the front desk, then emerged with a bundle of letters and a package. "Did you have a good trip? Was Chicago successful?"

"No, it was a wretched trip, and Mr. Melnik required that we fly. I was miserable. But I'm home now."

"Welcome back. Would you like breakfast?"

"Send up my usual at noon. I first need some sleep. Please have the kitchen call before they arrive."

"Certainly, Miss Durant. Anything else?"

"No, that will do, Cecil." Holding the bundle of mail, she turned to the bellhop who had followed her from the entry and carried her bags. "Juan, home."

"Yes, ma'am," the bellhop answered.

The two of them proceeded to the elevator. Durant leaned against the paneling as Juan and the elevator operator discussed boxing at the Legion Hall in Hollywood.

"Please stop that, you two," Durant said to the pair. "It's a barbaric sport."

"Sorry, ma'am."

"That's okay. I'm just tired."

"Yes, ma'am."

Durant followed Juan down the hallway to her suite. He opened the door and placed her two bags in the bedroom and then walked back to the small kitchen that was a part of the suite. She placed the mail and the small package on the ornate iron and marble ledge in the entry.

"Anything else, Miss Durant?"

"No, Juan, that will be all. Please confirm that my breakfast order was placed. No need to call."

"Of course, Miss Durant."

Juan shut the door behind him as he left.

Durant picked up the package, crossed the living room, and sat on the couch. The sun was a finger's width above the rooftops. The light cut diagonally through the back blinds as she lit a cigarette. A letter opener lay on the glass coffee table; she carefully slit open the package and removed the small bundle wrapped in newspaper and secured with Scotch Tape. She smiled and peeled away the newspaper. A bundle of fifty-dollar bills was secured to a larger bundle of twenty-dollar bills. A note wrapped them both.

> *M.D.,*
> *Your share of the last two months' sales. Business has been hot, to say the least. You were right, those girls you sent over were easy, even a few eagerly participated. We are expanding distribution to Chicago and St. Louis. The films are being carried by girls in their luggage. Let's have lunch soon.*
> *D.*

Durant walked to the window and looked out over Los Angeles from her ninth-floor apartment. She was poised to star in a new Sierra film; she was holding in her hands a substantial share of her now lucrative partnership; and the one woman who could have thrown a wrench into the whole enterprise was lying in a morgue two thousand miles away. Yes, the future was looking good.

8

The following Monday, a week after Kitty Hill's body was found, Alfano stood at the murder board and considered the new slips of paper and photos that McDunnah had pinned to the cork. Three headshots of the LA3, as McDunnah called them, had been added to the right side: Melnik on top, then Durant, then Roberts. Notecards with personal information were pinned next to each photo: age, Los Angeles addresses, notes about movies, and criminal records (as much as could be found). Alfano had wanted the addresses just in case these fellow employees of Kitty Hill became suspects; knowing their whereabouts in advance would make it easier for the LA police to bring them in. He knew this was just a hope; nobody wanted to deal with interstate extradition these days. And the chance of the Bureau getting involved was slim at best, not that he wanted them involved. He dictated to McDunnah the biography Roberts had narrated while with him in the car. That was added to the cards next to Roberts's photo.

The picture in the center of the board was a headshot of Kitty Hill. Two photos, placeholders really, for the dozens of others in an envelope in his desk, showed her body on the white rug along with the red scarf. McDunnah had strategically placed a small piece of paper effectively hiding the dead naked woman's assets. A typed card gave Hill's backstory as well as personal information.

The lower portion of the board included a floor plan of the twenty-fourth floor of the Palmer House. Four rooms had notations: *Hill's Body Here* read a card tacked to the space indicating the northwest corner room, and for the adjacent room, *Melnik*. The room on the opposite corner: *Durant*. Three doors down, toward the elevator: *Roberts*.

Alfano leaned in, his hands clasped behind his back, and read the details about the woman on the white rug:

> *Kitty Hill, formerly Katherine Mooney. Singer and dancer in Chicago nightclubs from 1916 to 1923 . . .* (That's why he'd thought he'd recognized her.) *Drake and Simmons nightclubs. Did burlesque for a time; that's when she changed her name to Kitty O'Neal. Husband, Allen O'Neal, killed in gang shooting in 1923. The manager at the Chez Paree nightclub said she left Chicago and headed West in 1923 or '24. Her last known address was 1228 Brockton Avenue, Los Angeles, California.*

Sergeant McDunnah came to join him.

"Good job," Alfano said. "How did you get so much information since last Tuesday? And the Chez Paree only opened last year."

"Much of that was cribbed from the *Tribune* article. The news story was put together by one of their beat writers who covers the Loop. He remembered Kitty from the old days. And I got a guy on the Los Angeles police force, name's Gil Tuttle, a detective sergeant. He's the son of a gal who was married to a neighbor's brother that I grew up with in Bridgeport. I even dated his sister. That was long before Moira. He quit the Chicago force about twenty years ago, packed up everything, and moved to LA."

"You Irish, just one big family. I'll take your word for it. Again, good job."

"I'm fleshing out the details on the others—might take a few days," McDunnah told him. "Thanks for Roberts's life story. I'm having Tuttle check it out. But they are public people, so I'll get what I can. Seems that Kitty Mooney, or O'Neal, left an impression with some of the nightclub managers, especially the current manager at Chez Paree. He worked with her at a club on Rush Street about ten years ago. She was all Irish, great looks and voice, could dance. She wasn't from Bridgeport. After her husband was gunned down, she changed her name from O'Neal to Hill. I also found out that the night her husband, Allen O'Neal, was slain, her brother, Ian Mooney, was also killed, both shot dead, execution style, at close range. I'll add all that to the board."

"Maybe she was killed over those two murders?" Alfano suggested.

"That was ten years ago. My guess, anyone involved is either dead or in prison. Besides, they couldn't pin the deaths on anyone. It was outside a local Irish bar on Halsted."

"Maybe she knew the killer or killers?"

"Right now, anything is possible," McDunnah said. "I've got Tuttle chasing a few leads."

"Don't they have crime in Los Angeles? Tuttle got that much time on his hands?"

"You are paying him a hundred bucks for this."

"What?"

"Information costs money."

"What about the brotherhood of the police?" Alfano said. "Scratch my back, I'll scratch yours."

"The key word is scratch, the one spelled with a dollar sign."

"Cynical Irishman."

"A good Irishman is always cynical; I'll find the funds

somewhere."

McDunnah walk back to his desk. Alfano knew without looking that the sergeant still walked with a slight limp from the gunshot wound to his leg a few months earlier. The sergeant's job wasn't unlike a concierge at a hotel. Everything was filtered through him, walk-ins, phone calls, mail, and interdepartmental communications. He assessed and then passed it onto the right person or team. Even before the gunshot, he seldom walked the streets. For Tony Alfano, Sergeant McDunnah was both his right and left hand.

Alfano turned his full attention back to the board. He studied the photos of Kitty Mooney-O'Neal-Hill. The kill shots had come from a reasonably large-caliber weapon, possibly a .32, suggesting her assailant was most probably a man. Guns could be found anywhere. These days, it was easier to get a Colt revolver than a vial of cyanide. The scarf, sex either consensual or forced, the bruises on the arms, and the bullets themselves were confusing. And if she were a heroin addict, one more layer of suspects might be added. There were the two champagne glasses, one with Hill's prints, the other wiped clean. The bottle of 1930 Moet & Chandon Brut had also been scrubbed. The door had been locked from the inside. And the watch— the Cartier watch. Expensive, Los Angeles bought, too easily traced, Polo Club logo—was it another clue, or a plant, or a misdirection?

Alfano heard the welcome sound of a coffee cup tap the top of his desk. "Thanks, Sergeant. I'd have gotten my own coffee."

"Your favorite mayor just called. Eleven at his office," Mc-Dunnah said.

"Really, can't he just leave me alone?"

"I'm beginning to worry about you. You spend too much time in that downtown office, you don't know what will rub off. Rumors will start."

Alfano picked up the coffee. Weak or strong, the sergeant's coffee was always hot.

"I have a question," Alfano said. "Why would someone go to all the trouble to make this look like a cheesy *True Detective* story—even to the locked door?"

"It's possible the killer left through the connecting room door—it wasn't even locked—then through Melnik's room. All the other clues? Maybe they are not clues at all, but misdirection."

"Yes, maybe," Alfano said.

"Specifically, what do you mean?" McDunnah said.

"The scarf: Is it Hill's, or did the killer bring it? Did she know her killer? The two champagne glasses and expensive champagne suggest it. The room next door was Melnik's. Roberts says he was fifteen miles away in Evanston when Hill was murdered. Where was Durant?"

"I'm chasing it all down. The young lady says she was with Roberts but is dodgy on the details," McDunnah said. "I'm also checking Melnik and Durant's whereabouts and where they went that morning before the meeting with the mayor. They had nine hours since leaving the Evanston theater. Now, it may be impossible to know where they were."

"It still pisses me off that they took off," Alfano said. "They knew they were leaving but said nothing."

"We could try and extradite them back here for questions."

"At the moment, it's not worth it. I'll let the mayor know when I see him. He was, when I first met this trio, blissfully unaware of any of this."

"Blissfully unaware, yeah. That just about sums up our mayor," McDunnah said.

Alfano sat in the overstuffed corner chair in the mayor's outer office. He lit a cigarette. The secretary's desk had been unoccupied when he arrived. Halfway through his first cigarette, the secretary walked through the office door and stopped, startled at the sight of someone in the chair.

"You are ten minutes early," she said, sounding more like a third-grade teacher than a mayor's secretary.

"And you were not at your post, Miss Sarah Jean Alcott. Anyone could have just waltzed in and gotten to your boss. Tsk-tsk."

"I was out for just a moment. And whatever my schedule, it's none of your business, Detective. Too much tea," she added under her breath.

He grinned at her. "Some of that quaint Nebraska charm is beginning to turn to nasty Chicago grit. I like it."

"You are incorrigible." Sarah Jean leaned across her desk and pressed the lever on the intercom. "Detective Alfano is here."

"Please let him in," came the mayor's voice. The door buzzed. Alfano stood.

"Until we meet again, Duluth."

Her reply was to wave him toward the door.

"Tony, Tony, come in, Detective," Mayor Kelly said. He was sitting behind his desk, a cigar in the ashtray to his right.

Alfano looked around. The mayor was uncharacteristically alone.

"Good morning, Mayor. What can I do for you?" Alfano said.

"Well, this will be short and sweet. I have the bishop, three nuns, and three honor students coming to visit me in about twenty minutes. So, I'll get right to the point. I need you to represent the city of Chicago on a very important assignment."

"I'm right in the middle of the Palmer House killing. I can't break away."

"This is possibly connected to the murder of that unfortunate girl. In fact, I may be able to help you while you help me."

"Really?" The thought of the Trojans and the Greeks and

a horse came to mind.

"Hines Melnik called me this morning. It was early here, damn early in California. You do remember Mr. Melnik?"

The photo of Melnik on the murder board flashed across Alfano's mind. "Of course."

"Well, it seems he needs you."

"That little shit torpedoed my investigation. The dead woman was his employee; she ran his production company. And then, without a word, he and those two actors got on an airplane and fled Chicago! If they were here, I'd throw them all in jail. If for nothing more than being smug Californians with tans."

Kelly smiled and took a pull on his cigar. "Mr. Melnik needs you to provide your professional assistance while they film his movie. He called you a technical advisor. He wants you to make sure that the characters and the story work—'make it true to life,' he said."

"Not a chance. There's too much to do here," Alfano said. "Besides, what do I know about making movies?"

"He's paying for two weeks of your time, all expenses covered, and a donation to the Police Orphan's Fund."

"How generous."

"And he needs you in Los Angeles by Thursday," Kelly said with a smile.

"Thursday, this week? The train will take almost three days as is. I'm too damn busy. I have the Hill murder, and two others—the Herrington killing and the Jane Doe in Jackson Park. My office is close to breaking them open as well. I just can't walk away and leave the other detectives high and dry."

"They are all good boys. Pass these other cases on to someone else. Use your time in Los Angeles to work on the Hill murder," Mayor Kelly said. "You said yourself these LA people are your prime suspects. So, get up close. If one of them did it, I'll back the extradition. And don't worry about the timing or the train—they are paying for your plane ticket. You leave Wednesday morning; you will be in Los Angeles the next afternoon."

"Plane ticket? I am fucking flying?" Alfano said, the color draining from his dark Italian face.

"Detective Alfano, are you afraid of flying?" The mayor sucked on his cigar, exhaled. "I'll be damned," he said into a cloud of smoke.

9

That afternoon and Tuesday, Alfano worked the case, trying to put Wednesday's departure out of his mind. The body of Kitty Hill was unsurprisingly left unclaimed. McDunnah called Sierra Films and waited a full day for Hines Melnik to finally return his call. Melnick said he was sorry, but he was not interested in having the body shipped to California for burial. And no, he did not know if she had any next of kin. He would send a hundred dollars to help with the local funeral arrangements. Alfano was disappointed with the response by Kitty's Los Angeles associates. It was another reason he wanted to tell the mayor to take the idea of him flying to California and stuff it in his snoot. Alfano convinced the coroner to hold the body until he got back from California.

The inevitable arrived at 8:05 AM Wednesday morning. As Detective Anthony Alfano quietly recited his rosary, the airplane rose gracefully, albeit very noisily, off the runway at Chicago's Municipal Airport. They had assigned him the first row, starboard side, the first of the eighteen passengers. There was more leg room, though he was sure his seat assignment was intended to torture him; it was a longer walk to the toilet in the tail of the plane. He tried to convince himself that he was made of sterner stuff, especially considering that five of the seats were occupied by women who were all atwitter over their adventure. He was hardly able to keep down his breakfast.

He was pissed at himself; he knew he was made of sterner stuff. In 1915, as a beat cop with two years on the streets, he'd been at the pier helping recover bodies from the *Eastland* ship disaster. He'd taken on the gangs and bootleggers through the 1920s. He was there the day they walked Al Capone out of his hotel to the bus to take him to jail. During his twenty years on the job, he'd worked for Mayors Busse, Harrison, Thompson (twice), and Dever. The two shortest terms were for the assassinated Anton Cermak and his interim placeholder, Frank Corr. And now it was Edward Kelly. To be honest, he hadn't liked any of them—and he'd only personally met three of them. Sure, they shook his hand when he was awarded three citations for distinction in the line of duty, but Kelly was the only one with whom he'd had more than a two-minute conversation. Alfano was not a politician. He was a simple soldier in the never-ending battle between the not-so-good and the not-so-bad. He understood, but he never turned his back on the wronged and the powerless. He was no avenging angel, like Bureau agent Eliot Ness, a heroic figure in the unfolding gangland stories and deeds. After Capone was taken down for tax evasion, Alfano sat in on a couple days of the trial. It was an event—a circus—though it resulted in Capone's conviction. He hoped the man would rot in hell.

Alfano tucked the rosary beads into his pocket, looked out the window, and was hypnotized by the landscape that passed under the Curtiss T-32 Condor. His stomach had settled, the coffee stayed down, and the stewardess smelled delightful. The flight plan was due south to Memphis, six hours ahead of them. Then west through Little Rock to Dallas, and around midnight, weather permitting, El Paso, Texas. Then through the night to Tucson, Phoenix, Glendale, and eventually the United Air terminal in Burbank, California. All this was beyond him; he had never been west of the Mississippi River in his entire forty-two years.

Late that day, after flying back and forth over the Mississippi River, they finally headed west. He ate lunch during the short layover in St. Louis, and had dinner in Texas, and breakfast in Glendale, before the last leg to Burbank.

Late the next morning, twelve miles north of Los Angeles, Alfano walked through the recently completed Burbank United Air terminal and saw a woman in the lobby holding a sign with his name on it.

"I'm Alfano," he said, looking down at the incredibly beautiful young woman.

"Good morning, Mr. Alfano. I am Gloria. I am your escort today; our driver is out front. Mr. Melnik told me to tell you that the day is yours. He knows you will be exhausted. However, you don't look too exhausted to me, if I may say so. They say that flying can be so stressful."

"Thank you, I'm surprisingly not, Gloria. I've had stakeouts that were tougher and more uncomfortable."

"Stakeouts? Are you a G-man or a detective like Sam Spade? I've never met a true-to-life private eye."

"It's worse than that, Gloria. I'm a cop," Alfano said.

"Golly, a real cop. And Mr. Melnik is doing a detective picture. What a coincidence."

"More than you can imagine. My bag?"

"They will bring it there." She pointed to a long counter near the lobby area.

"I assume there's a hotel or something in my near future?"

"Yes, you are at the brand-new Georgian Hotel on the cliff above the beach in Santa Monica. I was told by Mr. Melnik that you should have the best. It's quite a place."

"How long is the drive?"

"With the traffic, maybe an hour, maybe less. You never can tell here in Los Angles. He said for you to relax, enjoy the day. Go to the beach. I am at your disposal."

Alfano looked at the girl; if she were twenty, he would have been surprised. Auburn hair, nice tan, athletic—if he were only fifteen years younger. Unfortunately, right now all he could imagine was that the girl's father couldn't be much older than himself.

"Lead on, my dear. Adventure awaits," he told her.

They found Alfano's one bag and met the driver at the curb in front of the terminal.

"Detective Alfano, this is David Baine, our driver," Gloria said.

"David," Alfano said.

David opened the back door to the limousine and Alfano discovered he had the back seat to himself; Gloria took the front passenger seat.

The drive across the San Fernando Valley was a dusty mixture of small towns, tract homes, and farmland. David then took them up and over the San Gabriel Mountains via Sepulveda Boulevard and drove west on Sunset Boulevard to the coast.

"This is the most scenic route, Detective," Gloria said as they cut south through the mountains. "Along Sunset is where all the swell and rich folks live. Me, I've got a small apartment in the Sawtelle neighborhood. It's not far from Sierra Films' production lot. I don't mind. I think I've got a chance at getting a spot in a picture coming up—maybe even Mr. Melnik's newest, a walk-on spot."

The driver harrumphed when he overheard Gloria's expectation.

"You never mind him, Detective Alfano. He wants to be an actor, too. I dearly believe half of LA wants to be in the pictures. So, I work where I can."

"Mind if I smoke?" Alfano asked.

"Oh, please. I don't mind. Thank you for asking."

"You want to be an actress?" Alfano asked "Where are you

from?"

"Denver. After my folks died, I took off. Hopped on the train here. I'm taking acting and dance lessons with some of the money they left me. I got dreams."

Again, the driver harrumphed.

"David, you stop all that noise. I swear I'm going to make it."

"Detective, if I had a dollar for the times I've heard that . . . well, I could probably buy one of these limos and make real money," David said. "That's why Hollywood is here; it's all fake. We all got dreams and live in a land of smoke and mirrors."

"Pay him no mind—and this is the Pacific Ocean," Gloria said, pointing out the front window. "I remember the first time I saw it, I nearly cried, I did, nearly cried. I'd never seen anything so wonderful."

"Looks like Lake Michigan," Alfano said, "but with palm trees."

The Georgian Hotel in Santa Monica fronted Ocean Avenue; it sat high on the bluff overlooking the ocean. David took Alfano's one bag and carried it into the lobby; Gloria walked in with the detective.

"I've changed my mind," Alfano said. "It's almost three. I'm going to take a bath and get some sleep."

"You need some lunch," Gloria said.

"I'm good; I'll get room service. Is David going to take you home, or somewhere?"

"I was going to do some shopping, then take the trolley home. It's not far, maybe twenty minutes."

"Tell you what—be back here at six and I'll take you to dinner. You can tell me about Los Angeles, California, and why you left Colorado. And I'll tell you all about Chicago. That a deal?"

Gloria broke into a big smile. "That is a deal, Detective. Six o'clock, right here."

"You know a good place to eat?"

"The best seafood is about a block from here."

Alfano looked at the desk clerk, who nodded. "She's right, Mr. Alfano."

"It's a date. Six o'clock," Alfano said.

"Do you need some help with your bag?" the clerk asked.

"No. I'm good."

The clerk slid a key across the counter. "I have you for two weeks, excellent. Top floor, corner room. Just sign here." He spun a large ledger to face Alfano.

After signing, Alfano grabbed his bag and turned around. He was surprised that Gloria was already gone. And so was the driver, David.

"I hope that you enjoy your stay, Mr. Alfano. If there is anything you need, just let us know," the clerk said.

The elevator attendant was a woman, something Alfano had never seen in Chicago, at least in the hotels. He walked the hallway to his room, slipped the key into the lock, heard a slight muffled cough from behind, and then the lights went out.

10

The ringing wouldn't stop. The pain throbbed behind his ears in time with the thumping of his heart. Alfano tried to open his eyes, but a cloth covered his face. He tried to move his arms. They felt frozen, unmovable.

"Lie still. It will only hurt more," a voice said. A man's voice, strong, one that had experience giving orders.

"What . . ." Alfano started to say.

"Just lie there, you're good. Just a little more time, Detective. Try to get some sleep. That's the best thing right now."

Alfano wanted to say something, but the darkness dropped like a warm blanket.

The next time Alfano woke up, a cool, damp cloth lay over his face. "I could use a cigarette."

"All I got are Lucky Strikes," the voice answered.

"They will do."

"Feel like sitting up? Let me help."

Alfano felt two strong hands grab his shoulders and pull him forward; he felt pillows being stuffed behind him. Then the strike of a match, the smell of sulfur, the taste of a cigarette. The cloth fell away from his face; he slowly opened his eyes.

"That guy clocked you good. Damn, you went down like a sack of potatoes."

Alfano squinted at the owner of the voice. "You Gil Tuttle?"

"At your service, Detective."

"Thanks, I guess. What happened?"

"Lot of balls on that guy, knocking you down in the hallway of a hotel in the middle of the afternoon. I wonder what his game is?"

"Someone sapped me?"

"Yeah, I just got off the elevator, turned the corner, and this guy whacked you on the back of the head. You dropped like the aforementioned sack. I pulled my piece, but the guy bolted—ran to the stair door and disappeared. I dragged you into the room—could see it was just a love tap, a little cracked skin—I've had worse. I dropped you on the bed. That was an hour ago. I thought Chicago detectives had harder heads."

"I've been called stubborn, not hardheaded," Alfano said.

"I'd say you were lucky. Not sure what that guy had in mind. Once you were down, I wonder what he was thinking of doing. He wasn't a big guy, couldn't have carried you down the stairs, or used the elevator."

Alfano nodded. "Too public, too many questions."

"Right. And he didn't take anything. Maybe if I hadn't showed up, he would've stripped you down, taken your money, your bag, maybe your pistol."

"Just clothes. I travel light. My gun?"

Tuttle nodded toward the bedside table. "I pulled it from your holster. Nice piece; that Colt 1911 would blow a man's arm off."

"Chicago is a rough town." Alfano swung his legs over the edge of the bed and pushed his feet into his shoes. Then slowly felt the back of his head. Took another drag. "That why you left?"

"Boyo, I can take rough. I can take any of it. My dah was a cop. I knew what I was getting into. McDunnah and me grew up together in Bridgeport. I spent five years on the force there."

"He told me. Why did you leave?" Alfano slowly stood, holding onto the iron bedstead to steady himself.

"Look, Detective, I took on the gangs that prowled the city. I made my bones in those days before Prohibition, even took a bullet in a bar from a kid who believed he was immortal. The asshole wasn't. So, I can take it and put out even more. Even got married. That's what changed me life. I had a bunch of time saved up and used it on my honeymoon. Took the train here to California. We was married in December, just before Christmas. Fact is, we celebrated the holiday going through the Rockies, then we arrived in Los Angeles."

Tuttle finally took a breath and handed Alfano another cigarette. "You want a little stimulant? They put a nice setup for you on the dresser there."

Alfano, for the first time, looked around his room. A tray on the dresser held a couple bottles of bourbon, a carafe of water, and another with a yellow liquid.

"What's that on the right?"

"Tequila."

"Bourbon."

Alfano shot the liquor back; it helped.

"So, me and Dora arrived in Los Angeles; it was eighty wondrous degrees. When the train pulled out of Chicago, it was fucking five below zero. Both of us decided, right then and there, to move. Now, I got a nice home, two kids, a good job on a very corrupt and racist police force. And, Detective Alfano, I am your Hollywood liaison while you are here. Didn't think I'd have to be a nurse. Does this happen often, Detective Hardhead?"

"No. I'm usually better at seeing behind me." Alfano looked at the alarm clock on the side table: 5:13 PM. "I have a dinner date at six. Do you want to join me?"

"You feel up to it?"

"Might help take my mind off the lump on my head. Let me take a quick bath, put on a clean shirt, and then I'll tell you. And thanks."

"Welcome to LA, Detective."

At 6:00 PM, Alfano and Tuttle walked out of the elevator and into the lobby of the Georgian. Standing in the middle of the lobby, in a flowery dress and soft cap, was Gloria. She waved at Alfano and made a face that said, ". . . and who the hell is this?"

"Gloria, this is Detective Gil Tuttle with the Los Angeles Police Department. He is helping me while I'm here. Gil, this is Gloria . . ." Alfano stalled, trying to remember her last name.

"Gloria Downs," she said, unflustered. "Detective Alfano never knew my last name, or actually my stage name. Everybody in LA has a stage name. Don't you think so, Detective Tuttle?"

"Sometimes we call them aliases. That all depends on what or who you are trying to hide from."

"You are kind of funny and kind of cute," Gloria said. "Don't you think so, Detective Alfano?"

"I wouldn't know, Gloria. Tuttle looks like the usual Irish cop to me."

"Before I forget, Mr. Melnik will pick you up at 9:00 AM tomorrow. Here is his phone number. He said to call him when you get back to the room, anytime tonight. He will be up."

"Thanks," Alfano said, taking the slip of paper she held out. "Where's this restaurant?"

"Two blocks from here. It's on the pier. It will be loads of fun."

Alfano could tell Gloria was disappointed that Tuttle came with him. His intuition, such as it was with women, said as much. They never mentioned to Gloria what had happened in the hotel hallway. After a couple of drinks, served in teacups, he felt himself relax.

"Prohibition? What's it like here?" he asked Gloria.

"Well, my opinion as someone who has never had a legal drink, is that it is all a bunch of foolishness. My view, sitting here with two police officers illegally drinking, is that I am sorely sad to see this fine experiment in morality end. I dearly believe it has made American better. Don't you think so, Detective Alfano? Hasn't it made America better?"

"The lady is a politician," Tuttle said. "But, of course, it's all bullshit."

"Oh, Detective Tuttle, how could you say that?" Gloria said, feigning indignation.

"And an actress," Tuttle said. "Alfano, one thing you will learn here is never listen to an actor or actress. Prohibition has raised a whole new generation of criminals and led to the deaths of hundreds if not thousands of wannabe gangsters, thugs, and quick-buck artists. And that money has spread to all sorts of other dour human proclivities—gambling, drugs, and if you'll excuse me, young lady, prostitution. And look around, the Depression has knocked this place for a loop. Half the stores in Santa Monica and across LA are shut down or close to it. Crime is rising, and I think it will only get worse. In Los Angeles, the one bright spot is the picture companies. A lot of money comes through those concerns."

"And dreams are dreamt, and hearts broken," Gloria said.

"There's that, too," Tuttle said. "Here's to your dreams, Gloria." He raised his teacup.

"I'm exhausted. It's been a long two days," Alfano said as he stood. "Where's home?" he said to Tuttle.

"The Los Feliz area, if the traffic's not bad," Tuttle said. "I'm parked on Ocean. I can be home in forty-five minutes—promised Dora I would be home tonight, and it's still early. Gloria, I enjoyed the evening and the company. Alfano, here's my card if you need to get me."

"Can I have one, Detective? A girl might need a cop some-day." She winked as she smiled at Tuttle. "Detective Alfano, I'll walk you home."

At his car, they said goodbye to Tuttle and watched him drive up Ocean and turn onto a wide street that Gloria said was Santa Monica Boulevard. "He can follow that all the way across Los Angeles to within a few blocks of his house."

They crossed the street, and Gloria said goodnight to Alfano. She snuggled in close and gave him a peck on the cheek. When Alfano didn't readily respond, she said, "I guess you really are tired."

"Gloria, you are a great kid and fun to be with, and I hope we have a few more of these dates over the next few weeks. However, I am tired—exhausted, in fact. And tomorrow will be a long day."

She shrugged. "It's still early though. We could have a little fun."

"I need sleep, Gloria, not fun. I'm going to call Melnik. You go home and be a good girl."

"LA is full of good girls . . . girls who are good at a lot of things." Her smile was dazzling. "Sleep tight, don't let the bed bugs bite, Detective." She winked again.

Gloria turned, whistled loudly through her teeth, and raised her hand. A taxi pulled directly to the curb. She turned back to Alfano and smiled. "It's on my expense account."

He watched the taxi turn onto Santa Monica Boulevard and follow Tuttle's route east.

As Alfano crossed through the hotel lobby, boarded the el-evator, and walked down the hallway to his room, he did some-thing he should have done earlier: he looked over his shoulder at every turn. He made it to his room unscathed and unmo-lested, though the thought of Gloria Downs bounced around in his head. Fun, yes; trouble, also yes. Old enough to be her father, yes.

He looked at the address card for Melnik and called the number. "Thanks for the—"

"Forget that shit," Melnik broke in. "I've got a bigger problem. It has serious impacts on the production. Grab a cab, come to my house, now. I know it's late, but Jesus, we need to talk."

"Mr. Melnik, I'm beat. I haven't slept for two days. What can't wait until morning?"

"Someone sent me a photo of Kitty. She was dead, nude, on the floor—it was sickening. On the back is scribbled *YOU ARE NEXT.*"

11

Alfano gazed wistfully at the large bed. "Well, fuck," he said after he hung up the phone. He went to the dresser and poured an inch of bourbon into a glass and tossed it back. Out of habit, he pulled his Colt, ejected the round in the chamber, inspected the magazine, and pushed in the ejected bullet. He looked longingly at the bed again, sighed, put on his jacket, and left. It was 10:45 PM.

A yellow cab waited at the curb in front of the hotel; a woman sat in the driver's seat.

"How long will it take to get to 1003 North Crescent Drive, Beverly Hills?" Alfano asked, reading from the scrap of paper that had Melnik's details.

"This time of night, twenty minutes, tops," the driver said as she pitched her cigarette out the window. "Classy, high-hat neighborhood—I've made a few runs up in that part of the hills in the last month. Late-night party?"

"No," Alfano said as he pulled open the back door and slid into the seat. The driver dropped the lever on the clock and pulled away from the curb.

"Don't I know you from somewhere?" she said. "Aren't you that actor, no the director, who did that movie *Wait Until the Rain*? Just came out—great picture. You were great, the cast was great, that broad Sheila Linquest, she was great. Yeah, you're that director, name is . . ."

"No, I'm not. Mind if I smoke?"

"Sure, no problem. Yeah, you certainly are. I know it."

"I am not. In fact, I just got into LA this morning. Don't even know the movie."

"It was just premiered. I try to go to all of 'em—if I ain't driving. Saw it at Grauman's Chinese in Hollywood. Where you from? Saying you just got in?"

"Chicago."

The driver whistled. "That's a long train ride."

"I flew."

"Like in an aero-plane? Jesus Christ, really? Wouldn't get me up in one of those, no siree. By the by, my name's Ruby. If you need a tour guide or a driver, grab a card from the back of the seat. I'll take you anywhere." She craned her neck and looked back at Alfano. "I know Los Angeles like the back of my hand."

Alfano obligingly slipped a card into his jacket pocket.

"I check my service five or six times a day; you need me, just call," Ruby said. She looked again at Alfano. "Damn, you look just like that director; the name will come to me. What's your line of work—banker, attorney? You look like a serious professional; I get a lot of them. Yeah, I'll go with attorney."

Alfano leaned back and sighed. Exhaustion, the five drinks during and since dinner, and the chatter from the cabbie was about to knock him down. "I'm a cop."

"Well, damn. I'd never have guessed that," Ruby said. "Local? No, wait, you said you just got in from Chicago. Must be a big case if you came out here? Big case—like in the movies? Hey, did you see *Midnight Mary*? All crime and gangsters and cops . . . *That's it*. Damn, I knew it. You look like William Wellman, the director. Don't I have a great memory?"

"I'm not Wellman. I am not a director. And I haven't seen

Midnight Mary."

"Well, you should. Loretta Young, Ricardo Cortez—you will absolutely love it," Ruby said.

Alfano rubbed the back of his neck. "Look, I'm tired. I need a few minutes of shut-eye. Can you give me that? Wake me when we are almost there."

Looking in the rearview mirror, he could see her eyes focused on his. "Sure," she said. "It's about fifteen minutes. That enough?"

"That will do."

"What's your name?"

Alfano closed his eyes. "Tony Alfano. Detective Tony Alfano."

"A fellow wop. I knew it. Me, I'm Ruby Lombardi."

"Ruby, a few minutes?"

"Right."

Alfano leaned back against the seat and pulled his hat over his forehead. Even with his eyes closed, he was aware of the streetlights flashing by; the lights were mesmerizing. He faded in and out, half conscious of the rolling countryside passing below as the road wound upward, the mountains, the lights of towns eventually lost in the blackness of night, the drone of an airplane.

"We're almost there, Detective." Ruby's voice startled him awake. "Two blocks."

The soft light of streetlamps climbed up the road ahead of them, round bright dots that disappeared with the curve of the street. The taxi slowed; Ruby whistled softly. "Nice castle, Detective. This the place?"

Alfano looked through the iron gate that crossed the drive, which swept up the hill. A massive house, lit up like Christmas, filled the horizon. Ruby wasn't far off calling it a castle.

"There's a phone on the column over there. Maybe you have to call up to the house to open the gate?" Ruby said.

"What time is it?" Alfano asked.

"I got 11:25. Do you want me to wait? There's no cabs this time of night up in this part of Beverly Hills. Just five bucks more to sit tight."

"Wait. I'll see what's up."

Alfano climbed out of the taxi and walked to the double gate. He saw the phone and opened the panel door in the column to use it, but when he took the phone receiver in his hand, the cord fell loose and away from the box. He heard a whistle from the taxi.

"That's not a good sign, Detective," Ruby observed.

Alfano went to the closed gate and pushed. The right side swung open.

"That's not good, either," Ruby said.

"If I'm not back in ten minutes, get to a phone and call the cops. This is probably nothing, but . . ."

"I saw something like this in a movie."

"This is not a movie, Ruby."

"It's beginning to feel like one, Detective."

Alfano pushed the gate open enough to walk in, then quickly hiked up the limestone-paved drive to the front door of the mansion. Light poured out of every window; the courtyard drop-off area was lit by overhead lamps. A sleek blue Pierce-Arrow sedan was parked to one side of the turnaround. He continued up the seven marble steps to the double bronze-and-glass front door; the right-hand side was ajar about one inch. Alfano peeked through the open slot, took a step back and to one side, and pulled out his Colt. Using the toe of his shoe, he silently pushed the door open about two feet, enough to look straight into the large foyer. A small alcove sat off to the left, about ten feet ahead. He took a deep breath and slipped his way through the open doorway and quickly made his way across the checkerboard-patterned floor to the alcove. There he waited; no reaction, nothing. No sound, no radio, nothing except a methodical clicking, from the far end of the hallway, courtesy of an exceptionally tall oak grandfather clock. Working his way along the wall, Alfano slipped past the clock and into a larger room that looked out onto the backyard. The room was stuffed with gilded furniture, landscape paintings, and a massive fireplace that filled one wall. He guessed the room to be the front parlor. Beyond the French doors, the blue luminescence from the swimming pool eerily illuminated the entire deck and terrace.

Alfano made a thorough search of the ground floor and found nothing, especially no Melnik. Returning to the foyer, he regrouped. Ahead down the hallway was the kitchen, and off to one side of the hallway was a dining room that also looked out onto the pool area. He so wanted to yell out for Hines Melnik, but his detective habits muzzled him. He went to the French doors off the dining room and used his handkerchief to push down the latch. With a click, the door opened. Soft music came from a radio on the far side of the pool where an oriental tentlike structure had been erected. The fabric glowed from an incandescent light on the inside. Alfano cautiously crossed the pool deck and stopped at the tent. It sounded like someone had left a radio on somewhere just beyond the tent. Standing close to the fabric, he strained to hear the music: it was a Tommy Dorsey swing tune, and it was ending. He slowly looked around the corner of the tent; the chaise lounges near the pool were empty.

A radio voice said: "And tonight, brought live and direct to you from the Apex Club on Central Avenue, we have a special presentation of Los Angeles jazz. We are open until three o'clock, brothers and sisters. Why don't you come on down and enjoy the Avenue? It's a great night for a stroll."

Alfano clicked off the safety on his Colt, then raised the weapon and guardedly looked around the rest of the terrace. He circled the pool. Nothing. The radio began playing another

Dorsey tune.

He went back into the house and headed up the circular stairway that spiraled its way upward from the foyer. He stopped at the landing on the second floor. The hallway split and went left and right. A thick, light beige runner laid over the oak parquet flooring crossed the stairs and down hallways that headed left and right; the carpet going left was clean, the right carpet had the faint outlines of dark footprints, in two distinct sizes. They led to a room on the left, the side facing the pool; the door was open.

As he had done downstairs, Alfano walked along the thin strip of wood flooring that paralleled the runner, the footprints leading the way. He stopped at the open door to the first room. He took a chance and quickly looked in, then stepped back. What he'd seen was an office with a large desk, chairs, bright lamps, bookshelves, a far wall of windows, the blue light from the pool below, and what looked like a man's body sprawled in the middle of the room.

He entered, holding close to the doorframe. The office was cluttered; stacks of papers and books filled every tabletop and horizontal surface. There were a dozen oil paintings on the walls, and movie posters flanked the doorway he'd just come through. A baby grand piano took up one corner of the large room. On the far wall, to the right, a large door hung on its hinges. It was the door to an open and empty safe.

Alfano went to the body. The man lay on his back, his chest soaked with blood. What looked like two holes were punched through the fabric of his elegant white silk shirt. Blood covered everything; a large pool extended outward from the body and across the oak floor in all directions. It stopped where it met the edge of an oriental carpet. Alfano placed his fingers against the neck of Hines Melnik. Nothing. Then he stepped back, his gaze taking in the entire room. Three glasses sat on the top of the desk—two were empty, one contained about an inch of gold-colored liquid in the bottom. A bottle of bourbon, two-thirds empty, sat next to the glasses. A bottle of champagne sat in a silver bucket, water beads on its exterior. He crossed the room, looked in the safe, and confirmed it was indeed empty. Papers were scattered on the floor outside the safe. They looked like legal documents; one lying faceup read *Will* at the header. There were two empty watch boxes, one printed with the jewelry firm name Laykin et Cie. No money, bonds, or other negotiable paper. On his mental list of what happened, Alfano posted the first obvious thought: robbery.

His second thought was the similarity to the Kitty Hill killing: body in the center of the room, two bullets to the chest. Unlike the Hill murder, where all the doors were locked, Melnik was fully dressed and the house was as open as a church on Sunday.

Alfano decided not to use the phone on the desk. He remembered seeing a phone box hanging on the wall near the double doors in the dining room. He went back down the stairs to the terrace and removed a business card from his pocket. He dialed.

"Gil? Tony Alfano here. Sorry for the late call. I got a situation here. Is Beverly Hills in your jurisdiction?"

"No, it has its own police force," Gil Tuttle said.

"Well, I got a male body here at a house on North Crescent Avenue. Looks like gunshots to the chest, killed in the last hour."

"Do you know who he is?"

"Yeah, my meal ticket."

12

Alfano watched the lady cab driver walk up the dead man's driveway. He'd forgotten about her. She walked over to where he stood at the foot of the marble entry steps talking to Gil Tuttle.

"Do you want me to hang around? Your fare's been adding up," she said and pointed over her shoulder. "It's been almost an hour, and people are starting to gather out there."

Seeing her really for the first time in the blare of lights from the house, he was impressed. Her brunette hair was hiked up under her cabbie's hat, the starched blouse she wore was well fortified, and her dark eyes didn't look too bad over the small nose and newly lacquered lips.

"Jesus, you're still here," he said belatedly.

"Detective, you said to wait, I waited. Now there seems to be a party, and you didn't invite me. Nonetheless, I still need my fare paid and you did promise me a five spot."

Alfano nodded but made no move to reach for his wallet. His mind was still on Melnik and the bloody scene inside the mansion.

"What the hell happened?" the cabbie continued. "The whole Beverly Hills police force is out there, and nobody is saying nothing. One flatfoot questioned me about why I was sitting out front waiting. I told them I was waiting for a cop. They said it wasn't funny. Then you came out, and they let me come up to see if you're ready to go."

"Gil, this is my driver, Miss Ruby . . . ?"

"Lombardi," she reminded him.

"Lombardi," Alfano repeated. He usually would have remembered. "She was my ride here," he said unnecessarily to Tuttle.

"And the detective still owes me my fare—and five clams. Don't you, honey?"

Two men in suits walked out the front door and down the steps to Alfano and Tuttle. The first was medium height, slicked-back black hair, smart suit, polished shoes. He sported a thin mustache that accented his dark complexion. A gold shield hung on the pocket of his vest. Alfano's first thought a half hour earlier had been that this guy would have made a good movie cop. To keep the universe in balance, the second guy was the direct opposite. Short, creased face; everything about the guy, including his suit with mismatched pants, was scuffed. His shoes were well worn and dull. A cigarette hung limply from his lips.

"Alfano, who's this?" the first detective asked.

"Detective Tuttle, Los Angeles Police," Alfano answered. "He's the guy who called you."

Detective Dominic Suarez was the lead detective with the Beverly Hills Police. His scruffy backup was veteran Buddy Loomis. Alfano was waiting for them at the top step of the marble steps when they arrived. He introduced himself and told them why he was there.

"Glad to see you two have met," Tuttle said.

"Who's this?" Suarez asked, looking at Lombardi.

"I'm the one who is wondering if he's gonna pay me," Ruby said.

"Beat it, sister," Loomis said.

"I leave when I'm paid, buddy."

"How'd you know my name?"

"What name?"

"Buddy."

"Your name is Buddy? Damn weird," Ruby said.

"That's enough, Loomis," Suarez said. He looked at Lombardi. "Why don't you wait out by your cab? I might have a few questions for you."

"Ruby, hang in here for a few more minutes," Alfano said. "I'll make it worth your wait."

"Yeah, right. I've heard that before."

"Please wait. I'll be there shortly," Alfano said. As Ruby walked back down the drive, Alfano turned to Suarez.

"A little out of your jurisdiction, ain'tcha, Alfano?" Loomis said. He crushed his cigarette on the driveway.

Alfano looked at the scuffed-out butt and shook his head.

"Cool it, Buddy. And welcome to Los Angeles, Detective," Suarez said, getting around to niceties. "The first patrolman on the scene said you found the body. That true?"

"Yes."

"Why didn't you call Beverly Hills Police?"

"Detective, I haven't a clue where the hell I am right now. Gil Tuttle here was and is the only person I know in this whole fucking town. I called him; he called you guys. I hung around. Professional courtesy, you might say."

"That a crack?" Loomis said.

"Really, Buddy? Cool it. I understand where he's coming from," Suarez said. "Why were you here?"

"The dead guy, Hines Melnik, invited me out here to Los Angeles as a technical advisor for his next movie, a cop picture. I flew in today. Tonight, after dinner, I called Melnik from my hotel, the Georgian in Santa Monica. That was ten thirty-five. I was told by the woman who picked me up at the airport that Melnik was going to meet me at the hotel at nine tomorrow morning."

"Her name?" Loomis said, making notes in a notebook.

"Gloria Downs."

"Then why the call?"

"I was told to call him to confirm the pickup. Melnik told me that someone was trying to blackmail him. He was upset and wanted me to come over to his house tonight."

"This was when?" Suarez asked.

"As I said, ten thirty-five. I caught a taxi out front of the hotel about ten minutes later. The doorman there will confirm that. And Ruby, down there in the yellow taxi, will give you the same story. I came here. It was eleven twenty-five when I went through the gate."

"How do you know what time it was?" Loomis said, scribbling.

"I asked Ruby . . . Detective Loomis," Alfano said.

For the next few minutes, Alfano went through the entire process of entering the house and then finding the body. The one small detail he left out, for now, was the comment that Melnik made about a photograph, the photo of Kitty Hill. A photo that he didn't find.

"Then I came outside to wait for you guys. The first cops arrived about twenty minutes after I hung up with Detective Tuttle."

"It took twenty minutes for your guys to get here?" Tuttle said to Suarez. "Good God, I hope I don't get mugged in this town."

"It was late. It's Thursday, slow," Suarez said. "There were only four patrolmen out, and they were down on Wilshire, a problem at a bar—drunks. How long are you in town, Detective?"

"With Mr. Melnik's unfortunate death, I'll probably head back to Chicago in a day or two. No reason for me to stay here."

A uniformed patrolman came out the front door and walked down to the foursome.

"Yes, Smith. What do you need?" Suarez said.

"We found something you might want to see."

"And what's that?" Loomis said.

"You have to see this for yourself, Detective."

"Lead on."

"May I tag along?" Alfano asked.

"Sure, what the hell? After all, it's your party," Suarez answered.

They followed the patrolman up to the front door, then stopped and backed away as two men in white coats carried a stretcher with Melnik's body through the door. Another older man followed; when they cleared the door, the older man took Detective Suarez off to one side. They talked for a moment, and then Suarez returned to where Alfano, Tuttle, and Loomis waited.

"The coroner will perform the autopsy in the morning," Suarez said. "We will know more then. Preliminary report is lead poisoning."

"Bada boom," Alfano said unsmilingly.

They followed the patrolman back into the house and proceeded through its labyrinthian hallways to the far back. A door at the end of the hall stood open. Another patrolman stood outside the door.

They could smell the room as they gathered together just inside. Alfano had lost count of the bordellos he'd been in during his career. Some had been nothing more than stink holes made all the worse by unwashed sheets, beds, and the collective sweat of johns and hookers. Others were high-class, even elegant. The smells of lilacs and sex mingled together. This room said lilacs, sex, and film production. A large bed with satin sheets and fluffed pillows was against one wall. Nice pictures hung on the walls, and the furniture was contemporary. What took the romance out of the scene were the two movie cameras on tripod stands, both on wheels. Lights hung from the ceiling on brackets, others were mounted on stands. Folding chairs were set up behind the cameras, and electrical cords snaked across the floor. On a bench were two handheld cameras; boxes of film were stacked on shelves. On the far side, beyond the cameras on their tripods, was a dressing area with a cloth curtain.

"Well, I'll be damned," Suarez said. "This is a first."

"For Beverly Hills, maybe," Tuttle said. "We've rousted a bunch of these over the last three years, mostly in the Valley. One of the seedier sides of the movie business."

"Valley?" Alfano said.

"The San Fernando Valley, over the mountain behind us. There are moving picture firms there as well, and pornography seems to just fit in nicely. Right now, there's a never-ending supply of girls, guys, and experienced cameramen. Stag films are big moneymakers. They pay well if you're an unemployed actor."

"We pick up a few cans of film during raids in Chicago," Alfano said. "But they go out the door as fast as they come in. The market is never satisfied."

"This one looks to be high-class," Suarez said, giving voice to Alfano's earlier thoughts.

"Better than most," Tuttle said. "Some are just downright disgusting. Is this the reason Melnik might have been killed?"

"It does throw a twist into the killing," Suarez said.

"It certainly does," Alfano said.

13

The phone on the bedside table rang three times before Alfano pulled the receiver off the cradle.

"Who the hell is this?" Alfano mumbled.

"It's me, Gloria. I'm downstairs, and you are late. Not really, except that Mr. Melnik changed the time to seven. He said he would tell you that when he talked to you. I'm sorry, but David is waiting. We need to go."

"What time is it?"

"Five till."

The fog was clearing from Alfano's head. "Melnik said for you to pick me up?"

"Yes, he changed it last night. We need to get going. I can't be late."

"I'll be down in fifteen minutes," Alfano said. He dropped the receiver back onto the phone, slowly extracted himself from between the sheets, and wandered into the bathroom. After the usual morning rituals, he dressed, slipped his pistol into its holster, and took the elevator. He walked into the lobby at 7:20 AM. The one thing that nagged him was the way Gloria was acting. Obviously, she did not know about her boss's untimely demise.

"Good morning, Detective. The car is out front," Gloria

said, a bit too chipper for Alfano this early.

"I am going into the restaurant to have breakfast and coffee, then we can go."

"That is impossible—we are already late. Mr. Melnik insisted that you be there well before eight. We can just make it. There will be food there."

Alfano took a deep breath, then turned and headed into the restaurant.

"Detective, please, I need this job."

Alfano raised his hand and waggled a finger in a follow-me motion. He took a seat in the nearly empty restaurant that overlooked Ocean Boulevard. The morning marine haze obscured any view of the Pacific Ocean. Beyond the edge of the cliff that overhung the beach, the rooftops of the buildings on the pier were just visible.

"For Christ's sake, Detective, help me out here, please," Gloria said as she followed him to the table.

He pointed to the chair opposite his. "Sit." He looked at the waitress walking toward their table. "Coffee, please—two."

Gloria looked around as if hoping to find something that would make Alfano understand her predicament.

"Sit," Alfano repeated.

She sat.

Alfano looked her over. She was dressed in a loose-fitting cotton dress, a string of large faux pearls, her hair was neat and nicely cut, and she wore a comfortable-looking summer hat. For a girl who lived hand to mouth, she looked very good. Two different outfits in two days? Yes, she spent her money wisely, he thought, and she cared for herself.

"Detective Alfano, I understand, I really do, but they usually have a spread of food at the studio, even eggs sometimes. You could eat there, and I will have done my job and kept my job."

"And your job is exactly what?" Alfano asked as he watched

his coffee cup being filled.

"To get you to the studio on time. If I'm there, I have a better chance to get picked for a cast role or even a walk-on part. In this town, it's all about opportunity and being in the right place at the right time. I believe I have Mr. Melnik's eye and trust. Maybe I can make something of this."

The waitress came to stand next to the table, a small pad in her hand.

"Simple. I'll have bacon and eggs, over hard. And wheat toast. Gloria?"

"Detective, please."

"She will have the same thing. Thanks."

The waitress walked away.

Alfano looked directly at Gloria. "What did you do after you left me last night?"

Gloria's back stiffened. "I caught that cab and went directly home."

"What time did you get home?"

Gloria thought for about ten seconds. "I walked into my apartment building around nine thirty. You didn't want me to hang around . . . if you remember. I called Mr. Melnik from the hallway phone as soon as I got home. He asked about you. I told him you'd call. That's when he told me to pick you up earlier, so I called David and told him the new time. Didn't Mr. Melnik tell you all that?"

"Did Melnick seem anxious, concerned?"

"About what? But yes, he wasn't his usual talkative self."

"Did you talk to anyone else about what you did yesterday?" Alfano asked.

"No, I went to my apartment, opened a bottle of wine, and took a bath."

Alfano smiled.

She read the thought on his face and scowled. "You had your chance last night, Detective. After the wine, I crawled into bed and read for a while. I turned out the light about mid-night."

"You didn't get any phone calls? Can anyone verify that you were at the apartment?"

"Of course not. I told you I don't have a phone in my apartment. Not having a phone is cheaper. I use the one in the hallway. And I saw none of the other tenants. Why the third degree?"

The waitress dropped the plates of bacon and eggs in front of Gloria and Alfano. The toast arrived a minute later.

"Really, Detective, what's going on? I'm getting a little spooked."

Alfano took a sip of his coffee. It was strong, tasted good. "Last night, Mr. Melnik was murdered."

Alfano watched as the news sank in. He had dropped this bomb many times over the years. He looked for the reactions, trying to see behind the eyes of a loved one, a suspect, even the killer. The real killer often just stared, most probably reliving the moment, the act; for some, the pleasure of it. Others screamed, especially the women. Some denied it, declared it wasn't true. Some wanted the particulars: when, how, did he have a suspect? In Gloria's case, he watched her face turn ashen white, her eyes glaze over, and then she fainted face-first into her bacon and eggs.

As the waitress helped Gloria to the ladies' room to recover from the egg on her face, Alfano talked with David, the driver, who had come looking to see what was taking so long. Alfano told him what had happened and asked him a few of the same questions. David, who lived with two roommates in West Hollywood, said that he'd spent the evening prior at his apartment and his roommates helped him wash the limo. All were hopeful actors. One even had an extra spot in *King Kong*.

"Who told you to pick up Gloria so early before coming here?" Alfano asked.

"She did," David said. "She called last night around ten thirty. I said sure, then hung up. So, you're telling me that little round shit is dead? Wow! I expected him to drop dead from a heart attack long before somebody knocked him off. How'd he die?"

"I don't know," Alfano lied. "I heard it through a friend on the police force. You know, it's all hush-hush."

"Does it have anything to do with the death of Miss Hill?" David asked. "When I heard she was killed, I was shocked, she being a nice person and all. Things have been in an uproar since Mr. Melnick and the others returned from their tour. Go, go, go, tight schedules and all. That's why Gloria was in such a rush."

"Who told you about Kitty Hill?"

"It was Adam. He told me—when I drove him home from the studio on Tuesday—that he saw her dead, all laid out at the coroner's. Were you the detective he was talking about?"

"Maybe," Alfano said.

"Well, it really hit him hard. He was close to Kitty, and I think she liked him."

"Did she have a lot of friends?"

"Yeah, I think so. I drove her a couple of times to parties in the Valley and up in the hills. Actors' and actresses' places, fancy parties. I was never asked to stay. I would just drop her off and come back three or four hours later. She was great, always gave me something extra. She said once, 'Been there, kid, I understand.' You can ask Gloria about her. When Gloria came to LA, she stayed a few weeks with Kitty before she got her own place. They were friends."

"Thanks. Where did Kitty live?"

"A small courtyard apartment off Wilshire in Beverly Hills."

Gloria rejoined them at the table. She looked only slightly worse for wear.

"Sorry about that," she said to Alfano. "It was a shock to hear that Mr. Melnik was dead, murdered. I'm still shaking. Do the police know who did it?"

"I really don't know," Alfano said. "I only just learned of it myself. So, are we going to the studio?"

"Really, you want to go after what happened? Why?" Gloria said.

"I need to see what it's like to make a movie."

"I don't know, Detective," Gloria said. "The whole studio might shut down. Without Mr. Melnik, I just don't know."

"Gloria, they have J.J. running the show now that Kitty's not here," David said. "He's a son of a bitch, but there's too much money already in this thing. If anyone will keep this going, it's Jorge Jones."

"And he's what, exactly?"

"The producer, the man behind everything. Some would say he was number one on the movie behind Mr. Melnik. Before J.J., that was Kitty's job. Melnik picked him up from RKO. My guess, he offered him big bucks or a piece. You know the old saying: the show must go on. J.J. probably invented the term."

14

Alfano was surprised at how close the picture studio was to his hotel. The street traffic was light on Santa Monica Boulevard; in less than ten minutes, David piloted the limo into the studio driveway. A high sign arched over the entry read *Sierra Films Productions.* From the back seat, Alfano looked through the windshield at the sprawl of large warehouse buildings beyond the sign. A man in uniform stood at the gate and waved them in.

"Good morning, Joe," David said through the open car window.

"Nothing good about it at all. It's a circus." Joe pointed to the driveway that split the alignment of buildings. "There's police everywhere. I don't know what's happening—they never tell me anything."

David nodded in understanding but didn't offer an explanation.

"Park at the first open stall," Joe said.

David did as directed and pulled the limousine into the first open space. Across the driveway, a low, long building hugged the side of a much taller warehouse structure. Windows lined the front of the lower building. Hanging over the only door, a sign with neat lettering read *Office, Sierra Films.* Three patrolmen stood outside; each wore a different uniform.

Wonderful—cross-jurisdictional issues, Alfano thought as he and his companions exited the car. To his surprise, Detective Gil Tuttle walked out of the office; behind him was the Beverly Hills detective, Dominic Suarez.

"Why are you here?" Alfano said to Tuttle. "We are still a long way from LA."

"That's my exact question for you," Tuttle answered. "So, you first."

"I'm here because this is where I was supposed to be," Alfano answered. "I was to start my work with Melnik this morning. I have a few days to kill, so to speak, and I thought I'd a least do what I was being paid to do—hang around and watch a movie being made. You?"

"It appears that Sierra Films studio is in Los Angeles," Tuttle said. "I'm now working with Detective Suarez on this case. That came down from city hall."

"He has a lot more resources than we do," Suarez said.

"You told the crew?" Alfano said.

"Yes, it hasn't hit the newspapers, yet, but it will," Tuttle said. "Probably this afternoon. A reporter was sniffing around soon after you left last night. A high-profile murder like this will have every nose stuck to the front page. The mayor wants us ahead of this."

"Great, and I thought only Chicago had these problems."

"Yeah, so did I, until I got here," Tuttle said. "We should be getting the preliminary autopsy report from Suarez's guy by the end of the day."

"I'm going with massive gunshot wounds to the chest," Alfano offered.

Gloria gave a little squeak of a scream. David paled through his tan.

"Probably; we need to confirm. It's getting hot. Let's go back inside. September and October are scorchers, Tony."

"Good to know. I'm beginning to think of buying a train ticket home."

A short angular man with a Latino complexion and thin black mustache burst out of the office door. He wore an open white shirt and a gaudy checkered sports jacket, a buff-colored straw boater set back on his head. A large gold chain wrapped his neck, and he carried a riding crop. Alfano was sincerely bemused.

"I need to get production going or lose the whole day," Mr. Gold Chain stormed. He pointed to Gloria and David. "You two get off the lot. I'll call you if I want you." The man then turned to Tuttle and pointed at Alfano. "Who the hell is he? Another cop? He looks like one." The guy was in constant motion, hands waving, cigarette ash flying.

"I'll tell you when you can start, Jones. I might have a few more questions," Tuttle said. "This is Chicago detective Tony Alfano. He's the guy Melnik wanted on-set to help coach Roberts. Isn't that right, Tony?"

"Yes, Gil, that's the story."

"Well, shit. You finally arrived and blessed us with your fucking presence. You were supposed to be here at seven. It's now fucking nine. Jesus Christ, the whole fucking day's schedule is shot."

"Tony, this overexcited and insensitive piece of Mexican is Jorge Jones, the executive producer of *State Street Killers*," Detective Suarez said. "His few friends call him J.J. He's taken over for the unfortunate Mr. Hines Melnik. It seems that the time to mourn has either been put on hold or is over. Not sure which."

"We'll mourn the poor bastard after we get this picture in the can," Jones said. "If anyone would understand, it would be Hines. Why are you standing here, Alfano? I need you inside. Seems Roberts can't find his prick with both hands in his pants. See Laurie K., first office left side. She'll give you a script. Read it and let me know what you think—first twenty pages will do. I want your comments and answers in two hours. Then find Roberts and kick him in the ass. And go find Vlad. He's the director; introduce yourself."

Gloria, still standing there watching the show, leaned in and said, "That's Vladimir Nabinsky, just off the boat from Yugoslavia or some such place. We call him Vlad the Impaler. This is his second film in a month."

"Jones, I'm leaving tomorrow," Alfano said. "I'm taking the train home. I can't stand all this good weather and sunshine. The excitement is killing me."

"Like hell you are," Jones said. "I read the agreement Melnik made with your boss, the mayor. I got you for two weeks, then you can go home to mommy. If you quit, you can pay for all your own expenses; in fact, I'll sue you and Chicago if you jump on me." With that, Jones snapped the crop on his palm, spun around, and walked back through the open office door.

"He always like that?" Alfano asked.

"That was him being a pussycat," Gloria said. "When he really gets going, you look for a door. It's the stuff of legends; they say the gorilla in *King Kong* was afraid of him."

Alfano said nothing.

"David, can you drop me off?" Gloria asked.

"Absolutely. Will you need a ride back to your hotel later, Detective Alfano?" David asked. "I can come back."

"What would be the best time?" Alfano said.

"I'll be outside the gate parked at the curb at six. J.J. should be through with you by then. Meet me there."

"Tony, I could give you a ride," Tuttle said, "but I'm not sure where I'll be at six. Take his offer."

Alfano nodded his assent.

"You be careful with those guys in there," Tuttle added. "There's a lot of strange things going on. Don't forget their idea of reality is a lot different than yours—and last night was round one. This will get a lot dirtier before it's over."

For the rest of the day, Alfano bounced back and forth from the studio office, where he read lines from the script, to sorties onto the set to review furniture placement, jargon, and police procedures. He quickly learned it was more about noise than substance. Roberts and Durant, who showed up on-set well after the local detectives left, were pleasant enough but didn't volunteer anything about their whereabouts Thursday night. Their remarks were vague.

Later, Alfano and the two actors sat to one side of the set as the crew moved furniture for the next scene.

"Where were you two last night?" Alfano finally asked.

"Detective Suarez came to my apartment early this morning. I told him everything I knew," Durant said. "He told me not to talk with anyone. If I remember anything, I am supposed to contact him." She held up a business card.

"I talked to him here. Last night I was home with a friend," Roberts said. "How did you enjoy the flight? We hit some turbulence over Arizona. Max got sick." He smiled.

"So did you, asshole." Durant lit a cigarette and blew a cloud into the air.

"The flight was way too long, Adam. The train's more comfortable," Alfano said.

"And the Georgian Hotel is good? I've heard it's nice," Roberts said.

"Yeah, for the few hours I've seen it, it's okay. Last night was a long night."

"You were there, at Melnik's house?" Durant asked.

"Yes," Alfano said, looking directly at her. She met his eyes briefly before looking away.

"Did they find anything else in the house?" Durant asked as she knocked the ash off her cigarette.

"A very dead body, a strange crime scene, the place lit up

like Christmas," Alfano said. "Mum's the word, as we say in the detective business."

"We are the embodiment of discretion," Roberts said.

"You haven't been discreet since you fell off that hay truck from Fresno," Durant said. "Detective, I was asking about a rumor I heard, and mind you it is just a rumor, even though vicious and cruel. Now that Melnik's dead, it can't really hurt him."

"Vicious and cruel? And what rumor is that, Miss Durant?" Alfano answered.

She leaned in. "The rumor is that Hines was into all sorts of kinky stuff, girls, guys, films. The rumor was that they would go to his house—"

"I hate to break this up, but the next scene is ready. J.J. needs the both of you."

The man interrupting Durant was narrow—thin was too good a word; he was narrow like a board edgewise. He had a mop of unruly long black hair, thin wiry arms under a black silk shirt, his slacks hung like they covered two black sticks, and his shoes were two-toned, black and white. His accent was so thick, Alfano wanted him to repeat everything again, slowly, then write it down.

"It's the bedroom scene. Miss Durant, change into the negligee. Adam, you're good. Alfano, I want you to watch this closely and tell me if it seems right."

"And what would I know about a bedroom scene, Mr. Nabinsky?" Alfano added. "We Americans do it the same as in Europe."

Nabinsky stared at Alfano as the remark was slowly disassembled and reassembled in the man's narrow mind. "Oh, yes, of course. It's that I want Roberts, in the roll of Detective Matt Long, to be . . . more detective-like, not her lover."

Alfano reconstructed the garbled words. "Mr. Nabinsky, we detectives, lovers or not, do it the same as normal humans."

Durant sniggered. "Oh, that's not what I've heard. I demand proof."

"Just shut up, Maxime. Go change. I'll meet you on the set." Roberts got up from his chair, set his fedora, and walked to the opposite side of the warehouse where the bedroom scene had been set up.

"He's a little moody," Alfano said to Durant.

"Hines's death hit him hard. They did a lot of films together. And the old sot made him rich. My guess, he's wondering what's going to happen to him now that the rabbi is dead."

"And you, I understand that you did a lot of work with Melnik, too."

"True, I did," Durant said as she stood and started to unbutton the top of her shirt. "And you never answered my question."

"And that question was?"

"Did you find Hines's little porn studio where dark and steamy deeds were filmed? I understand he was one of the best. His . . . endeavors . . . were a constant and growing source of income for him and a few others." By the end of the question and the comment, she'd reached the fourth button. Alfano was becoming impressed; she wore nothing under the shirt.

"Best what?"

"Silly boy, use your imagination." She turned and walked away toward her dressing room. When she reached the door, the shirt slid off her shoulders.

15

The Saturday noise from Sunset Boulevard was muffled by the jewelry store's air-conditioning unit humming through the vents. Alfano stood at the glass counter at Laykin et Cie; for a hot afternoon, the showroom was surprisingly cool. Outside, the limousine sat at the curb; David leaned against the car smoking a cigarette. The man behind the counter stared intently at the gold watch in his hand, a jeweler's loop held to his right eye. He methodically rotated the instrument as he examined the watch.

"Of course, Detective, I know this watch well. It is a fine design, don't you think? The Swiss can do magical things, especially Cartier. We are the only jewelers on the West Coast to carry this particular model. Many of our customers are movie folks. Innovative and elegant, this is a Swiss delight."

"Do you know who the owner of this specific watch is, Mr. Laykin?" Alfano said, tapping his fingers on the countertop.

"Well, as I told your sergeant last week on the phone, I cannot give out such information. We need to keep these things private. So many of our items are given as gifts, gifts that are not necessarily—"

"Look, I get it, privacy, special interests, possible personal embarrassment. Right now, I need a name. As my sergeant also said, that watch is an important piece of evidence in a murder, do you understand? I know who probably owns it; I just need confirmation."

"As I said, Detective—"

"Let me ask you a question, Mr. Laykin," Tuttle said. He was standing two steps behind Alfano. The detective badge secured to his vest flashed under the store's lights. "How would you like some police security? I can have a squad car park right out front all day. Do you think that would help your customers feel safer? How would you like that?"

Laykin quickly considered his options. "Let me check my records," he said weakly.

"You as much said you know who the owner is," Alfano said.

"I want to be absolutely sure, Detective. This is a sensitive matter."

"Why sensitive?"

"Please give me a minute, then you decide."

The jeweler walked behind a low partition in the back of the store. It was situated so that someone sitting could see the entry, but the desk surface was hidden from view of anyone in the outer room. Laykin took a key from his pocket and unlocked the top right-hand drawer; he then removed a thick ledger and brought it to the counter. He paged through the handwritten entries, then stopped and ran his finger down one of the columns.

"Yes, here it is. It was purchased last December, two weeks before Christmas. A Mr. Wells Barker paid cash for the watch."

"Wells Barker? That's the name?" Alfano said.

"Yes, Wells Barker. He also had it engraved with the logo and date. We have added this logo to other items as well as a silver presentation cup last year."

"I know the logo is from the Will Rogers Polo Club," Alfano said, not hiding his impatience.

You were expecting another name, Detective?"

"Frankly, yes."

"And that name was?" Laykin asked.

"Not important. Do you have an address for Mr. Barker?"

"Of course." Laykin looked at Tuttle, who coughed. "However, I do not believe that Mr. Barker was the final recipient of the watch," the jeweler said.

"How so?" Alfano asked.

"When Mr. Barker returned to pick up the watch, he was not alone. The actor Adam Roberts was with him. He is well known, you know. Mr. Barker made a big scene of securing the watch to Mr. Roberts's wrist. It was quite touching. Then they left together."

Alfano put his hand out to take the watch.

"If you don't mind, Detective," Laykin said. "Let me place this in a felt pouch. I wouldn't want it scratched. Just give me a minute."

As the store owner walked away, Tuttle leaned in. "That make sense?"

"Yeah, to a point. I don't know who Wells Barker is, but he knows Roberts and I'll hazard a guess they got something going on between them."

"There's a lot of that going on north of Wilshire Boulevard," Tuttle said.

Alfano sighed. He felt peckish. First the early morning call, the overbearing movie director, and now this unexpected turn with the watch. "Is there someplace good to eat near here?" he asked Tuttle.

"The Chateau Marmont hotel is five minutes away. Food's okay, the bar is great," Tuttle said.

Shortly, they pulled to the curb near the hotel. David said, "I'll wait here."

"No, join us," Alfano said.

After Tuttle showed his badge to the waif of a girl at the

reception desk, they were herded through the crowded bar to a corner table. The windows were open, the heat drifted in and out, the view was up and down Sunset Boulevard.

"Three bourbons, Canadian Club if you got it," Tuttle said.

"Sir, liquor is still restricted," the young woman said.

"Look in the back, let me know what you find," Tuttle added, then opened his jacket; his badge flashed in the sunlight.

Two minutes later, the waitress returned with a bottle and glasses.

"It's nice to know the local customs," Alfano said.

"To crime—it never pays," Tuttle said, lifting his glass.

Alfano looked at a confused David Baine. "Yeah, cops breaking the law. Go figure," he said.

"No," David said. "It's not that. I'm interested in what we were doing at the jewelry store. Did it have something to do with Mr. Melnik's murder?"

"No. It has to do with a crime I'm working on in Chicago. A woman was killed, Kitty Hill. You knew her, didn't you?"

David paused for a moment and took a sip. "Sure did. She was nice, always treated me swell. Even got me a few acting gigs, nothing special but enough to put a page in my resume. I was knocked flat when I heard she was dead—murdered was the rumor."

"It wasn't a rumor," Alfano said. "Two slugs to the chest, just like Melnik. Now I'm wondering if these two murders may be connected. Detective Tuttle is handling Mr. Melnik's killing. I'm trying to piece together Kitty Hill's."

"Too strange, if you ask me. I liked them both. This town's full of weird people, even to the point of being bizarre. Maybe it's the money, but I think it's a magnet for the just plain peculiar. People who can't cut it where they grew up, loners, misfits, even deviants. Many find a place here that tolerates their behavior and proclivities. And, like magnets, they stick to each other."

"Ain't that the truth," Tuttle added. "When I left Chicago, me and the wife believed we left all that crap behind us. Not a chance. It was here in piles, and I've been shoveling it since. Job security, I guess."

Alfano clicked Tuttle's glass.

"May I ask then what you were doing at the jeweler's?" David asked them. "It's one of the high-end stores. They cater to a lot of movie stars, celebrities, even politicians."

"A watch was found at the Hill murder scene," Alfano said. "The watch was purchased at that shop last Christmas."

"May I see it?" David asked.

Alfano looked at Tuttle, who shrugged. He took the stiff black felt pouch from his coat pocket and removed the Cartier watch. He laid it on the felt bag.

"Very nice. May I?" David said.

"Sure, kid," Alfano said.

David picked up the watch and turned it over, then clicked the timepiece, which flipped the face. He looked at the inscription, then clicked it back. "I know someone who has a watch like this."

"Who is that?" Alfano asked.

"Adam Roberts. He wears it on his right wrist. He is left-handed. He is quite proud of it; it was a gift."

"From who? Do you know?"

David slipped the watch on his own wrist for a moment. "Nice, but too expensive for me. I'd be afraid of losing it. Roberts's boyfriend gave it to him. His name is Wells Barker."

"So, Roberts really is a fag?" Tuttle said. "Really? Damn, the wife's going to be very disappointed. Can't wait to tell her."

"Not exactly," David said. "As they say around here, Roberts drives on both sides of the road, and fast, and where he parks at night varies."

"I get it—weird analogy," Alfano said.

"The city of Los Angeles is an analogy," David added.

After lunch, they walked back to the limo.

"All this is new along here, Tony," Tuttle said. He pointed up and down the street and at a couple of the taller buildings. "Ten years ago, this was nothing. "Just a dirt and sand road that went to the beach. That's why it was called Sunset Boulevard. For the last ten years, people up there in the Hollywood hills have been building houses on the sides of the cliffs and infill-ing the canyons. You can't see it from here, but there's a huge sign—me, I call it an eyesore—that reads in white letters and is lit up at night: HOLLYWOODLAND. All to sell lots. Soon all this will be packed in. And this boulevard is becoming a real problem for us—gambling joints, speaks, hookers, even dope fiends. Like me, the gangsters from Chicago like the weather here. They run a few of these operations."

"You really thought California was going to be different?" Alfano said as they climbed into the car.

"One can wish," Tuttle said. "David, drop me at the Bev-erly Hills city hall. I parked there."

"Yes, sir. Detective Alfano?"

"Do you know where the Will Rogers Polo Club is?" Al-fano asked.

"Yes, sir. I do."

16

After they left the Beverly Hills Police parking lot, David drove up into the hills above Santa Monica and pulled the limousine to a stop in front of the Will Rogers Polo Club. An attendant seeing the limo jogged to the rear door and opened it for Alfano. When the attendant did not recognize him, Alfano was asked, "May I help you, sir?"

"Kid, just here to look around," Alfano said. He held up his star to the attendant. "David, stay with the car. I'll be right back."

The pungent aroma of horses, manure, and freshly cut grass hung in the warm air. Beyond the building, the steady pounding of horse hooves on sod filled the canyon. They had passed the polo field as they drove up to what they thought was the clubhouse. A dozen men dressed in white attire galloped back and forth on horseback.

Alfano headed to the doors of the strangely shaped building where a weathered man, about fifty years old, stood just inside the wide opening. He was shorter than Alfano—a greyish mop of hair hung down his forehead. The face and the man were the most famous in America, and probably in the world.

"I can spot the law from a country mile, even if they arrive in a limousine. May I help you, sir?" Will Rogers said.

"Maybe you can, Mr. Rogers. I'm Tony Alfano, a detective with the Chicago Police Department. I'm investigating a murder. May I ask a few questions?"

"I haven't been in Chicago since June or July—had a polo tournament there. We took home the trophy. So, if this killing was during the last week or so, I got an alibi." He laughed. "Anyway, it's a pleasure to meet you, Detective. That driver of yours, he okay out there in the heat? Have him come in and sit."

Alfano waved to David. "Come into the shade while I talk with Mr. Rogers."

"Call me Will, everybody does." The famous cowboy introduced himself to David.

They walked into what Alfano thought was the Polo Club, which turned out to be a large barn; off to each side of the round central hub were stables and paddocks. A groom was leading two horses into the stable from the large pasture opposite the drive.

"I can see you're surprised; most are when they come up here. The horses are the most important part of this here rodeo. All the rest of the fall-de-ra we set up during the matches we do down at the house. We are country laid-back, you might say. What was it you wanted to ask me about?"

"Do you know Adam Roberts? He's an—"

"Actor, sure do. He's connected to Sierra Pictures. They asked me to work with them on a western. I said no, I have other contracts and obligations. This isn't about the Hines Melnik murder, is it—the one in the afternoon paper? Now, that was a shock, I'll tell you that."

"Tangentially," Alfano said as he stepped over a pile of horse shit. "I'm working a Chicago killing connected to Melnik, but it was a couple of weeks back, a woman. She was his executive producer."

"And you came out here to follow it up?"

"Not exactly. I'm here as an expert on police procedures, Chicago procedures. I'm supposed to be helping with a film."

Rogers threw back his head and laughed. "Nice ride, all the fun and no responsibility. My guess, you're like a prize stallion. They just want to show you off, but you don't get the privileges. What about Roberts?"

"A watch was found at the scene; it's been identified as his. It's inscribed with the logo of your club. I'm just checking."

"May I see it?"

Alfano took out the pouch and handed the watch to Rogers, who carefully looked it over.

"Pretty thing, seen a few like this in Europe. They flick the face over so it don't get broke when you play. I never coddle to such finery; a good pocket watch works just fine. Besides, who needs to know the time during a match? The logo, I don't have control over that. Anybody can scratch that image on anything. It's nice to know that Roberts likes it enough to put it on his watch."

"Is he a member?"

"Yeah. He can ride well, too. If I remember, he's from Fresno, a farm or ranch, not sure. But he can ride. He's a three-goal player, average but durable, even tough. Seen him a take a fall or two; as I said, tough. He is a hit with the girls, tell you that. They love a man on a horse. I know that for a fact. Hope that helps, Detective. I've got to get down to the house to see a man about a horse."

"Yes, thanks, anything helps."

Another groom, leading a saddled horse, came out of the stables. He stopped near Rogers. Alfano watched Rogers mount so easily that one second he was standing, the next he was on the horse and waving goodbye.

David walked over to Alfano, stopped, and began scraping something from his polished right shoe.

"So, that's Will Rogers. I thought he would be bigger," David said.

"Interesting guy. Big things often come in small packages."

Alfano asked if David knew where Kitty Hill lived.

"Yes, sir. The apartment is about ten minutes from here, just off Wilshire Boulevard. Small and comfortable. She didn't like the pretense of a big Beverly Hills house. She lived alone, so I don't think anybody is there to open it up."

"I've got her key, or at least what I think is her key."

"How did you get that?" David said, then paused. "Of course, I get it."

They went back down to Sunset, then east to Kenter Avenue to San Vincente Boulevard, to Bundy Drive to Wilshire. Hill's apartment was three houses south of Wilshire Boulevard on Brockton. David pulled to the curb in front of the one-story apartment complex.

"Plain, I'll say that," Alfano said.

"Kitty's apartment is in the back. There's parking off the alley."

"How many units?" Alfano said as he got out of the car.

"Maybe six or eight. I never counted. She liked the quiet of the back."

"She own a car?"

"I don't know. Never saw her driving one, if she did."

They went up the short walk to the opening that split the horseshoe-shaped complex, then through the interior courtyard to the far corner unit.

"This is her apartment," David said and stood to one side.

"Did you come here often?"

"No, just a few times. I drove her home after a couple of parties, had a drink or two with her. Then went home." David stopped and turned to Alfano. "And we never got involved. I certainly thought about it though. She was sweet and fun, but honestly a little too old for me, and she never left an opening. I liked her, Detective; she was a good person. We were friends, nothing more."

"She was pretty," Alfano added.

"Don't remind me of that."

Alfano took the key and unlocked the door.

"Hey, you," a woman's voice, shrill like a parrot screaming for a cracker, cut through the courtyard and echoed off the one-story stucco. "What the hell are you doing there?"

A full-figured woman in a housecoat the color of well-worn yellow socks was hurriedly bouncing across the thin strip of dried Bermuda grass in the central court. Her hair was up in rollers. Long pieces of masking tape held curled bangs in place across her forehead like bandages. Intermittently, the house-coat sprung open, revealing too much pasty skin. Her house slippers reminded Alfano of small, dead rodents.

"Hey, what the hell you two doing at Miss Kitty's apart-ment? You better have a damn good reason to be here or I'll call the cops."

That's when Alfano saw the two-foot-long black pipe she carried. He raised his star with his right hand and with his left pushed the door in as he turned to the woman who, thankfully, had good brakes.

"Detective Alfano, police, ma'am. I'm looking into the death of Miss Kitty Hill. This is her apartment, isn't it?"

The woman, clenching the open top of her housecoat with her fingers, glared at the two men as she lowered the pipe so it pointed to the ground. "Can't you just leave the dead alone? It's a damn shame, sad as hell. At least it was in her hometown. She'd go on for hours about Chicago."

"Your name?" Alfano asked.

"Candice Longacre. I own this complex. It's the only thing of value my bastard husband left me when he died. That man either really loved me, or hated me, leaving me this piece of crap. Every day I'm reminded of him: something breaks, or clogs, or leaks. But it does pay enough to stay out of the poorhouse." She adjusted her glasses and took a step toward him. She squinted, took in Alfano with a long perusal, then smiled. "You can call me Candy, honey."

Alfano took a deep breath. He heard David snicker under his breath.

"If you don't mind, I need to look around the apartment. Has anyone else been here, Miss Longacre?"

"Oh, please, Detective, it's Candy. And no, or at least for the last few days. Miss Hill had lots of friends come and go." She finally seemed to notice David. "I remember you—you was one of them. But no one since . . . last Monday, when someone knocked on my door. He said he was from the studio where she worked. He said she died. Not much else, but he did mention Chicago. I asked him, how and where. He said he didn't know, only that she was murdered. Kind of put me on edge, he did. But he had a key. He said he was here to of-ficially inspect her place and make sure there wasn't anything from where she worked. I know she was in pictures. So's I said, sure."

"Such a trusting soul," Alfano said.

"How much did he pay you?" David said.

"You're an impertinent kid, how rude," Candy said.

"Never mind him. Did the guy give you a name? Can you describe him?" Alfano said. He was already reaching in his pocket as Candy held her hand out; the front of her robe sprung open a few inches. Alfano took a five from his roll of bills and handed it to her.

"Of course, Detective. He was a short round man with a fancy-schmancy car, blue—robin's-egg blue. Don't know the type, but sleek and real modern like. His name was Miller or Mannik or something. I let him in; he spent no more than ten minutes. I stood around outside and waited. He left with a brown bag. I asked him what was in the bag, he opened it, I looked—just papers. He said thanks and then drove up to

Wilshire and turned left."

"Damn, you are a trusting woman," David said. "He could have stolen anything."

"Can you put a muzzle on your pet, Detective?"

Alfano turned to David. "Be nice to the lady. Don't bite her; she's too tough, you might get sick." Then back to Candy. "And he was the Monday guy?"

Alfano stepped inside the apartment.

"Let me think—Monday, yeah, Monday. That's trash day. I remember the truck driving by his fancy car. As I said, he said thanks and left. Nice enough, didn't say ten words."

"So you really don't know what exactly he took?"

"No. Weren't my business, honey. He seemed to know all about her, had a key. But I never seen him here, not like your boyfriend here."

"No other police stopped? No one else looked around?"

"No, you are the first."

"Thank you . . . Candy. I'll only be a few minutes."

"You want me to come in? Maybe I can help," Candy said.

"No, it's best if I go in alone to preserve the scene."

Candy looked impressed. Alfano smiled at her. "David, why don't you entertain Candy while I look around."

David gave Alfano a pained look.

Alfano shut the door behind him, then stood in the center of the living room and slowly took everything in. The venetian blinds were pulled down so that light slashed across the room. He peeked behind the blinds; the corner windows had iron grid frames about one foot square that gave at least some amount of security. A dark grey velvet settee, two chairs, and a coffee table filled the center of the room. A large desk and office area were off in the side corner. The kitchenette had a small range and refrigerator, a new one. The counters were clean, and neat. Kitty had cleaned up before she left for Chicago. A thin, dull grey-green carpet covered the main part of the room; a smaller matching piece lay under the desk chair. One wall had a dozen black-and-white photographs of city scenes. Alfano assumed they were from around Los Angeles. However, one, directly behind the desk, was of the Water Tower building on Michigan Avenue in Chicago.

The bedroom was dark and unremarkable other than the bed was very large—king size, he thought they called it. The bedspread was a buff-colored chenille; three pillows were arranged against the padded headboard. The single window, also with the same iron framework, was covered with a heavy roll-down shade that cut out almost all the light. He clicked on the wall switch. A lamp on the right side of the bed filled the room with a soft aura; the shade was red silk and glowed. He went to the bedside table and looked in the drawer: some ointments, a comb, a nail file. When he pushed it closed, he noticed the drawer from the outside was about six inches thick, inside only about two inches deep. He tapped on the inside drawer bottom; it sounded hollow. He removed the drawer and overturned it on the bed. A false bottom fell out as well as four dildos made of wood and bone; maybe one was ivory, the other rubber. There were other ointments, jells, a glass container with a white substance inside, and a leather satchel about six-by-eight inches. He opened the zipper and found hypodermic needles, matches, a small candle, and a large metal spoon. A small divider held packs of more white powder in glassine envelopes.

"You doing okay in there, honey?" Candy yelled into the apartment.

"I'm fine, Miss Longacre. Another ten minutes."

After replacing everything, he pushed the drawer back into its place in the dresser. He then looked in the closet: the clothes were expensive, and elegant. He was surprised by the men's suits, shirts, and ties, but the sizes were all petite and would have fit Kitty. The men's shoes on the floor were stylish, well made and polished. None were larger than a six or seven; he wore a size twelve. He knew he couldn't afford them even at their size.

In the back of the closet, he found two small studio lamps on tripods and what looked like a tripod similar to the ones he'd seen yesterday in the Sierra Films studio. They were smaller versions of the ones in Melnik's playroom.

He turned to the dresser. The clothing inside the drawers was a tangled mess. At least Melnik had closed them. There was a small jewelry box on the top of the dresser. It was empty. He guessed that the asshole had looted it.

The bathroom had also been cleaned out. Only Band-Aids, soaps of many kinds, and a large powder bowl remained. He opened the bowl and smelled the perfumed powder. He was certain she wouldn't keep her cocaine and heroin in the bathroom; the drawer did nicely. Obviously, it worked since Melnik probably inspected the drawer but didn't find the secret compartment.

He went back into the living room and went through the desk. It had been rifled, most probably by Melnik. The top drawer looked as though it had been tipped, then the pencils, pens, notepads, and other miscellaneous items dumped back in. The side drawers held files. Their labels dealt with humdrum personal items, rent receipts, utilities, and taxes. If anything had been taken, it would be hard to discover what. Kitty had been an organized and neat woman.

Alfano sat in the desk chair and looked around. He pushed back and rolled across the thin carpet. The wheels caught briefly, then again as he rolled back the other way.

"Your time is almost up, Detective."

"If you walk in here, Miss Longacre, you will spend the rest of the day in a jail cell for impeding an investigation. They will love you in that outfit."

He heard David laugh.

Alfano stood and pushed the chair away from the desk. He grabbed the corners of the small rug and methodically rolled it up. The oak boards of the floor under the carpet were surprisingly clean and dust free. Where the wheels of the desk chair had caught, he saw the outline of a four-wide board panel that had a nearly imperceptible gap in its seam. He took his penknife and carefully ratcheted up the panel of flooring and gently removed it. Inside the hidey-hole were a dozen six-by-six-inch film boxes, two leather-bound ledgers, another jewelry box, and a walnut-handled Colt Police Positive .32 revolver. He took his handkerchief and removed the pistol; it smelled like it had been recently fired. He checked the cylinder; four empty casings were still inside.

He put the gun on the desk and turned his attention to the film boxes, squinting as he looked at a length of 8-mm black-and-white film. He smiled wryly. "The actors jump right in. No foreplay here," he muttered. He placed the reel back in the box and then back in the hole. The journals were pages of shorthand notes about expenses, income, and profits—he guessed business books. He placed them back next to the film boxes, then laid the revolver back on top of the journals. He replaced the floorboard panel and rolled back the carpet. Cute Miss Kitty Hill had many secrets.

He went to the door and opened it. David stood between the apartment door and Candy Longacre.

"She give you any trouble, Officer?" he said with a smile to David.

Looking a little surprised by the address, David responded, "No trouble, Detective. She was a good girl."

"This punk kid is a copper? Well, I'll be diddled."

"That thought will stay with me all day. Thanks," David said.

"Miss Longacre, this apartment is a crime scene. The police will be here in about an hour. One of them will be a Detective Suarez. Do not let anyone else in. If you do, and I will know, you will be arrested for tampering with evidence. I will also see that you are arrested as an accomplice in a murder. Do you understand, Candy?"

The robe dropped open to full retreat. David blanched. Alfano was impressed.

17

Alfano walked back to the small table where David sat. The limo was parked at the curb just beyond the window of the diner. The midafternoon heat filled the un-air-conditioned room populated with booths and tables and few patrons. Fans spun overhead. A thin Latino girl stood over David with an order book in her hand.

"The hamburgers are good here, Detective," David said.

Alfano smiled at the girl. "Burger and fries?"

"Got it. Something to drink?" she asked.

"Cold Coke?"

"That is about the only thing cold today." She smiled. "Two burgers, fries, and Cokes. Be right back." She walked behind the counter and stuck the order slip on a steel ring and spun it toward the kitchen

"Did you get ahold of Suarez?" David asked.

"Told him everything. He is sending a few of his guys to check it out."

"What did you find?"

"Sadly, David, even though I temporarily promoted you from limo driver to cop, I have to keep this information to myself. There's many interconnected moving parts."

"If you found something, why didn't you take it?"

"There are two murders: Kitty's in Chicago and Melnik's here. The evidence must be managed. If I took everything, it all could be questioned—assuming we arrested someone at some time. Suarez will have control over it now. We came to an agreement."

"Agreement?"

"It's a cop-to-cop thing. He'll discover on his own what I found, no problems."

"You think Longacre will stay out of the apartment?"

"If she's smart she will, but then again, smart ain't on the menu today. Somebody did something stupid back there, and I need to see where it leads."

Alfano stood under the spacious walk-in shower in his hotel room. The only time he'd had this luxury during the last few years was at the YMCA when his apartment was being fumigated. This hotel had everything: air-conditioning, beautiful furniture, a well-appointed bathroom with a glorious shower. As he dried himself with the lush towel, trying to think of a way he could coerce his landlord into installing one in his apartment, the phone rang.

"Alfano."

There was a pause, then came a woman's voice, loud and penetrating: "Detective Alfano, Maxime Durant here. Are you free for dinner? My treat. We haven't had much time together and the days are such chaos with the filming and all, and besides, I think we didn't hit it off in Chicago. So, I believe we should spend some time together."

Alfano, standing naked in the middle of his room, said, "One second, Miss Durant." He shook a cigarette loose from its pack and lit it. "Now, dinner, that right? Tonight? Where?"

"Of course, tonight. I want to show you some of Los Angeles; the best restaurant is Musso and Frank Grill on Hollywood Boulevard. I have a standing table at nine. I assume you are free; I will pick you up at eight thirty?"

"Eight thirty, I'll be out front. You know where I'm staying?"

"Of course, Detective. I know everything."

The line went dead.

"Well, this ought to be fun," he said to no one in particular.

Thirty minutes later, Alfano had his shorts on and two fingers of bourbon in a glass. The phone rang, again.

"Thanks for the heads-up, Detective," Suarez said. "We found the hole under the floorboards and the other items you mentioned. The gun is at the lab being checked. We will see if it matches the rifling on the slug pulled from Melnik. The caliber is the same. Any idea on why the gun was stashed in Hill's apartment?"

"No, not now. Someone had to have a key. There was no break-in, and the windows were secure. Candy Longacre—"

"Now that one's a prize."

"Not one you want to win, Suarez. Besides, she's such a snoop, if someone broke in, she'd have heard them. Someone could have parked in back and dropped the gun—but they would have had a key. Maybe in and out in less than a minute, and they had to know about the hidey-hole. And they'd have to be close to Kitty, real close."

"We are going through the journals and the films. Porn, stag films, nothing fancy, just a lot of screwing—usual stuff. A couple of the more religious guys have issues with all this. Hell, I got issues with all this, especially when two slugs are pumped into a man's heart. You still available for dinner?"

"Sorry, Suarez, I've got to break it," Alfano said.

"That's okay. The wife hasn't seen me for a couple of days. Says she misses me. Hope she's cute."

"She has a way about her. She's taking me to some joint on Hollywood Boulevard. Musso and Frank Grill."

"Lah-de-dah," Suarez sang. "She's going all out. First, she'll ply you with liquor, then fill you with the best prime rib in LA. Anything on the dessert tray is delicious."

"Theirs or hers? And you know all this on a detective's salary?"

"I get out. This is LA, after all. The restaurant is also full of actors, writers, and other dregs of society. Some are from your part of America; some should be in jail. Be careful."

"Yes, Mother. Let me know what you find out about the gun."

Alfano was standing at the curb when a bright yellow convertible coup, top down, skidded to a stop. Maxime Durant was at the wheel. Her dress, coat, and hat matched the car's color. It was a new Packard and looked remarkably like the one he drove in Chicago. Aside from that, nothing else about the massive chunk of Indiana steel reminded him of Chicago.

"Climb in, Detective. I do not want to be late."

Alfano did as ordered and was immediately jammed back into the seat as she accelerated.

"I drive one of these!" he yelled over the roaring of the engine. He took a quick glance at the speedometer; it was tapping 60 mph on a city street.

"I love it. It's fast, comfortable, and screams, 'Get out of my fucking way!'"

"I don't want dinner at the morgue."

"Spoilsport, you take all the fun out of being bad." She reached over and squeezed Alfano's upper thigh hard enough to hurt.

Again, Alfano watched the scenery along Santa Monica Boulevard clip by. This time he noticed a few buildings that were little more than rubble piles, the debris pushed back from the sidewalk.

"What happened to those buildings?" he yelled.

"About six months ago, we had a big earthquake. Shook

the bejesus out of the whole city; the most damage was down in Long Beach. I was working in a studio doing final scenes. It hit just as we were shutting down for the day. All sorts of lights and shit fell from the ceiling. Couple of the grips were hurt, lucky no one was killed. But right here, on Santa Monica Boulevard, a brick wall collapsed and killed a couple of people sitting in a restaurant. Fires and earthquakes, hand of God shit, that's what you get here, Detective. Exciting, yes?"

Alfano held tight to the edge of the windscreen. Exciting? He wasn't sure if he'd be the next one screaming.

"Less than fifty years ago, this was all farmland and desert," Durant said as she wove in and out of the traffic. "We don't get rain for months at a time, then it comes washing down the hills, and mud covers the streets. Then there are the fires, holy Jesus, the fires. Another reason I live down here in a hotel. It's safer. Every few years, those hills burn."

She pointed left and waved her arm. The evening blackness had swallowed the ridgeline. A few lights danced along the face of the mountains, then the garish HOLLYWOODLAND sign dominated the skyline.

"A couple of years back, the fires covered most of the hills up there. It was something to see, something to be fucking scared of, too. My friends lost their homes. Burnt to the rocks they were built on."

Alfano looked up at the dark shadow of the ridgeline. She squeezed his thigh again.

"Ouch." Her idea of foreplay was giving him bruises.

"I suppose you got a nice house, maybe a wife, kids. I peg you for a family man," Durant told him.

The scenery outside the car changed again. Now the storefronts flew by; new buildings sat in between not-so-old buildings. People walked about; they gathered in front of restaurants, bars, and liquor stores. Like Chicago on summer evenings, music spilled out onto the sidewalks. A record store had set up speakers near the door. The Mexican versions of jazz filled the street. As they waited at one of the infrequent stoplights, Alfano watched what young couples did everywhere: dance to the music.

At the next light, he answered, "No wife, no family. Close a few times, but no cigar. Where are you from? Nobody I've met is from Los Angeles."

"Lover, I came about as far as you can get in these here United States," Durant said. Her accent shifted from bland, toneless Angelino to a thick Brooklyn accent. A nasal sound he knew well from criminals that had moved on from New York and made Chicago their new haunt.

"I ain't saying anything no one knows here, but my mother, a dearly sainted Irish girl, got knocked up by a big, brawling, dues-paying Brooklyn Jew," Durant told him. "He honorably married her—I'm sure my grandfather put a gun to his head. They named me Hildegard Karpinski. I have two younger brothers. They are still in Brooklyn, work at a bank. Mom is well; Dad was killed in the war. I did some stage work in New York. Melnik saw me nine years ago. He offered me a contract, I came here, and have no desire to go back. I'm having a good time and making a few bucks."

Until they reached the next light, it was impossible to talk over the roar of the wind and the motor.

"So Melnik's death hit you hard," Alfano said at the stop.

"Yeah, I guess it did. He was no saint, I'll tell you that. I understand you found his body. You've seen his place—his playroom, as he called it. There are few secrets in this town, but everyone knows to keep their lips tight. We all have secrets, and we think we can keep them hidden. We also know, at the right time, they are as negotiable as a bank bond or a quickie. Melnik was okay. He wasn't as kinky as many in this town, kept to his side of the road. Sure, some of his parties got out of hand; they often do up there in the hills."

She followed Alfano's gaze out the window toward the dark hills. "Lover, if those hills could talk, the stories they could tell," she said.

18

They drove another ten minutes in silence, then Durant turned north to Hollywood Boulevard and made a right and then a U-turn in the middle of the street, forcing oncoming traffic to slam on their brakes. She pulled to an abrupt stop right at the curb. Two valets jogged to the car.

"Good evening, Miss Durant," one of the young men said, helping her from the car. The other valet opened the door for Alfano; he got out on his own.

"Freddie, would you be a dear and wipe her down. We'll be a few hours," Durant said.

"Yes, ma'am, will do." The valet walked with her to the arched entry. She slipped him a bill; with the bill was a small glassine envelope filled with something white. Alfano wished he hadn't seen the not-so-secret transfer.

A man in an odd-looking uniform stood at the door and opened it for them.

"Good evening, Miss Durant. Pleasant evening."

"Yes, Louis, very pleasant. The usual crowd tonight?"

Durant looked at Alfano, smiled. Alfano's thought was it was like that cat in *Alice in Wonderland*, knowing and mischievous. He wondered if he'd passed the grin test.

After they elbowed their way through the crowd at the

door, a middle-aged tuxedoed man with a thin mustache, thick eyebrows, and even thicker head of black hair met them.

"Full house, John?"

"We will have a good evening, Miss Durant. Please follow me."

Holding two massive menu cards, John maneuvered through the tight aisles between the tables. Durant followed closely; Alfano took her six. Their objective was a booth in the far corner that overlooked the smoke-filled room. The din made conversation, and eavesdropping, difficult. As hard as he tried, Alfano could not help but stargaze. He saw three faces he knew from films but couldn't remember their names. But he did recognize Dick Powell and Joan Blondell.

Durant stopped abruptly; Alfano rear-ended her. She turned and looked up into his eyes, then took her finger and pushed up his chin. "Stop being a tourist, Tony. These are normal people having a good time. So, close your mouth."

At the booth, Durant slid in first, Alfano to her right. She exchanged a few pleasantries with John. The maître d' took their drink orders and left the menus.

"Just people in this new industry enjoying themselves," Durant said as she removed her gloves and placed them on her yellow lacquered handbag.

"It reminds me more of a fraternity party, where Daddy picks up the bills," Alfano said. "But I'm not here to judge."

"Lover, we are all here to judge."

Two men walked up to the table. Alfano recognized the smaller of the two; it was Will Rogers. His companion was taller and dressed in the most outlandish all-white cowboy outfit that Alfano had ever seen.

"Damn, Detective, you do get around," Rogers said. "Twice in one day. I'd think you were following me." He stuck his hand out to Alfano, who half stood in the gap between the table and the booth and accepted the handshake. "And with Miss Maxime Durant. What do they teach in Chicago? You're here less than two days and you have one of Hollywood's biggest stars on your arm." He nodded at the actress. "Miss Durant."

"Will, be kind," Durant said. "Detective Alfano is a friend and my guest."

"Well, collecting police officers would have been the last thing I'd have expected from you, Maxime," the overdressed cowboy said. "Changing tastes?"

"Detective, this rude man is Tom Mix," Durant said. "I enjoyed him more when he did silent films."

"Mr. Mix," Alfano said. He half stood again, reached across the table to shake the man's hand.

"Los Angeles Police, Detective?" Mix asked.

"No, Chicago."

"Seems both of us are a long way from home," said Mix. "Pleasure to meet you, Detective. Miss Durant, as always, a pleasure."

"How do you know Will Rogers?" Durant asked as the two cowboys walked away from the table. They waved at a few gushing patrons seated at nearby tables.

"We met earlier this afternoon at his club," Alfano told Durant. "I still have another murder to solve."

"Kitty, yes. I forgot." Durant lit a cigarette.

"Miss Durant, I find that hard to believe. I don't think you forget anything. There are similarities between Melnik's death and Hill's—I'm sorting them out." He looked across the room at the two famous cowboys. "It seems you can't go anywhere in this town without tripping over a real or pretend actor or actress. I'm a big fan of Mix's. I've enjoyed his serials. Maybe I should have had them both sign my menu, something to remember this evening."

"I was hoping for more memories than two cowboys at the table," Durant murmured.

Alfano put his hand on his thigh to deflect her fingers.

Their drinks arrived.

"So, prime rib, Yorkshire pudding, and . . ."

"Don't get ahead of your horse, cowboy," Durant said. "Are you closer to finding Kitty and Hines's killer?"

"You assume there is one killer, interesting," Alfano said and took a sip of his Canadian Club.

"The way you said there were similarities, I thought that was why you are here in LA—to catch the killer."

"I'm here because my boss, the mayor of Chicago, sent me here. Hines Melnik asked for my professional expertise to help on the film. Now I've got a dead studio mogul, a bump on the head, a grand tour of LA, a few decent meals, and a not-so-subtle proposition. I am beginning to feel more like a tourist or a john than a cop."

"Oh, poor boy."

Alfano jumped when she squeezed his left thigh again.

"Stop that!"

"Stop what?" she offered with a grin and sipped her martini.

Dinner was delicious, probably the best prime rib that Alfano had had in years, maybe in his life. The liquor served was the real McCoy, and the wines, all Californian, were some of the best he'd tasted. To watch the celebrity table hopping and the high-quality liquor pouring, he'd forgotten for a moment that Prohibition was still officially the law of the land. After three days, he was beginning to suspect that California believed it was a country unto itself.

"You were with Melnik a long time?" he asked Durant.

"For my second tour. The first was three years. I was made an offer, left—it was an unmitigated failure. I went back to Hines. Four years is a long time in this business, so yes, it was a long time. When I came out from New York, I was twenty-six. I had my shit together better than most of the girls that arrive at the train station. These girls are lambs for the slaughter, twenty, twenty-one. Hell, I met one girl—she said she was nineteen—I knew for a fact she was really sixteen. By the time she was nineteen, she looked thirty: a dope addict, sexually abused, and one or two abortions behind her. They found her dead on a bench in the train station with a ticket back to Tulsa in her purse. This town is not kind to young women or men. There are predators everywhere. This city draws them like flies to a corpse."

"And Melnik, his place in all this?" Alfano asked.

"I saw him as a mentor, though he did have his idiosyncrasies. He helped me. Got me into pictures, got me acting lessons, taught me poise, things I didn't learn in Brooklyn. I did what I had to, and he put me together with some of the best leading men. I've done okay, but I watch everything that happens."

She moved as if to grab Alfano's thigh again, laughed when he caught her by the wrist.

"Hines was a doll," she said. "We had a fling for a few years. The man wasn't married, never was. He was from Poland, came to America as a kid, maybe eight or nine. I know his story—I'm half Jewish—Karpinski is Polish. We hit it off, then he started screwing around; he had the attention span of a gnat and the sexual appetite of a bull. The son of a bitch would screw anything, and I know for a fact he did. Anyway, he grew up in Boyle Heights, a Jewish enclave on the east side of downtown—it's gone Mexican and black now. The Jews moved on to Hollywood and Beverly Hills, depending on whether you had money and how much. Melnik had a group of friends. Some drifted into crime and a lot of other unsavory things. The Jewish Mafia, he called them. Said he was lucky to get away. Some of his friends from the Heights are dead now. Others scattered, left town when things got hot. I think what goes on in Chicago is not much different than here."

"He got back into his old habits when the porn business

took off?"

"That's not a bad guess, but I honestly don't know, and I don't know where he got his money. There has to be a hundred film studios here in LA and in the San Fernando Valley."

"Why there?"

"Rent is cheaper, more young girls, bodybuilding guys . . . it's all about the ego and sunshine and films," Durant said. "Everybody wants to be a star."

"Make-believe . . ."

"Detective, to us, it's real. It's hard work, and one out of a thousand makes their bones. Most get fucked, literally and figuratively."

"So, Melnik was one of these predators, as you called them?"

Durant looked genuinely thoughtful. "Yeah, but not as bad as some," she said slowly. "There are some very bad people here, all dolled up, dressed to the nines, and they will do anything to protect their secrets. And they have the money to grease the skids. Here, like everywhere, it's *who* you know and how much you have, not always what you know."

"Graft, corruption, police? That does sound like my home-town."

"Most hometowns have a little of it; big towns just have a lot more," Durant said. She saw the waiter and pointed to her wineglass. He came over and filled it.

A dapper man, late twenties, in a slick grey silk suit, brilliant white shirt, and French tie walked up to their table. It was, surprisingly, a face that Alfano knew.

Durant smiled. The man leaned in and kissed her on the cheek.

"Tony Alfano, this is John Roselli. He is involved with the film industry. In fact, John was the executive producer on Hines's last two films."

Roselli extended his hand. "Mr. Alfano, a pleasure. And

this is Frank DiSimone." He indicated the man who had come up beside him. "Frank is an attorney I'm grooming for the future."

Alfano shook both men's hands. "The pleasure is mine, Mr. Roselli."

"Maxi, I'm so sorry about Hines; he was a great guy and friend," Roselli said.

"Thank you," Durant said. She finished her wine quickly.

"And you know Miss Durant through films?" Alfano asked.

"Yes."

Alfano said nothing more; he kept looking at Roselli. He'd never directly dealt with Roselli—hopefully, Roselli hadn't recognized him.

"As always, Maxi, love you. And a pleasure, Mr. Alfano," Roselli said.

Alfano watched the two men walk away. They stopped twice at other tables and shook hands.

Durant slipped on her gloves and slid out of the banquette. Alfano followed as she followed Roselli out.

"Yes, Detective, it is a menagerie. Yet, here you are, sticking your nose everywhere, even meeting the most famous man in America. You've got balls, Detective, I'll say that for you."

Alfano wanted to know where Durant got *her* balls. Outside, he watched Roselli climb into a buffed-out maroon Cadillac. He knew the man. Roselli—previously known as Filippo Sacco—was born in Lazio, Italy. Even at his young age, he was a close friend of Frank Nitti and Al Capone. Roselli had disappeared about eight years earlier from the Chicago scene. Once a mobster, always a mobster was Alfano's creed. And once Capone's friend, you ended up either rich or dead.

19

Alfano stood at the window of his room looking out on the Pacific Ocean; the open window permitted the sounds and smells of the sea to wash through the room. He heard Sunday church bells. He took in a deep breath; the fogginess of his brain and his actions testified to the fact that he hadn't had a decent sleep in three nights. The night had not gone the way he'd planned. He looked over at the bed. Maxime Durant Karpinski lay coiled like a kitten near where he'd slept. She didn't snore; at least that was a blessing. He blew smoke out the open window, then crushed his cigarette. In the predawn light, the ocean was a grey blue; not a wave roiled the surface. In a few ways, it reminded him of Lake Michigan. A long purr came from the bed. He looked—she still slept. He lit another cigarette.

He had never been one to overthink a situation, and this was one he was sure needed a lot of thinking. She was good, even adventurous. She hadn't mentioned dinner or a quid pro quo. Liquor and a good-looking woman were forever Alfano's great weaknesses. When combined, they became dangerous. The soft curve, the warmth, the afterglow—he would save the rest of his guilt for confession.

Another purr. "What time is it?"

"Seven thirty."

"I need more than five hours of sleep. Wake me at nine," the kitten purred.

"The phone call from J.J. said we need to be at the studio at nine."

"What phone call?"

"The call at six this morning."

"So that's who called," Durant said.

"Yes, it was J.J.," Alfano said.

"It's Sunday. J.J. says a lot of things—fuck him. Crawl back into this bed and tell me I'm a bad girl, or at least try and convince me."

"Self-criticism is good for the soul."

She rolled over, her nude body slowly unwinding itself from the tight curl she'd been in. In the brighter light of day, Alfano was impressed. Maxime Durant was nicely assembled; he'd enjoyed the evening exploring the structure.

"You look good in that light," she said. "I like tall men."

"I'm a little above average."

"Sweetie, I've had average from both ends. Don't cut yourself short."

"I'm not one for self-criticism," Alfano said. He took a drag.

"What's good for the goose is good for the gander. Come back to bed."

"I'm buying breakfast. Go take a shower, get dressed. You need to get back to your apartment and change. Showing up in evening clothes at nine in the morning is not proper. You'll make the hired help jealous."

"You always this bitchy and commanding in the morning? That won't work—only I can be bitchy and commanding in the morning. Besides, I have plenty of clothes at the studio. This isn't the first time I've come in late or early, depending. Order coffee with a roll or something. I'll be ready in a half hour."

She stood, stretched like a cat, smiled, licked her lips, and capered across the room to the toilet. The look Alfano gave her said he was reconsidering going back to bed. She smiled again and said, "Too late, lover. I've lost the mood."

With Maxime driving, Alfano found himself traversing Santa Monica Boulevard yet again. It was a grand total of three and a half miles of nondescript one-story shops, diners, boarded-up buildings, homes, empty lots, and apartments. Some side streets were paved, others just sand. In some lots, tents were set up, many of which looked half-collapsed. Fires were burning, and small groups of men, women, and children huddled around pots that sat over the fires. The children were thin, drawn, and in rags; the parents were not much better. Except for the palm trees, it all reminded him of Cicero near the tracks on a good day.

After an unhurried breakfast, they arrived at the studio on time at 9:15 AM. Jorge Jones was not impressed.

"You're late," he said to Alfano, who had followed Durant past J.J. and into the studio.

"I'm a hired hand, not a babysitter," Alfano said. "Besides, it's Sunday—other than cops, who the hell works on Sunday?"

"We are behind schedule. You kept my girl out. She's your responsibility," J.J. said.

"What are you going to do, fire me?" Alfano saw the caterer's table full of food and made a sharp right.

"Today, Mr. Detective, being Sunday, we work a half day," J.J. announced into a microphone at the retreating cop. "I wanted a full day, but Roberts has a polo match this afternoon. So, our 'star' is not available. You break any body part, and I'll kill you—you hear me, Roberts?"

"Thanks, J.J.!" Roberts yelled from across the studio.

No shooting; the day was too short. Alfano spent the morning sitting at a large table in a windowless room off to one side of the studio. The room was near the main entry, giving him a view of who came and left. The director, script writers, and actors sat around the table preparing for the next week's schedule. Three times Alfano offered suggestions about language, scene intent, and proper procedures. J.J. said they'd stick with the language but adjusted the scene (a shoot-out in an alley between Roberts's character and a young tough) to show that Roberts shot back in self-defense. The original had the detective shooting first.

"While I get the part about vengeance," Alfano said, "don't you think he'd wait until the bad guy tried to kill him first?"

"Sometimes bad guys need killing, Tony," Roberts said. "I get what you are saying, but this guy needed killing, bad."

"No one needs to be killed—not shot down in cold blood," Alfano said, taken aback.

"My experience says there are some that do," Roberts answered.

"Your experience? Really? Your whole ten years of Hollywood experience? In my twenty years of police work, I've met only one man who needed killing. Yet today, he's still alive."

"And who's that, Detective?" Durant said from the far end of the table.

"Alphonse Capone."

"Come on, Detective, Capone wasn't all that bad," Roberts said. "I understand he helped a lot of people in his community. He was a folk hero, a Robin Hood kind of guy."

"More like the Sheriff of Nottingham. Al Capone was directly involved in or ordered the killing of over a hundred people. His thugs bombed bars, polling booths, and shot down citizens in the street. He personally beat his competitors to death with a baseball bat. He ordered dozens of shootings, including in restaurants full of patrons; he shot down competitors on public streets full of bystanders. And he was, I believe, directly involved with the machine gunning of seven of his rivals on

Saint Valentine's Day. I'm sure you heard about that one. Right now, the son of a bitch is sitting in a Georgia prison making shoes, while syphilis and gonorrhea eat him out from the inside. Serves the bastard right. The man was, is, and forever will be pure evil."

"Jesus Christ," Durant said. "I'd have liked to meet him for a character study or something."

Alfano leaned forward and looked down the table to the pussycat. "He wasn't very nice to the ladies, either. His brother ran the biggest bordello in Cook County."

"From what you just said, they got even," Durant answered. That brought a laugh from the others.

"See that, Roberts?" J.J. said. "See Alfano's passion, that commitment—that's what I want from you. You are the leader of your men. You don't just carry the sword of justice—sometimes it's the sword of vengeance. I want that when you are driving your officers, especially just before the scene when you break into the church where the hostages are held. You are God's instrument."

"Really, J.J.?" Durant said.

The director was unfazed. "You, sister, need to stop going through the motions," he told Durant. "You are the reason that our detective is hesitant. He loves you, but you don't love him back. He knows it, and you're making him think twice about leading the attack. For him, it's all or nothing. His reputation is on the line."

"Well, fuck, J.J.," Roberts said. "I get it, really. Thanks, Tony. I get it now."

Alfano looked at Roberts; he wasn't sure, but there was something a little off about Adam Roberts.

David Baine was waiting on what was called Main Street within the studio's complex of buildings and trailers. The street roughly divided the complex in two. He waved to Alfano as the detective left the building.

"Need a lift? I'm free this evening," David said.

"I'm running on empty. Tell you what, give me a ride back to the hotel. Then go have the afternoon to yourself. Pick me up at five. I want to see downtown LA and a few places on a street called Central Avenue. I was told there's good music there."

"You won't exactly fit in there. In fact, neither of us will fit in."

Alfano nodded. "Same in Chicago, but I've learned that's where the good music is. Jazz and swing don't fit with so-called civil society."

"Detective, I can't tell a sharp from a flat. Can't sing a note, but I'm game."

"That's the attitude," Alfano said.

"I hope it's not an attitude that will get us in trouble."

20

Adam Roberts walked west on Santa Monica Boulevard after leaving the morning session at Sierra Films. After two blocks, he turned left on a residential side street and there was Wells Barker, leaning against the hood of a deep green Cadillac Coupe. Barker pitched his cigarette as Roberts opened the passenger door and climbed in.

"Went late?" Barker said, sliding in behind the wheel.

"Yes, sorry," Roberts said, and leaned over and kissed Barker on the cheek.

"That's okay. You sure you want to do this?"

"Yes, I need the money—we need the money. I told Jones that I have a polo match this afternoon, and since the asshole's afraid of horses, it's the last place he'd be, not that I give a fuck."

"You sure about the address? San Fernando Valley?"

"Yes, take Sepulveda to Ventura, and put the top down. I need the sun."

Sepulveda Boulevard cut north through a new tunnel carved through the San Gabriel Mountains that flanked the whole northern side of the Los Angeles Basin. The mountain ridge separated the farm fields and orange groves of the San Fernando Valley from the urban sprawl of Los Angeles with its islands of high-rises, one-story neighborhoods on gridded street patterns, and skeletal, stinking forests of oil derricks. It was a ride that took you back a half century to an age before the derricks, the stench, and cheap hustle that Los Angeles had become. Fresh and sanitized-looking stretches of tacky homes with six-foot palm trees lined the streets of neighborhoods like Sherman Oaks and Van Nuys, though the Valley was too much like Fresno, Roberts sometimes thought. The farm towns had, fungus-like, spread into a seamy boredom of cheap housing, cheap stores, and cheap people. The towns of San Fernando and Burbank, being the two largest, showed potential to continue the infection and metastasize into real cities. Looking down into the Valley from high up on Sepulveda Boulevard, the haze convinced you that it all went on depressingly, forever. And it was here where the porn industry of Southern California had truly sunk its cheap dyed roots.

They reached their destination, a concrete block building with a sign that announced *La Dolce Vita Films*. Roberts leered: such blatant advertising for a less-than-acceptable business. He was well known in the film industry. The unlamented Hines Melnik had made him a star, one that could no longer participate in the more interesting and enjoyable aspects of the industry, at least on film for public dissemination. Six years ago, soon after he'd arrived from Fresno, someone told him about a way to make a few desperately needed dollars. He certainly wasn't a virgin. He'd lost that when he turned fifteen and a few high school buddies took him to one of the more well-known shacks on the south side of Fresno. Her name was Juanita. It was over in seconds and barely worth the three dollars, but he got better at it. It became more than a desire, it became a full-blown need—some take to alcohol when young, he took to sex. He also discovered he was what he called "nondiscriminatory" in his partners and liaisons, a true Lothario.

He asked around and ended up one afternoon at an address

in the Valley. He bedded three of the most beautiful women he'd ever slept with, did what was directed, never failed his duty, and smiled for the camera—and made fifty much-needed bucks. These clandestine operations moved around the Valley, and even into Los Angeles proper. Soon Roberts got a reputation, a solid reputation. It was at one of these shoots that he had been handed an invitation to a party at the home of Hines Melnik. He came for the drinks and food and stayed for the fucking. Melnik said he'd make him a star, and Melnik was true to his word. The only change was that he'd have to give up this secret parallel life, a small price in exchange for the dollars Melnik paid him.

It was during this time that he met Wells Barker, who, three years later, quietly moved into the Beverly Hills house. Barker, even though once called an Adonis by a film fan magazine, was not as lucky career-wise, though Roberts and Barker were a known thing within the industry, and thus were cut some slack. Many actresses, known for their insatiable appetites, were given the same latitude. The seamier rumors about many of these queens of the cinema would curl Grandma's hair. Many young men and women came to Hollywood for their chance to be in pictures; many remained because they were trapped in places like La Dolce Vita Films.

Nowadays, Roberts stayed off to the side, off-camera, even did some directing of two of the shorts. He did miss the excitement of the couch and bed. He had reasons for not screwing up his deal with the newly departed Hines Melnik and Sierra Films. His contract was with the studio and not a personal services contract. Someone would be taking over the studio, probably for ten cents on the dollar, and Roberts wanted to be there when it happened. He would become somebody in this industry.

Barker was the film star that afternoon, and Roberts was mildly jealous. Job done, it was dark as they drove back over the San Gabriel Mountains. This time they took Mulholland Drive to Benedict Canyon. When they reached Beverly Hills, they were five blocks from Roberts's house. Ten minutes later, they walked in the front door, and Roberts vented his pent-up vigor on Barker, who did little to stop the onslaught.

About the time Roberts and Barker were departing the Valley to return to Beverly Hills, David drove the limousine east on Pico Boulevard to the dizzy white lights of Central Avenue.

"How do you know about this street?" Alfano said.

"I asked around. Everyone said, 'Stay the fuck out of there.' But they did say the best jazz, out of a dozen places on Central Avenue, is at the Apex Nite Club. It's next door to the Dunbar Hotel."

"Look, kid, if you don't want to go, just tell me. No big deal. I got the word from friends in Chicago that this was a great place for music."

"Are you nuts, Detective? We'll give it a try. It's an adventure, and as warm as it is, the joint will be packed."

They turned right off Pico onto Central. It looked like every man and woman in this part of Los Angeles had come to stroll, posture, display, and preen on Sunday night. To Alfano, it was no different here than on a warm evening in Chicago. As they drove slowly down the avenue, the music came at them in waves, as if bouncing from one side of the street and then the other.

David slipped the limousine into a parking lot where hand-painted signs advised *All Night—$5.00*. The other fifty or so cars jammed into the lot were sleek and elegant. Five dollars would do that, separate the wheat from the chaff.

"What can I do for you, mister?" asked a lanky black man sitting on a stool near the entry.

"I need a few hours," Alfano said from the passenger side

of the front seat.

"I might be able to find you some room."

"Would twenty dollars find me room?"

"Mister, for twenty dollars, I'll dust her off and spit shine the lights."

Alfano got out and waited as David parked the limo in a spot behind the attendant. He saw a cornet leaning against the back of the man's stool.

"I saw Louis Armstrong play that same model at the Grand in Chicago last winter," Alfano said. "You play, or is it just for decoration?"

A smile came over the man's weathered face. "You know your shit. I played with Satchelmouth in New Orleans, maybe fifteen or so years back, during the war. We was playing cornets in them Storyville honky-tonks. The kid was self-learned; he got his own style of playing and singing and was good. Those were the days after he got out of that school for delinquents—but that's another story—and that kid weren't no delinquent. I could go on all night. I knows that kid, love him like a son. He's gone uptown with the trumpet nowadays. When he split from New Orleans for Chicago, I came here, needed warmth for my bones, not that wet heat New Orleans got. I taught him a little, but the kid was his own man. When he comes through here, we talk about the old days. So, you know Satchmo?"

"No, I wish. I have friends in Chicago who do. I go to the jazz clubs on State Street and elsewhere. I've seen him play but never met him."

Alfano stopped talking as a fresh burst of music could be heard from across the street.

"That's the Apex," the guy told him. "It's a good trio there tonight, from New York—you might like them. They are some fellas from Duke Ellington's band who are out here for a few weeks. Rumor is they's working on a picture over there in Hollywood or someplace. That's their rental Auburn over there."

"Thanks. You ever get to Chicago . . . ?" Alfano looked into the man's eyes.

"I'm Edgar Dassault, New Orleans born."

"Mr. Dassault, Tony Alfano. Do you happen to know a man called Deacon Smith?"

"Shore-do. We played together, too, but that was—oh, shit, let me think, maybe twenty years ago. You know the Deacon?"

"Absolutely. He has a café on State Street in Chi-town, just opened. In fact, Mr. Dassault, I saw him two weeks ago."

"No fucking way. I'll be damned and go straight to heaven. How is he?"

"Wife, kids, good Baptist, has a small stage for new kids."

"That's the Deacon. When you see him—wait a fucking minute. What the hell are you doing here?"

"I'm chasing down a murderer."

"You a cop?"

"Detective."

"No shit. Nice fancy car, got a fancy white chauffer, hopping all over the fucking country—well lah-de-dah. What's this old world coming to?"

"Mr. Dassault, for that I have no fucking answer."

Dassault laughed. "I start playing right here in about an hour, make a few dinero. I split the rate on the cars with the guy who owns the lot. Listen for the sound."

"You bet I will."

"It's a pleasure to know you, Detective Alfano."

Alfano shook Dassault's hand, then he and David crossed the street and walked the one block to the Apex Nite Club. The sidewalks were packed, and more than a hundred people were waiting outside in the evening heat for a seat inside. Alfano guessed that inside was even hotter.

"I'm thinking twice about this, David. It's way too hot—and heat, booze, and jazz—well, that's a strong concoction," Alfano said as he lit a cigarette and looked up the sidewalk.

Four young black men in long colorful jackets and balloon pants were strolling toward them. People stepped aside and watched them parade by.

"We're starting to see zoot suiters in Chicago; it's showing up in the clubs and dances," Alfano said.

"It's big here and getting bigger every year," David said. He took the cigarette Alfano offered. "Mostly the pachucos, though. But the coloreds are picking up the vibe."

"Pachucos?"

"Here in LA, it's more the Mexicans and Latins that dress in zoot; they call themselves pachucos. The coloreds also wear the style. It comes from some of the black musicians who are wearing the costume. It's an attitude thing as well. It does strike a look. On me, I'd be all jacket."

"In two days, Baine, I've gone from the beaches, to polo clubs, to pachucos. Los Angles is an interesting place." Alfano rubbed the back of his head; he still felt the welcome knot from his first night in town.

The four zoot suiters skipped down the sidewalk in style, almost prancing. When music spilled from the open doors of one of the clubs, the boys broke into an impromptu dance. A girl from the crowd joined in. Two more girls came out from the club and joined the dance, partnering with a couple of the guys. The crowd stepped back and into the street while some of the best dancing Alfano had seen in a long time worked its way up and down the sidewalk. A saxophone cut through the night and added to the sounds from the club. The crowd clapped and danced. Vehicles stopped as the dancers moved into the traffic lanes.

The blast of a police siren broke the rapture.

The police car stopped in the street, opposite the dancers. A megaphone appeared through the open front window. "Please clear the street. This is an illegal assembly. Please clear the street. No dancing in the street."

The crowd ignored the order. Another saxophone, a tenor, joined the first.

"This is an official order by the Los Angeles Police. Please clear the street. This street must be kept open."

Two beer bottles sailed over the crowd and crashed onto the hood of the police car; the bottles dented the black metal and sprayed beer over the windshield. More bottles followed.

"David, we need to get out of here. That patrol car has a radio. He'll have backup in minutes, and this place will light up."

People spilled from the club; more bottles flew through the night. Alfano and David crossed in the middle of the street, weaving between the stopped cars. The drivers leaned on their horns; the honking seemed to come from everywhere. More sirens filled South Central Avenue. The double flashing red lights on the roofs of the incoming police cars could be seen between the cars on the street.

Alfano looked back at the original police car—a dozen more bottles arched through the air and exploded on and around vehicle. The cops wisely stayed inside.

As if mysteriously transported to Central Avenue, a dozen uniformed policemen appeared and marched two by two toward the action. They pushed and jammed batons into the crowd. All the officers were white; all the crowd was black.

"Not good, Detective, not good at all," David said as they reached the far side of the street. Edgar Dassault was standing next to his stool when Alfano and David ran into the parking lot. Alfano noticed that Dassault's coronet was missing.

"You see what the hell the police are rousting about over there?" Dassault asked.

"Someone threw a bottle of beer," David said.

"That's how it always starts. Some fool tosses a beer or a firecracker, and holy shit comes down. Go out the back, then take a right on Hooper. It'll be fucking crazy here all night—

and tell Deacon he still owes me ten bucks."

David did as directed; they drove for what seemed like miles to Alfano. Block after block of one-story buildings, dreary storefronts—half-empty, abandoned, and derelict. Soon they were passing one-story cottages and bungalows. Some of the streets were paved, most not. To Alfano's surprise, they ran back into South Central Boulevard at a Y-intersection.

"This is depressing," David said. "And I'm lost, Detective. I think we are headed the wrong way, but fuck, I don't know."

Alfano looked at the clock on the dashboard of the limousine: 1:33 AM.

"Which way is the ocean?" he asked.

"I think it's to the right."

"Then, David, at the next street turn right. We will find out together."

21

The next morning, Alfano rolled out of bed, poured himself a wake-me-up, took a luxurious shower, and dressed. He walked out of the shower at eight forty-five. He was hungry. There were three sharp knocks on the door; he looked through the small peephole and saw the grin of Detective Dominic Suarez. He was still in the hotel bathrobe.

"It's Monday morning, Detective, a little early?" Alfano said as he backed away from the door and Suarez followed him in. Suarez was flying solo, no Detective Loomis. Alfano took another sip of breakfast.

"Little early for that?" Suarez said, pointing to the glass.

"Leftovers, cold leftovers. Besides, I was going to call you to find out the latest about Melnik. Buy me breakfast; I'm starved."

"There's a pancake house a block from here. You game?"

"After last night, I'm game for anything. I need to make a call."

As they walked to the diner on 2nd Street, Alfano told Suarez about his adventure on South Central Avenue. The detective told him what an idiot he was for going to the neighborhood; so far, Alfano realized that he had done nothing, since arriving in Los Angeles, to disprove the Beverly Hills cop's assessment. They were given a table in the corner away from the windows. The diner was small, packed, and the coffee strong.

"Aren't you working at the studio today?" Suarez asked.

"That's the call I made; I'm taking the day off," Alfano said.

"That producer will be pissed."

Alfano shrugged. "Anything on the gun?" Alfano said.

"Yes, it's the one that put two slugs into Melnik," Suarez said. "After canvassing Hill's neighborhood, *nada*. No one saw anyone that night hanging around the alley or the complex. Based on our timeline and the coroner's numbers, it would have been sometime around midnight. Of course, you could have shot him, then stashed the gun, then called Tuttle—all to take any heat off you."

"Nice. I came to the same conclusion. The only part that blows it all is that I didn't do it."

"The guilty always say that."

"This time I'm telling the truth."

"Yeah, and I've heard that, too. A thousand times."

"Moving on," Alfano said as he poured syrup from a tiny white pitcher over his cakes. "What I see is that my Chicago victim, Kitty Hill, was running a number of games out of her apartment—and most had to do with the sex business and porn films. She also was good at her job working as a producer with Sierra Films and Melnik. If she was making money, she was hiding it somewhere—maybe get a warrant to look at her bank records. You might check the apartment for other hidey-holes."

"We only found the one, even searched under the building. Nothing. You said she was originally from Chicago?"

"Yes, she danced, sang some, worked at a few of the better clubs. Her brother and husband were gunned down; my people say she saw it. Afterwards, she took off and ended up here. That was about ten years ago."

"Maybe because she knew the killer?" Suarez said, plastering butter over his cake.

"Possibly, but more likely who sent them—and there was only one gun used on both men. Whoever did it was good. After Hill escaped to LA, Durant told me she worked her way into legit picture making; she found a place here. She was hoping for a bigger future, which means money, more money."

"She was also in the stag film business and—how do I put this so my mother would understand—playing on both sides of the street," Suarez added. "The films bear that out."

"Your mother would be pleased with your discretion," Alfano added.

"My mother is a saint. So, for now, I will leave it as playing in the street."

"I know, your mother thinks you are an insurance agent."

"My mother knows exactly what I am, and I love her for it. My father was a cop in Tijuana, got out when he could."

Alfano raised his coffee cup toward the waitress. "Miss Hill is found dead—two bullets to the chest—during a Sierra Films motion picture tour of the Midwest. There was nothing I saw, other than the bloody nude body, to suggest a connection to the sex industry. Maybe a kinky lover, maybe something got out of hand, but nothing that I saw was based on her proclivities."

"Shot?"

"Yes. Large caliber, close range to the chest, same as Melnik. My three lead suspects—Miss Hill was traveling with them—are Melnik, Durant, and Roberts. They quickly changed their plans, climbed aboard an airplane, and returned home before I could ask more questions. Then I'm invited here, all expenses paid, set up in a nice hotel, clobbered over the head, discovered the murdered body of my benefactor, and have enjoyed the on-and-off-again company of you, LA detective Gil Tuttle, and assorted lost souls for the last few days."

"You failed to mention an evening and morning with one of Hollywood's most promiscuous leading ladies," Suarez added.

"Are you following me, Detective? Shame on you."

"Actually no, we were following Maxime Durant. You just happened to get in the way."

"So, I'm not her first?"

"If, according to the tabloids and rumors, and the simple fact that Beverly Hills is a small town, you are not even on the first three pages."

"And I thought I was special. She fits the image, doesn't she?"

"And there is Mr. Melnik's playroom to consider, and the rumor of Durant's involvement in the porn industry herself. She wasn't on the films, and there's nothing we can put a finger on, but a few others are well known in the Valley."

"Ah, the Valley."

"The San Fernando Valley, where Hollywood dreams go to die or be screwed—literally."

"Fun town you got here, Detective."

"Ain't that the truth."

"Can you send a copy of that ballistics test and photos to my sergeant in Chicago?" Alfano said. "By airmail; I'll cover the expense. I want to check it against the report on the slugs found in Miss Hill. If they match, my list of living suspects is down to two."

"That list had the same two names on it Friday morning— there is no way that gun could have gotten here faster than being carried in a suitcase."

"Call me old-fashioned, Detective Suarez, but I need a motive. Why was Hill murdered? How is she connected to Melnik's death, especially if the same gun was used? Why kill Hill in Chicago and not here? And then kill Melnik here, in his house?"

"And you are sleeping with one of the suspects, tsk-tsk.

They do do things different in Chicago."

They walked back to the Georgian. The lobby clerk pointed to Alfano and motioned him to the desk. She handed him a note.

"A woman called; I took the message," the clerk said.

Alfano opened the envelope and read the short note.

I heard you were taking the day off. Are you free at noon? Call me at 1378.
Gloria

"Fan mail?" Suarez asked.

"All work and no play makes Tony a dull boy, Suarez."

The detective gave Alfano a knowing look. "Durant?"

"No."

"Who?"

"You're the detective, you figure it out." He made the call.

Gloria drove up to the curb in front of the hotel. "Where did you find this?" Alfano said, looking at the car, a mid-1920s Ford Model T roadster, all shiny and black. Its driver was dressed in a loose orange tank top, white shorts, and white tennis shoes.

"A friend lent it to me for the day for gas. I need to be back by five to pick him up from his mother's place in Venice Beach. Until then we have the whole day, or what's left of it. First, we are going to stop at the best Italian deli here in Santa Monica, and then we are going on a picnic. Do you have a swimsuit?"

"I don't wear swimsuits," Alfano answered.

"Ooh, that's not acceptable, even in California."

"I mean I don't ever wear one."

"We will find one," Gloria said. "There's a shop inside the hotel. Buy a suit; I'll wait."

"As I said—"

"I really don't care, Detective. Go and buy a swimsuit—I'll wait."

Strong women were another weak link in Alfano's manly armor. He turned around and went back into the hotel; five minutes later, he returned to the car carrying a bag.

"That didn't hurt, did it?" Gloria said. "I have the perfect spot up the beach in Malibu. First the deli; do you like Italian?"

"Really? For a picnic? I would never have thought . . ."

". . . nothing better. And quit being such an ass."

Six blocks later, they pulled to a stop in front of the Bay Cities Deli on Lincoln. Alfano was intrigued. The place had the look and feel of a delicatessen you would find on Chicago's Taylor Street in the old Italian neighborhood. When they walked through the door, the aromas swept him off his feet. It was like he'd come home.

"Number thirty-two!" yelled a large man with a thick black mustache. He wore a white coat. When no one answered right away, he reached across the counter and took a white tab from a woman who couldn't have been four feet, ten inches tall. "Number thirty-three—you next, Silvia?"

Alfano looked at the man calling the numbers. He knew the face and the man, but why? Where?

"I'm going to get two sandwiches, potato salad, pickles, some cannoli, and four bottles of beer," Gloria said. "What do you want?"

"What?" Alfano said, still distracted by the counterman. "All that for you?"

"Yes, but I'll have the other sandwich for dinner. And you are buying."

"Order me the same," Alfano said, still looking at the man. Then he said, "Tony DiTomasi, is that you?"

The numbers man looked at Alfano. He could practically see the man's brain working, trying to put a name and a face together, then a big smile like a light bulb going on lit up his face.

"Well, I'll be damned," DiTomasi said. "Tony Alfano, what

the hell are you doing in this part of the world? I thought they'd never let you leave Chicago. Damn, you look good. Give me a minute."

DiTomasi finished the order, passed over a deli bag to Silvia, and came around the end of the long glass case. He gave Alfano a big hug. "What the hell?"

"I heard a rumor you were in Los Angeles," Alfano said. "But that was seven or eight years ago. You work in a deli?"

"Worse than that, Alfano. I own the joint." DiTomasi looked at Gloria. "Hi, Miss Downs. You with this guy?"

"I'm his babysitter while he's here in LA. It has not been dull."

"Alfano is one of the best—you still a detective?"

"Still a detective, on loan to Sierra Films here in Santa Monica. They're doing a cop and mobster movie—I'm the technical expert."

"Miss Downs, this guy—when I was with the Chicago police—was one of the best. Always had the back of the honest cops on the force. But then bad apples started going really bad, too much mob money. That's why I took off. Came out here, got as far away from all that crap as I could."

"I can't believe it," Gloria said. "You were once a cop?"

"Yes, dear, a cop." He looked at Alfano. "Sierra Films, that's Hines Melnik's studio. You involved in that murder? It's all over the papers."

"Indirectly. Production is still going on. The locals out of Beverly Hills are handling the case. I'm staying out of it."

"Don't be so modest, Mr. Alfano. Aren't you the unidentified officer who found—" Gloria started to say.

"Gloria, please," Alfano said. "Tony, I'm here for a few more days, then back to Chicago. Maybe we can get together to talk about the old days."

"Alfano, the old days are just that, old. Give me a call, sure. Let's talk. Miss Downs, take care of this goombah—so, what do you want?"

22

Alfano asked, "How far out of the way is Melnik's house?" as they drove north on Ocean Boulevard.

"It's a lot out of the way, but I get why you want to go there," Gloria said. "We can take Sunset Boulevard, then it's straight east. Have you seen where Adam Roberts lives?"

"No."

"It's on the way. We'll drive by. Then up the hill to Melnik's. Beyond Melnik's, further east, there's a great view from above the Hollywood Bowl; we can have lunch there. But you bought a swimsuit."

"Maybe I can use it later in the week."

"I'll hold you to that."

Gloria drove the flivver east on Sunset Boulevard like it was a European auto race. She wove in between cars, touched the harsh horn occasionally, and in general made Alfano squeamish. The Ford wasn't all that powerful; he wondered what she would be like with his twelve-cylinder Packard. Then again, maybe not.

"We turn here and go down Roxbury past Roberts's house. He's renting it from a director at Paramount."

"He lives there alone?"

Gloria didn't answer.

"So, he doesn't live there alone? One Wells Baxter lives there as well?"

She took a breath. "Detective, things and people in California are different, or they think they are different. People think different, act different, are maybe a little more tolerant—and certainly 'weirder' and 'unconventional' comes to mind. Adam Roberts does not live alone; he has a gentleman friend. No one talks about it . . . sort of a code of silence about things like that. He makes a lot of money for a lot of people. So, they keep his secret."

"So, he is a homosexual," Alfano said, seeking confirmation of what he already knew.

"Yes, but not exclusive," Gloria said as she slowed.

"The euphemism I've heard is that one plays on both sides of the street?"

"The rumors I've heard is that he plays on both sides of the boulevard, and it's a wide and very busy boulevard." She slowed the car to a stop. "That is his place on the right. I've been to a few parties there. Nice, roomy, a pool in the back." She lowered her voice. "A high wall encloses the backyard. It's very private."

"You know the layout of the house?"

"I took a personal tour when no one was watching. It's quite something, but the furnishings and decor are a little off, too butch for my tastes, or masculine depending on the point of view. Lots of nude male paintings, sculptures, and such. When things start getting comfortable at parties like that, I leave. Not that I'm a prude or even all that much a saint, but these mash-ups are more than I care to indulge."

"I don't see a garage or a driveway."

"There's an alley in the back for trash, parking, and utilities. It's as nice as the street out front. Seen enough?"

"Yes."

"Hines Melnik's place is up the hill near the Beverly Hills

Hotel, but then again you have been there."

"Gloria, the taxi driver could have taken me to the far side of the moon that night. It was late, you'd plied me with liquor, and I walked in on a murder scene. Not what I expected for my first night in California."

Gloria took two lefts—the second was Beverly Drive—then accelerated up the hill. Alfano recognized the sign for the Beverly Hills Hotel as they passed it. Melnik's house was close and on the right. A police car sat in the driveway; that was the only evidence of any crime at the house. The gate was open. Gloria parked on the street, and they both walked up to the patrolman in the cruiser.

Alfano said, "You are Smith. I met you Thursday night. You were the first car on the scene."

"And you are that cop from Chicago. Detective Suarez warned me about you; he thought you might stop by."

"I'd like to go up and take a look, refresh my memory."

"No can do, Detective. Suarez locked this place down as tight as a drum. I've had people wandering by for the last three days, just taking a stroll, they all said. All asking if this is where the murder was."

"You told them yes, of course."

"Didn't tell them nothing. It's none of their damn business. These people have more money than sense, I'll tell you—nosey and all."

"You hungry?" Alfano asked. "Thirsty? Did you have lunch?"

"Yeah, a little."

"So, here's the deal, Officer Smith. You know Santa Monica, Bay Cities Deli?"

"Absolutely. I always get something when I take the wifey to the pier."

"Well, Officer, this is your lucky day. I will trade you a triple Italian meat sandwich, with all the fixings, and a beer—of which I will never tell where you found it—for thirty minutes inside the house."

"That's bribery."

"No, it's a sandwich. Besides, all the evidence will disappear. I'll take the wrapping paper with me when we leave. It never happened—other than you will need a breath mint."

Smith didn't exactly drool, but he gave in easily.

Gloria was already walking back toward the Ford when Alfano said, "Get the officer his sandwich and one of the beers, and don't forget the napkins."

When the handoff was made, Alfano and Gloria started up the driveway.

"Hey, she can't go," the patrolman said.

"Who can't go?"

Smith looked at the two of them, shook his head, and chewed off another large piece of sandwich. "Get the fuck out of here. And don't forget, you only got thirty minutes."

The house was just as Alfano remembered it. He noticed that Gloria had gone quiet and a little hesitant once they entered.

"You okay?"

"Yeah, but it's all so creepy. I never liked this place. I always thought it was like some Polish castle moved here to Beverly Hills."

"Polish, interesting."

"At parties, Melnik would tell stories of growing up in Prussia or eastern Poland—I had to look that up. Then he'd tell about taking the boat across the Atlantic to New York, his new friends he met onboard the ship. He said it was the SS *Manhattan*. It was filled with a mixture of Europeans, Poles, Germans, even some Italians. Eventually his family reached Los Angeles—he'd go on for hours. And while he'd go on and on about his past, the liquor flowed, and the guests would pair off and wander off to some of the rooms." She turned and walked away toward the terrace.

"Is this where it happened?" Alfano asked.

Gloria stood in the French doorway that opened onto the pool. She stared out at the pool without seeming to see it.

"I had just turned eighteen. A friend of Melnik's discovered me at a Woolworth counter, honest to God, that's the truth. It was in my hometown, Denver. I was working that summer, just after high school graduation. I had plans to go to a secretarial school, then get out of Colorado. My dad was gone. He ran out on my mother when I was fifteen, and she went to live with her sister. I took a room in a boardinghouse for girls. It wasn't too bad; the job paid twenty-five a week. Life was good. Well, one of those movie tours came through town pushing a film—to this day, I can't remember the name of the movie. But a guy, a handsome guy, sat down at my station, looked at me, and said I had potential."

"And signed you up?"

"No, worse. He filled my head with a dream. He gave me his card and said if I ever came to California to call him. I made two mistakes that day: I took his card, and I believed him. Six months later, I stood outside the door to his office at some studio, now defunct, and reminded him about who I was. He said he didn't need me but gave me Hines Melnik's name and this address. 'Be there Friday night at eight,' he told me. He said Melnik was interviewing actresses for parts in a new movie. I believed every fucking word."

"I'm sorry," Alfano said.

"Detective, I don't want sympathy. I knew boys; I sure as hell wasn't a virgin. I knew a lot—or so I thought. Late that night, after most everyone had left, or found a room somewhere upstairs, I saw light in that window over there. I was deciding to call a cab or find a couch for the night; I was pretty well lit up."

She pointed across the terrace to a window that Alfano

remembered was one of the high windows in Melnik's porno studio.

"I'd had a lot of champagne by then. I wandered around a while trying to find the source of the light. That's when I walked into the studio. Melnik was directing two women and a man on the bed. I remember there were two others, a cameraman and Maxime Durant. I was drunk, shocked, and confused. I actually thought I was sophisticated. I watched a while and drank more champagne. Then I found myself on the bed. Durant was hovering over me, my clothes were gone, and that potbellied son of a bitch was standing next to her. Durant said to have a sip of this; it would relax me. All I remember was Momma's little girl was not in Denver anymore."

"I'm sorry."

"Why the hell are you sorry? I got myself into that. I was stupid."

"Why did you stay? Why didn't you go back to Denver?"

"Money. To be honest, they were nice to me—afterwards. They paid me one hundred and twenty-five a week to be a gofer. A lot more than a counter girl at Woolworth's. Melnik never asked to have sex with me again. Ever since I've been a gofer, assistant, take people around like you, show them a good time. I do what I want, no strings, no pressure, and certainly no tit for tat. I have a nice apartment." She looked at Alfano. "It's just all so fucking weird."

"They raped you."

"Yeah, I guess, technically. But all too outlandish, and here I still am two years later, and you are thinking I'm the girl who killed Melnik. That I got revenge on the son of a bitch. I know that's what you are thinking."

"Sure as hell, that's what I'm thinking," a voice said from behind them.

"Hi, Suarez, I wondered how long it would take you to get here," Alfano said. "Gloria Downs, this is Detective Suarez of the Beverly Hills Police. I'd shake his hand, but the sandwich he's holding tells me that I'm not having lunch today."

23

Downs, Suarez, and Alfano climbed the spiral stairway to Melnik's office. The blood had dried into ghoulish patterns where the actual shooting took place. The furniture was unneatly rearranged; there were black powder patterns and residues on many surfaces and drawers, the champagne bottle was still in the silver ice bucket. The bourbon bottle, now decorated with black dust, sat on the desk. The glasses Alfano remembered were gone.

"Did you find anything downstairs worth noting?" Alfano asked.

"Another champagne glass, no prints on it. That's not unusual," Suarez said. "No bullet casings—though if I had to guess, the revolver you found at Hill's apartment might be the same one used to kill him. I should know today."

"This is where you found him," Gloria said, looking at the mess on the floor.

"Why don't you go back to the car. I'll be right there," Alfano said.

"Detective, I'll be the one to dismiss her," Suarez said. "I have a few questions."

Gloria turned to Suarez. "I wasn't here that night. I was home. I had a nice dinner with Detective Alfano and another policeman—Tuttle was his name, I think. Then I took a cab home to Sawtelle. That was about nine. I took a bath, had a nightcap, climbed into bed, and read. I was asleep by eleven."

"She's good, Alfano. Practiced and everything . . . almost makes her a suspect."

"If you were to go from your apartment to here, what would be the quickest way?" Alfano asked Gloria.

"I don't own a car, but I could have borrowed that Model T, I guess. You can check with my neighbor. Since it doesn't have working headlights, I'd have to drive real slow. Santa Monica Boulevard to Beverly Hills, then left on Beverly Drive. So, it would take me at least forty minutes to get here. I also could have taken a cab. I like Yellow—I dated a Yellow cab driver for a few months. You might call them and confirm that I didn't use them."

Suarez said nothing.

"Detective Suarez, I did not like Mr. Melnik. I actually despised the asshole, but I didn't kill him," Gloria insisted. "He wasn't worth the trouble. And you mentioned a revolver. I'm from Colorado; I know how to shoot pistols, shotguns, long guns. To pin this on me, you must put me and that gun together."

"Cute and smart," Alfano said. "She's right, it would have been difficult."

"When are you going home, Detective? I could use the peace and quiet," Suarez said.

Alfano left Gloria to capably fend for herself and did a circuit around the house. He inspected every room, even the kitchen, which he paced off and determined to be twice as large as his whole apartment. He investigated Melnik's playroom; it didn't look any more innocent in the light of day. Upstairs was a collection of eight bedrooms, a lot for a confirmed bachelor. The office sat in the middle like a hub, with the bedrooms evenly spaced in both directions along the hallway. Other than the size and style, there was nothing remarkable about the house; it was not overly decorated, or, as Gloria said, butch. Melnik's office looked to be the most inhabited room in the house.

Through the office window he could see Suarez and Gloria standing on the pool terrace. Alfano lifted the books and papers strewn across Melnik's desktop and counters, looking for what, he didn't know. Three of the stacks of papers were scripts; he recognized them from reading his assignments from J.J. There had to be a hundred split evenly between the three piles, each with a neatly typed cover. A few were covered with handwritten notes. The handwriting was impossible to read; it wasn't English.

He turned in a slow half circle, taking in the details of the now familiar room. More books filled the shelves on one wall. Opposite, the door to the safe still hung open. Photographs in silver frames were displayed on almost every flat open surface or shelf; a dozen were spread across the top of the baby grand piano in the corner. He looked at all of them. Some were of a young boy; in others, the boy stood between two adults, a man and a woman. He recognized a young Hines Melnik in all of them. There were photographs as the family grew older and more children filled the frames. Then a teenage boy, again Hines, stood at a wooden railing, the beach, the ocean, and the side of a rustic building behind him. Next to him stood another boy, same age; they had their arms entwined over each other's shoulders. The boys were maybe fourteen or fifteen. There was a familiarity about the other boy, but then again, the graininess and discoloration made identification difficult.

"Find anything?" Suarez said as he walked into the room. Gloria was behind him.

"No, it looks all too normal, nothing stands out, no confession, no sinister notes left by the killer. I got bupkis. Gloria, does this look familiar?"

She looked at the photo. "That's Santa Monica pier. I recognize the side of the building; they sell hot dogs and drinks. It's still there—that's a young Melnik, maybe twenty-five years ago. I don't know the other fellow."

"We are chasing down some fingerprints we found. The glasses were wiped down. Nothing yet," Suarez said to Alfano. "You think the killer also killed Kitty Hill?"

"Yeah, maybe. But the revolver confuses it all. Why carry the damn thing halfway across the country and use it for another murder? The only suspects I got at the front of the line are two actors. And besides, guns are everywhere for fifty bucks, even in California, I'm sure."

"Two actors? Roberts and Durant?" Gloria asked.

"For the moment, not your concern, Gloria," Alfano said. "Why don't you head downstairs; I'll be right there. If that's okay, Detective."

Suarez nodded, and the two men waited as Gloria went down the stairs and they heard her shoes tap across the marble foyer.

"She's a handful," Suarez said.

"Another disillusioned actress, but she's okay. She didn't do it, I'm certain. But my track record with guilty women this year isn't good."

"And why is that?"

"Not your concern and all long stories. Just my luck in choosing women who turn out to be suspects and worse."

"I take it you are leaning toward Maxime Durant?" Suarez said.

"She is a good prospect. Did you notice that nothing seems to be trashed here? Even this room is still an organized mess. The front doors weren't busted in—no windows broken. Someone might have climbed over the wall or the fencing in the rear, but I don't think so. What gets me is that the front doors and gate were unlocked and open—not wide open, but open. And somebody cut the phone line from the gate. Anyone could have waltzed right in. I'm thinking that Melnik knew the killer, let them in, had a drink—then was killed and robbed."

"Yeah, my thoughts, too. Not a big help, but at least something. Them? Two people?"

"No, just not sure it was a him or a her."

"Got it."

"And he still had on his watch, a nice watch," Alfano said. "I saw one like it at a jeweler's shop. A real robber would have taken it."

"Yes."

"And they knew about Kitty's little hiding place in the floor. That makes it a smaller party, much smaller. Why did they keep the gun at all? The damn thing only weighs a pound and a half. With that short barrel, a strong woman could use it, if she knew how to shoot."

"We are trying to find out when it was made and sold and where," Suarez said. "That might give us a lead. You know as well as I do that there's no list of serial numbers for guns."

"Yes, maybe someday, but not now. Was the information sent on to my sergeant?"

"Yes. I put a copy of the ballistics on a United flight this morning. Your sergeant should have it tomorrow. He can check the grooves against what he has; if there's a match, then we will know."

"Yeah, that information and a dime will get you a cup of coffee."

G loria decided unilaterally to salvage their afternoon picnic lunch. Against Alfano's protests—saying he needed to get back to the hotel—she drove west down Sunset Boulevard and turned north onto the Pacific Coast Highway, telling the still protesting detective that they were going to a small and uncrowded beach she knew. A mile beyond the *Entering*

Malibu sign, Alfano gave in and changed into his swimsuit at a gas station. Another mile on, Gloria pulled to the side of the road near Malibu Road and parked. She pointed to the stretch of beach thirty feet down the bank. A sandy trail worn into the hillside gave them access. While Gloria set up the picnic, Alfano walked to the edge of the ocean and stood wiggling his toes in the wet sand as he smoked a cigarette. A hundred yards offshore, he saw something he'd never seen before.

"What's that? What are those guys doing?" Alfano said, pointing to a group of men drifting on the surface of the sea.

"It's called surfing. You've never seen it?" Gloria said.

"Seen it? I've never even heard of it."

Gloria walked up to Alfano and pushed her shoulder into his back, then passed him a beer.

"Those guys are sitting on long, flat boards made of wood. They wait for one of the bigger swells to run to the beach. If there's enough height and momentum, they stand up and ride the wave in. The surf's not high today, so most of the time they just hang out and talk to each other. I've been here when the waves are ten or fifteen feet high and crashing up and down the beach. Hundreds of guys, and even some girls, ride the surf. It's quite something."

"It looks like a perfect way to waste your time and get sunburned."

Gloria laughed. "Their tans are inches thick. A couple of actors I know are surfers—as they are called. It keeps them in shape for the camera. It's like skiing but on water. I tried it once with a guy I was dating; it was fun. The bitch is that the boards are huge and weigh a ton. I couldn't carry it down to the beach from the parking lot. Maybe that's why there's more guys than gals surfing." She grabbed his hand and hauled him back to the blanket. "Lunch is served."

A pod of pelicans, in a trailing formation, ghosted along the top of the waves and over the dozen or so surfers. The birds disappeared around the point of land to the north.

"It's almost perfect here," Alfano said. "Two people a long way from Denver and Chicago."

"I've decided to be a pal and share my other sandwich with you, since you used yours to bribe those cops."

"One was a bribe, the other was stolen," Alfano answered.

"Either way, I found the whole process at Melnik's interesting," Gloria said.

"I assume you knew Kitty?" Alfano asked as he sat on the blanket.

"Yes, I did, for maybe the last year and a half. Melnik introduced us at one of his parties. Later he had me deliver scripts to her at her apartment. I liked her; she was smart, been around the block as they say. And wasn't afraid to tell me about it. She gave me pointers like a big sister. She never talked about who she was before LA."

"Did you know she was from Chicago?"

"I thought so, maybe guessed it. She had a picture on her wall. When I asked, she said it was in Chicago. She never came right out and said, though. One evening we split a nice bottle of Scotch a friend gave her. It was the real stuff, Cutty Sark, fancy-shmancy, I thought. She started talking about a city she once lived in, back East. Cold all the fucking time, she said, noisy, lots of gangs, killings. I guessed Chicago or Detroit, maybe Milwaukee. Some friends of hers died, maybe were murdered? It sounded that way. She said she took off right after that, came to California. She told me to never tell anyone about what she said—makes no difference now, I guess."

Alfano sipped his beer. "She was a dancer and a singer in Chicago about ten years ago. Her stage name was Kitty Hall then; I guess she changed it to Hill when she got here. She had a good reputation, worked some of the swankier clubs. People said she was good, had a chance."

Katherine Mooney, her given name, had an older brother

named Ian, Alfano told Gloria. He filled in what he knew of Katherine's history: As children, the siblings came to America from Ireland with their parents. The parents were believed to have died around 1918 from the Spanish flu. By then, the kids were pretty much on their own. Kitty was singing in a church choir and performing at clubs. Ian got caught up in an Irish gang on the Northside run by a guy called O'Banion. Then Kitty fell for a guy, Allen O'Neal, who worked with Ian. They got married; she was maybe twenty-three. Life was good, she probably thought. The boys were running booze from Canada. A lot of the places where Kitty worked bought O'Banion's bootleg liquor. Then, as things usually go, they crossed the wrong man—Al Capone. One night, the guys were gunned down outside a bar in the Irish part of Chicago.

"I was told that Kitty saw it all, that she knew the killer, and knew she was next. She took off, came here, and started a new life. You know more about her second life than I do."

"That's a story that would make a movie, Detective. Maybe I'll write it."

"I'll be your technical advisor."

"Deal." They clinked beer bottles. "Kitty was into some pretty nasty stuff, you know that," Gloria said.

"I assumed—I saw the evidence in her apartment. Do you think somebody wanted her dead over that?"

"Who knows? There's big money in stag films and porn—or so I've been told. And I was told that the gangs back East are involved. A lot of the money comes through their affiliates here. There are rumors of money for films, money for unions, money for the right job and the right production crew." She smiled. "But to kill somebody, to shoot them down in cold blood?"

"I've seen people killed for their shoes, Gloria. It's not a nice world out there, and in some places, it is downright shitty and barbaric. And in the gangs, it's worse."

"How's the sandwich?"

"Like I was home in Little Italy."

They sat in silence, looking out at the water where the surfers still drifted on their boards. Gloria looked thoughtful.

"Every big city has an Italian district. Here in LA, we're a mongrel lot," she said. "People are from everywhere, Europe, Mexico, China, and from across the country. They bring their music and food, clothes, and their good ideas and bad habits. Right now, oil runs this town—there are oil wells everywhere. You probably saw some. There's a hill south of downtown that just prickles with oil rigs, ugly as sin. But it greases the wheels of the city; there's graft, corruption—what's not to like? You can find your poison anywhere in this town. There's a rumor that they are going to build those derricks out there in the ocean, goddamn them."

"The weather is nice," Alfano said as he laid back.

"You've been lucky. Wait a few days when it's a hundred and ten degrees and the dust blows in from the desert, and the hills, right up there, are on fire, and the smoke in the city is so thick you can't breathe, then you will change your mind. But, hell, last Christmas it was seventy degrees."

Durant had gone on about the fires, too, Alfano remembered. He didn't mention that to Gloria. He said, "It was bitter cold in Chicago; I worked that day."

"And in Denver, too, so I won't complain too much. I guess you need to get back?"

"I pissed J.J. off today. I need to be at the studio at nine. Perhaps I can go home at the end of the week."

"You should check with that friend of yours, Detective Tuttle. Maybe they could use a cop like you out here."

Alfano looked out across the water. A soft swell had developed, and the men and their boards rose up and down; the pelicans made a return trip.

"I like Chicago, been there my whole life, so I'll probably

pass. But I get why you suggested it."

"Never let an opportunity pass you by," Gloria said.

24

Monday night, after eating dinner alone at the diner on 2nd Street, Alfano bought a Cuban cigar from the tobacco store on the corner and strolled through the park that capped the bluff above the Santa Monica beach. The pier below was lit with colored lights that spun and flashed; hundreds of people walked along its wooden boards. The air was still, the ocean glasslike, the setting sun spit a fiery orange boulevard across the water's surface and directly at him. *Yeah, it would be nice here, walk away from all the shit in Chicago, breathe fresh air for a change. Yeah, maybe be a cop. Beverly Hills was nice, the LA Police looked professional, but then again there was a hard side to Tuttle, intolerant, rough, even for a Mick. Pull up stakes at my age, not likely. Then again, I can adjust to almost anything. I've done it on the force a dozen times. New captains, new sergeants, new mayors, all such bullshit. DiTomasi and his Italian deli, now there was an idea. Maybe the movies, acting? Anthony Alfano, just shut the fuck up—what the hell are you thinking? You got a limited future, and that future sure as hell ain't in California.*

The room phone woke him from the first good sleep he'd had in a week. He looked at the clock: 5:45 AM. He groggily remembered walking back to his room and collapsing into bed.

"Who the hell?" he said.

"Sorry, Detective. Suarez here."

"You getting to miss me at this time of the night?"

"I sure as hell would trade places with you right now. I got a body."

"I hate calls that begin, 'I got a body.' It never turns out well."

"Well, it didn't for them."

"Oh, bodies."

"Yeah, I got two. Both found in the swimming pool."

"Only in Los Angeles."

"Beverly Hills."

"Even better. Name or names?"

"Adam Roberts."

"Well, fuck."

"Yeah, there's that, too. I'm at his house. The coroner will be here in an hour. He was on a fly-fishing trip, got in late. Needed his sleep."

"There's a lot of that need going around. Give me the address; I'll catch a taxi."

"Thanks. My guy is getting coffee—black?"

"As black as possible."

Alfano sat back on the bed and lit his first cigarette of the day. He checked his watch, then lifted the receiver and made a long-distance call. After a ten-minute conversation, he dressed, secured his weapon, took the elevator to the ground floor, saw the closed restaurant, listened to his stomach yell, and then wandered out to the street. He had a tangible feeling that the approaching sunrise promised a hot day. A yellow cab sat at the curb, its windows down.

"That you, Detective Alfano?" a woman's voice asked through the open window.

"Ruby? You work night shift hours?"

"I get all the handsome men to myself then. Where we

going?"

"A few blocks from last Thursday. I got to see the man."

"I assume there's a murder or two involved?"

"An assumption?"

"Not really. The LA Police's newfangled radio transmitter—call letters KGPL—can be picked up on my car radio. It keeps me entertained and busy. You would be surprised about how many people want to go to the scene of a crime, or escape said scene. There was a call sent by the Beverly Hills Police for some help at a scene where two male bodies were found. LA broadcast the initial report at four forty-five this morning."

"So, you were waiting for me?"

"That would not be right, Detective—that would be called stalking or something. Anyway, what's the address?"

Alfano handed Ruby the slip of paper with the address he'd jotted down as he talked with Suarez.

"Yep, just a few blocks from that dead movie director. Fifteen minutes, if the . . ."

". . . traffic ain't bad," Alfano said.

"You are learning, Detective."

Ruby was on a mission; she took twelve-and-one-half minutes door to door on the mostly empty streets. His knuckles must have barely recovered their feeling when she slid the car to a stop in front of Roberts's house. Three patrol cars were parked on the street and along the curb. Snugged in between was a nondescript black Ford. Alfano knew it was Suarez's. A dozen people in bathrobes and various stages of dress stood across the street watching. Three of the uniformed cops stood in the driveway smoking.

"Do you want me to wait? Same deal as before," Ruby said as she backed up against the curb.

"Yeah, wait. What do you charge by the hour?"

"Normally ten dollars. For you, I'll make an exception—it's twenty. Hazard pay; there's guns around. And I think you still owe me ten from last Thursday."

"Cute, but twenty it is if you throw in the return trip to the hotel."

"Done. Do you want me to get coffee? There's a diner down the hill, open all night."

"I was promised a cup."

"Good luck with that. Just let me know if the police deal falls through. I'm going to get one and I'll bring you a backup."

"Thanks, Ruby."

Alfano walked up the drive to the cops.

"You Detective Alfano?" the sergeant asked.

"Yes. Detective Suarez, he inside?"

"Through that open door."

Alfano went as directed. Another uniform stood at the door. He held a clipboard, Alfano identified himself, the cop waved him in.

"They are in the back; coffee is in a thermos in the kitchen. Please don't touch anything," the cop said. He looked at least thirteen years old, all bright and shiny, his uniform a little too large, the hat a little too settled over his ears. Alfano smiled, nodded thanks, crossed through the house, and found the kitchen where an odd collection of cups littered the counter. A stainless-steel thermos stood on the counter. He picked it up—empty.

"Sorry, I tried to save you a cup. My back was turned," Suarez said.

"My day already stinks," Alfano answered.

"The bodies are next to the pool. This way."

The two detectives walked through the house to a rear-facing wall of windows. A French door was centered in the panels, and beyond lay a terrace and a pool. A diminutive oriental woman sat in a chair in the hallway; an officer stood near her. Alfano guessed she was Chinese.

"She's the maid and cook. Her name is Luanne. Her English is excellent," Suarez said.

The woman looked up and in perfect English said, "I went to USC, acting. I needed a job. Adam was kind. This all sucks."

"She comes in early to make breakfast for Roberts," Suarez said, "especially on shooting days. She usually goes directly into her work. She found this door open. She walked out, expecting to find the 'boys,' as she calls them, passed out on the lounges. It would not be the first time, she said. She saw no one. When she went to the edge of the pool to collect glasses and other things that needed to be cleaned from the tables, she saw two dark shapes in the lights. They were at the bottom of the pool."

A deep, caught-breath sigh came from Luanne. "Awful," she said.

Alfano looked out the windows; Suarez's partner, Buddy Loomis, and a second man stood next to two bodies neatly laid out on the paving stones a few feet from the pool's edge. The terrace was still wet around the bodies, both of whom were male, wearing bathing suits and colorful, loose buttoned shirts. Alfano went out to the terrace. Suarez followed.

"Good morning, Detective Loomis."

"Nothing fucking good about it. It is too damn early for this shit."

"Yeah, there's that," Alfano said as he looked down at the bodies. They appeared asleep; they hadn't been in the water long—his guess maybe a few hours. He studied the area around the terrace, the small tables, and what was on the tables. He went to the edge of the pool and stared into the water. He followed the wet terrace stains to the bodies, then noticed small shards of broken glass under one of the tables and across the deck—not good for bare feet, he thought.

"You might have your boys look and see if there are any larger pieces still lying around," he said, pointing. "I'm thinking these two were not alone. You never know, maybe a fingerprint."

"These were big men," Suarez said. "You don't hold their heads underwater and wait for them to drown. Maybe there were a couple of guys helping."

"So, you think murder?" Alfano said.

"Or, maybe they was drunk, one fell in, and the other tried to rescue him. Then the fags struggle until they both drown," Loomis said.

"That's helpful, thanks, Buddy," Suarez said tightly.

Alfano got down on one knee and looked at the faces. "I see no scrapes, no bruises, their hands show no cuts, and both have manicured nails—if either struggled, there would be marks or scratches. No obvious wounds. Neither was shot or stabbed. Sadly, I've seen a few drowned people in my career; they can be a mess if there was an attempted rescue—a drowning man will do anything to stay alive."

He looked at the bottoms of both men's feet.

"They did not cross this paving after the glass was broken. There are no cuts on the soles of their feet, either one. It's a bet they were in the water before the glass was broken. Interesting."

Alfano looked back to the doors. Two pairs of tennis shoes sat neatly next to each other on the stone paving. The exterior lights were still on, as were the pool lights. There were no liquor bottles, no pitchers, only two glasses. This small party of two had ended poorly.

"Do we know who the other man is?" Alfano asked.

"Luanne says his name is Wells Barker," Suarez said. "When she started working here a year ago, they were together. She says they were very close."

"I'm gathering that's not unusual," Alfano said.

"Thick as fleas on a dog here in Tinseltown," Loomis offered.

"So I'm learning. An actor as well?"

"Not unusual either," Suarez said.

"Strange town," Alfano said.

"No shit, Sherlock," Loomis blurted.

A commotion came from inside the house, preceding a man in a pinstripe suit walking out onto the terrace. He was tall, lanky, wore specs, and sported a thin, stylish mustache. His hat was a straw boater with a brown and orange band. He looked more like a banker than the coroner. Alfano knew who he was; they'd met at Melnik's four nights earlier.

"Not home six hours and already back to work. This town stinks," the coroner said.

"Dr. Goodspeed," Alfano said. "How was the fishing?"

The doctor lit up. "I caught a four-pound rainbow near one of the tributaries that feeds Big Bear Lake. In a canoe, mind you. With my son, nothing better. So, Suarez, what do we have?"

For the next half hour, the coroner studied everything about the bodies. He poked and prodded, opened their shirts, looked at the fingers and arms, even the toes.

"Preliminarily, I'd say they both drowned, and I agree with Detective Alfano about the lack of injuries. I'll know for certain after the autopsy. You are in luck—even with the weekend, there's no backlog. They are first on the list. I'll also look for drugs; that's a possibility. These actors and actresses have recently been doing some strange stuff, heroin, cocaine, so who knows? No obvious needle marks, but I'll look, of course. Anything else, Suarez?"

"No, Doc. When do you think?"

"Preliminary, midafternoon at the earliest. Just pray some of your partners don't step into line before you."

25

Instead of going back to his hotel, Alfano asked Ruby about a place to eat near the Sierra Film studio. He also asked her to join him.

"I don't often eat with the customers," Ruby said as she wolfed down a stack of pancakes and a side of bacon. "I drop them at some of the fanciest places in town, and pick 'em up there, too. But never go inside. I watch my budget—thanks for this, Detective, delicious."

She looked at Alfano with a warm smile, causing him to flatter himself with a rude thought.

"You are a Chicago detective. Why the hell are you out here?" she asked him.

"You have a good memory. I'm a technical advisor for a movie. So far, the producer and director of the movie is dead, murdered with two bullets in his chest. His executive assistant was murdered in Chicago two weeks ago, also two bullets. And back there in Beverly Hills were two men, also probably murdered, who were fished out of a swimming pool. One was the star of the film under production, the other was his boyfriend."

"There's a lot of that going around," Ruby said. She pointed to her coffee cup; the waitress nodded.

"So, I hear—homosexuality or murder?"

"Both, Detective. I read the papers and listen to the police radio. You would think this town was one bad movie itself. Riots, shootings, dead bodies, Sodom and Gomorrah stuff—it all makes you wonder about people and civilization."

"Yeah, twenty years scraping up people from gutters makes you kind of hard about them." Alfano finished his scrambled eggs. "You from here, Ruby?"

"Unless you are a Latino, Mexican, or Indian, all of us white folks are from somewhere else. This all was once a part of Spain, then Mexico, then the United States, and all stolen from the Indians. It's been fucked so many times its bastard children are wandering around like lost souls in the wilderness. I've seen a lot driving a taxi, sometimes too much. It's getting close to the time for this girl to get out. I like the heat, it's cleansing, so maybe Yuma or Phoenix. I was from Minneapolis originally, farm family. Came here twenty years ago."

Alfano resigned himself to another life story, though he had to admit he was interested in the events that landed people in this town of broken dreams.

"I was just a kid," Ruby was saying. "I needed to get away from a bad family situation before it killed me—or I killed it. I didn't know shit from Shinola. Jumped right in, fell in love with a guy named Lucky; he was from somewhere in the San Joaquin Valley, Modesto, I think. Beautiful man, and I loved him dearly. One day he walked out of a bar and into a streetcar. Cut him up into four pieces, so they say. That was enough connubial bliss for me. There was a little insurance—Lucky worked for an insurance company. With the money, I bought a taxi. Been my own boss since and will never go back to working for someone else. But, as they say, this town has a thousand sad stories. You staying in LA, Detective?"

"In about an hour they will shut down the movie I'm here for, fire whoever squawks and those who don't, claim the insurance if they bought some, and after pissing on everyone they'll pull up their pants and start something new tomorrow. I will, blessedly and with the grace of God, be on a train to Chicago tomorrow night."

"You will miss Los Angeles," Ruby said. "I know you will."

"Ruby Lombardi, I can assure you I will not miss Los Angeles. And send me a card from Phoenix—it will give me a reason to find it on a map."

An hour later, Alfano was proved prescient. Detective Suarez broke the news to J.J. Jones, while Alfano sat in a chair in the back of the production office. Alfano wasn't sure if Jones was happy or crushed. He just stared at the cop then stood, took a deep breath, and yelled: "Shut it down! Everyone out. We are done. This movie is over." He looked around the room. "Where's Durant? Where the hell is that bitch? Anybody seen her?"

It was an excellent question, one Alfano had wondered about since walking into the studio. Where the hell was the female star of the movie? He looked at Suarez and tilted his head toward the door; they walked out.

"One of three things has happened, Detective Suarez," Alfano said. "Maxime Durant is dead somewhere like her moving picture partner, she's hiding out waiting for this to blow over, or she knows what happened and is preparing to take off."

"You think that actress could put those two men in the pool?" Suarez said.

"If they were drugged, or unconscious, yeah, maybe. She'd just roll them across the deck into the pool and let nature do the job. That's what we call in Chicago a working hypothetical theory."

"We call them that here, too, Detective. By the way, a little more information. After you left Roberts's house, one of the neighbors—who most emphatically did not appreciate the activities of the residents of Roberts's house and the antics of his sometime guests—told me that someone who looked remarkably like the actress Maxime Durant—'that witch with a painted face,' she called her—was walking down the street a few houses down from Roberts's house late last night. This local informer and her husband were walking their dog, a white standard poodle named Fifi, I'm told. When they rounded the corner, Durant passed them in a hurry. She turned her head away when she saw them, but they were directly under one of the streetlights and the neighbor immediately recognized her. They didn't speak, but Fifi barked. The informer claims she isn't one of those nosy neighbor types. However, she also added that there was a yellow car parked at the curb the next street over. She'd never seen it in the neighborhood before. Her husband, who was all excited about the vehicle, called it a Packard coupe."

Alfano lit a cigarette. "I suggest we pay Miss Durant a visit, find out if she knew where her car was last night, and ask if she has an alibi."

The lobby of the Beverly Wilshire Hotel was busy. When Detective Suarez flashed his shield, the manager shrugged.

"I haven't seen Miss Durant for a few days, Detective," he said, clearly trying to act distracted. "If you would like to leave a message, I will see that she gets it."

Suarez leaned in, looked at the man's name plaque, and calmly said, "Mr. Grande, you are going to go quietly to the elevator with us, then we are going up to Miss Durant's suite, where you will knock on her door and tell her that you have an important message for her. When she opens the door, you will leave. Do you understand?"

"Well, I'm not sure; let me call her first. We respect the privacy of our residents."

Alfano leaned in next to Suarez and added, "I'm sure you do, but there is a chance that Miss Durant is injured, possibly dead. We need to find out. All on the QT, get it? And I'm sure you don't want the police and the coroner wheeling their gurney through here in about an hour, leaving a mess and all. It would not be good for business. So, shall we?"

The manager looked shocked. He did as told, knocked politely on Durant's door; there was no response. Suarez firmly moved Mr. Grande to one side and banged with his fist. The pounding echoed up and down the hallway. A door across the hall opened about an inch.

"Miss Durant is gone," a small, high-pitched voice said through the crack. "She left an hour ago, all in a hurry. Passed me in the hallway, didn't even say how do you do. Are you the police?"

"Open up the apartment," Suarez said to the manager.

"Don't you need a warrant or something?" Grande pleaded.

"There may be an injured party inside, so open the door. If not, I will bust it open—and you will wait till hell freezes over for reimbursement from the city. What will it be?" Suarez took a few steps back and turned his shoulder toward the door.

The manger hurriedly produced his keys and opened the door.

"Wait here," Alfano said to Mr. Grande before following Suarez into the suite. It was unoccupied. They did a cursory look around. An open bottle of bourbon sat on the kitchen counter along with a single glass that held a touch of brown liquor.

"Where do you think she went?" Suarez said as he eyed the glass. Fingerprints covered its surface. He wrapped a thin towel around the glass and slipped it in his pocket.

"I've got an idea. I need to make a call."

Alfano took out his wallet and looked at a card inside. He then picked up the phone. Nothing.

"How do I make a phone call?" he yelled out to the manager.

"Is it a local call?"

"Look, just tell me. You don't want Detective Suarez to ask you questions for the rest of the day at police headquarters."

"Double-click the cradle. Tell the switchboard the number you want; they will get you your party."

Alfano told the operator the number. It rang a few times; a male voice could be heard.

"Good morning, sunshine. Alfano here. I need the address of Kitty Hill's apartment."

"You could have asked me," Suarez said behind him. "You did send me there on an errand involving a gun."

"I'm old and tired; I forgot. Sorry, David." Alfano hung up.

26

S uarez drove, they hit Santa Monica Boulevard again. Alfano was beginning to feel at home; he recognized landmarks and empty lots. They turned north onto Brockton, the one-story apartment complex on the left.

"Take a lap around the block," Alfano said. "Look for a yellow Packard ragtop."

Durant's car was parallel-parked in the alley behind the building.

"Good call, Alfano," Suarez said.

"You would have gotten here," Alfano answered.

"Maybe."

"Drop me here in the alley, then you go around to the front. Take the walkway that splits the complex, box her in. You've already met Candy; I don't want to relive the pleasure."

"She did say you were a handsome guy, asked me if I knew your phone number. Want me to set you up? Could make for an interesting evening."

"You're so thoughtful."

Alfano entered the two-building complex through the open gate of the rear entrance and studied the door of Kitty Hill's apartment that faced the courtyard. He jacked his Colt and chambered a round. Obviously, Durant knew the back way in; she'd been here many times. Durant and Hill were in the porn business together; how far their other business dealings went, he had a few ideas, but nothing concrete. Hill was the financial and management side; Durant acquired the talent and handled production. They needed fresh faces, girls and boys who moved back and forth in the film industry. And they all needed a buck.

The door to the apartment was closed but not shut tight; a finger-width gap ran down the doorframe. Using his left hand, he slowly pushed the door inward. Daylight streamed through the high windows at the back of the front room. Durant was on her hands and knees, scratching away at the floor. The grey rug had been pulled aside and lay crumpled against the wall. A small chrome revolver lay on the floor a foot from Durant's right hand. Alfano watched her bang around on the floor with her fists, then she stopped and scratched with her nails at the floorboards.

"Fuck, it was here. I know it's here," she mumbled.

Durant paused, hooked her fingernails in a seam, and slowly pulled up the floorboards that covered the hidey-hole. She gasped, reached in, and waved her hand back and forth through the space. "Fuckers, shit."

"Looking for something, lover?" Alfano said.

Durant flinched, then reached for the revolver.

"Don't, just don't. It would be a waste to shoot you. I'd get nothing out of it. So just don't, Miss Durant. Just crawl back a few feet, slowly stand, and put your back to the wall. Be careful, very careful."

Durant looked furious but did as ordered. Alfano crossed the space between the door and the desk. Without looking, he kicked the small revolver backward across the floor toward the door behind him.

"Take a seat, Maxime. I have a few questions." He pointed to a chair to her right.

"You have no jurisdiction here, Alfano. Why don't you go home to bum-fuck Illinois and play with the pigs and cows— you got nothing on me." Durant hinted a smile, her eyes grew larger, her focus now behind him.

Alfano felt the muzzle of a pistol at the back of his neck.

"Is this the man you were expecting, dearie?" Candy Longacre said. She blew into Alfano's ear. He grimaced.

"He is a bit of a dreamboat, but shit, there's dozens in this town, a dime a fucking dozen. What do you want me to do with him, Miss Durant? Shoot him?"

Durant stiffened; a smile came over her face. There was nothing kitten-like about her now. She had the look a snake made before it struck. "That's a brilliant idea, but right now I'd rather take the opportunity to . . . Candy!"

Alfano heard the sickening thud of steel on bone. He heard, as well as felt, Candy Longacre's body as she fell against him and collapsed to the floor.

"Detective Suarez, I hope?"

"And not a minute too soon," Suarez said.

Alfano kept his weapon on Durant as he heard handcuffs being snapped on Longacre. She moaned.

"She'll live," Suarez said.

Still pointing the pistol at Durant, Alfano nodded at the chair. She sat. He grabbed another chair and placed it directly in front of her.

"That hole is an interesting place to put something. What were you looking for, Maxime?"

"None of your fucking business," the actress said.

"*Au contraire*, it is my business and that of Detective Suarez as well. What were you looking for?"

Durant's glare was acerbic, cutting. Her acting skills were good; the hair on the back of Alfano's neck rose like the hair on a dog's back. She crossed her arms, which had the effect of pushing up and accentuating her breasts.

"Look, Maxime, I want to go home to bum-fuck Illinois—get out of this sunny land of Sodom and Gomorrah. And my patience is gone, too, so I'll start. You can fill in where you want. Okay?"

"Fuck you," she said through gritted teeth.

"First of all, the gun, the movies, and the ledgers and note-book, and what looked like Kitty Hill's diary that were in the hidey-hole are now in Detective Suarez's possession. He tells me the movies are quite entertaining." Alfano turned to the now awake Candy Longacre. "The reviews are that your bits, *dearie*, are overacted and exaggerated. Somebody recognized you from your silent films from at least ten years ago."

Candy glowered at him but said nothing. Alfano turned back to Durant.

"Detective Suarez is getting warrants for the bank and the safety deposit boxes listed inside the books. His people are good at figuring out the codes that you and Kitty used. You shouldn't have used the bank directly across the street from the Beverly Wilshire; that made it too easy."

"I don't know anything about any banks or boxes," Durant said.

"Please, of course you do. Detective Suarez tells me that you have a little money in your bank account yet live well be-yond your means—living large, as they say. The porn industry is a cash-and-carry business; reminds me of Prohibition. Al Capone learned the hard way, and now you will, too. The IRS will want to look into all this. I'm sure the detective will pass on the information."

"I earned that money."

"I am certain you did—moving on. Adam Roberts and his boyfriend are dead. Detective Suarez tells me that what hap-pened was made to look like an accident. He believes it was, in fact, murder. His cracker-jack coroner tells us there was a barbiturate residue in the drinks, so after having their drinks they may have accidentally fallen into the pool and drowned. Me? I'm going with their being rolled into the pool while unconscious, but the betting money is even on that. We found a fingerprint on a piece of broken glass that matches yours. I'm doubling down on you drugging them and rolling them into the pool."

"Why the hell would I do that?" Maxime said.

"For the same reason people have been killing people since Cain and Abel," Alfano said.

"What?"

"Money, and to shut them up because you killed Hines Melnik, and Roberts saw you do it. With Roberts dead, you would be in the clear. You could keep all the money."

"I didn't kill Melnik. Melnik's the one who tried to kill us. We went there to get paid; he owed us, all legal and all. He pulls this gun out of the safe—"

Candy mumbled something.

"One second, Maxime. What was that, Miss Longacre?" Alfano asked.

"Maxime, you stupid bitch, keep your fucking mouth shut. They got nothing on you," Candy screamed. "Don't say shit."

"Good advice, Candy," Alfano said. "Maxime, that's the best advice you'll get today. But, since you just admitted that you and Adam were there Thursday night, and Detective Suarez needs a perpetrator for the murder, and now that Adam is dead, my guess is he's going to go with you."

"I insist," Suarez said.

"See, Maxime."

"What?" Suarez said, turning his head to the door.

Alfano heard footsteps; he looked past Candy, still on the floor, to Suarez. A uniformed cop had arrived and handed the detective a note. Alfano waited.

Suarez whistled. "This is all?" he asked the uniform.

"They are still looking; Detective Loomis says they have

three more banks to visit. May not finish until tomorrow."

"Thanks." Suarez walked over to Alfano and showed him the writing.

"Wow, interesting," Alfano said, then looked up at Suarez. "This was in the safety deposit boxes?"

"Yes, Detective, almost a quarter of a million dollars in fifties and hundreds; not new. It was like the money you'd find on the street, not in a bank."

"There's more in the other banks, I'm sure. What do you know about this, Miss Durant?"

Durant's face was wet from perspiration. "Nothing. I don't know nothing about any of that money," she said.

"Your boxes, your money." Alfano thought for moment, then smiled. "Unless it wasn't your money. Detective, do you know a John Roselli? He was called 'Handsome Johnny' in Chicago."

"Sure, he's been here eight or ten years. High-profile Hollywood type, listed as the executive producer on a few films. There are rumors about connections to the mobs back East— your town, too—Capone and Frank Nitti. But Roselli has kept his nose clean here."

"Yeah, that's where I knew him. I was with Miss Durant having dinner the other night at Musso's and . . . what was the name?"

"Musso and Frank Grill. Good prime rib."

"Right, so Saturday night Maxime introduces Roselli to me. I could tell they were more than friends. Well, I knew Handsome Johnny back in Chicago. He took off for Los Angeles during the Capone and the Outfit's best days. Now, why would he do that? There was nothing out here on the Coast at the time, just oil and movies. The oil didn't mean much to the Outfit, but LA had films, unions, cute girls, big budgets, entertainment, and things that go bump-bump in the night. All things that the mobs like."

Alfano was beginning to enjoy himself. He looked at Suarez and spoke to Durant.

"Maxime, you were John Roselli's bagman—I mean bagwoman—for the Chicago mob, weren't you? The money from their operations in gambling, booze, prostitution, and films needed cleaning, a way to make it legit. And after Capone was convicted of tax evasion, they really needed it washed. You got the Chicago money from Roselli, passed it on to Melnik for his film interests—all his interests—and then made sure it came back to them through the ticket sales."

Alfano could practically feel Durant's eyes burning a hole in his forehead.

"Don't say nothing, Maxie, don't. He's making up shit—aren't you, you dumb fuck," Candy said.

"The way I see it," Alfano said, "Thursday night you went to Melnik to extort him, make him pay to keep his mouth shut about what happened and to give you a bigger piece. He believed you were the one who shot Kitty—and Kitty Hill was in this up to her pretty little neck, too. When Melnik told you I was coming out here to LA, you believed that I was coming to arrest you for Kitty's murder. Am I right?"

"Melnik thought it was me," Durant said in a low voice. "I was on my knees next to her. She was dying."

"Jesus, Maxie, shut the fuck up," said Candy.

Durant ignored her. "When Melnick came through the pass-through door, he found me with her. Blood was everywhere; he went nuts. The gun was a few feet away. He tried to grab it, I got it first, and pointed it at him. He stopped. 'We need to clean this all up,' he said. 'I have a hundred thousand riding on the movie. I can't have my star wrapped up in a murder.' I told him I didn't do it. I found her on the floor. He told me to get out. He said if it wasn't me, then it had to be Adam who killed her. But I knew different—it was Hines."

"Sure you did. Then what happened?" Suarez said.

"I was in a daze. I loved her," Durant said so pitifully that Alfano almost believed her. "Hines took the gun and put it in his belt . . . locked the door," she continued. "I saw him lock it. It was strange that the door was unlocked to begin with, I remember thinking that. I took one last look at Kitty and followed him back into his room. He told me to go to my room and change into clean clothes—mine were covered in her blood. He would clean up everything; he told me to meet him in the back stairway in fifteen minutes, bring my bloody clothes so we could dump them. I did what he said."

"Melnik told you that Roberts shot Kitty—how did he know?" Alfano said.

"I don't know. He just said it. She was dying when I found her. All she said was the name Ian. I don't know who Ian is. Do you?"

"You were at Melnik's last Thursday night?" Suarez asked.

"Yeah, you were right. We both were. It was money, a lot of money. We were owed for six months of work, things that Kitty arranged. He owed me for the vig on the drop—Adam didn't know anything about that side venture. Melnik invited us over before we started on the picture, to have a clean slate, 'even-up everything,' he said. We went to his upstairs office. We talked, came to an agreement. He went to the wall safe. When he turned his back to us, he had the gun—it looked like the gun that killed Kitty. He was out of control. He pointed it at Adam and kept screaming, 'I'll kill you, you son of a bitch! I'll kill you for killing Kitty.' Adam denied it, said he didn't know what Hines was talking about. Adam began backing away. That's when I threw an ashtray at Hines. It was big. It hit Hines's arm, and he dropped the gun. Adam pushed him away, grabbed the gun, and shot him in the chest. Twice, I think. Then we ran."

"Who took the money?" Suarez said.

"Money? What money?" Durant protested.

"The money in the safe," Suarez said.

"You said he was going to pay you for your work in the porn industry. That's what it was for, right?" Alfano said.

Durant looked again at Alfano. "We earned every fucking nickel. It was ours."

"Yeah, but there was a lot more money than Roberts ever expected, right?" Alfano said. "A lot more than what was owed the two of you. You knew what the money was; it was the mob's money. You knew there were hundreds of thousands of dollars. What did you do? Tell Roberts that you'd make sure he'd get what was due him?"

When Durant didn't answer, Alfano continued. "He wanted half right then, and you panicked. So you and Roberts split the money, and both of you took off and left Melnik dead on the floor of his office. You made it look like a robbery?"

Durant stared at him but said nothing.

"So, Roberts killed Melnik," Alfano said. "Is he the one that sent the photo of Kitty to Melnik? The one he stole from the coroner's office in Chicago?"

Durant grinned. "Maybe? I don't know. Roberts took something from the desk as we left; it could have been it. Doesn't make any fucking difference. I saw him put two bullets in the man's chest. Said it served the asshole right for stiffing us. He laughed at his joke."

"Detective Suarez, how much money was in the safe in Roberts's bedroom?"

Durant's eyes widened; her face reddened.

"Someone failed to lock the tumbler," Suarez said. "We were going to get a safecracker, but we got lucky. The safe was as empty as a banker's heart. And there was a nice handprint on the top of the chair that sits directly under the safe; the safe was wiped, not the chair. The prints matched the ones on a piece of broken glass . . ."

"Do you think there was money or something else inside?" Alfano asked him.

"A reasonable guess is money. The number I showed you was from Miss Durant's bank, the one across Wilshire."

"You might also check the trunk of her yellow Packard."

"My thoughts exactly."

"I like your story," Alfano said to Durant. "You played your part exceptionally well, maybe worthy of an Oscar. Except it's all a fucking lie."

"Fuck you, Alfano. I liked you—you fuck like a pro, energetic, involved. I even thought about offering you a job out here. Handsome adventurous old guy, young girls . . . that shit makes lots of money in this industry."

"I'd want a piece of that," Candy said. "Ouch, that fucking hurt."

"Another word, and I'll kick in your teeth," Suarez said, removing his shoe from the vicinity of her left kidney.

"See, Antonio, you already have fans," Durant said. "But there's a halo around you; you just fucking glow. I'd be wasting my time, Mr. Goody Two-Shoes. You're a Boy Scout."

Candy sniggered.

Alfano also heard a chuckle from Suarez, which made him uncomfortable. More cops had arrived and were outside the door. One of them was Detective Tuttle.

Alfano watched Durant look past Suarez and the uniforms to where Tuttle stood in the doorway. Her expression changed only slightly, but Alfano knew a tell when he saw one.

"Hi, Gil," he said and turned back to Durant. "That's all bullshit, isn't it, Maxime? Maybe your bit about Melnik and Kitty in Chicago is true, maybe it's not—right now, we'll just leave it lying on the table. Maybe Melnik, like you said, believed that Roberts, for some reason, did shoot Kitty. What I am thinking is that Melnik and Kitty had meetings in Chicago, meetings you weren't involved in. Meetings with the money people you've been doing the bag work for. Melnik needed a lot of money for his movie and was there to get it. Maybe that farce you described in Melnik's office with Roberts was also real, to a point—but the only witness is dead, which is convenient. Maybe that's why all of you came back to LA in a hurry, because Melnik had a bag full of money—yeah, that might be it, too. And he also had the gun. It comes down to the gun."

"There's no way to prove any of this—no fucking way," Durant spat out.

"It was you, Maxime, who picked up the gun after Roberts knocked it out of Melnik's hand, and it was you who shot Melnik twice, point blank in the chest. It was you who convinced Roberts to keep his mouth shut—maybe you told him about the money, even gave him some to keep him quiet. Then you came here and hid the gun in the hidey-hole. You thought it was safe, and since you were paying Kitty's rent, you believed no one would find it. Roberts didn't know where you hid it, I'm certain about that. You would come back later and move it to a safer place or destroy it. However, you couldn't have Roberts holding Melnik's death over you, and you couldn't let him keep any of the money. So, last night, you went to his house, drugged him and his boyfriend, and rolled them into the pool—all to shut Roberts up. Then you conveniently cleaned out his safe—after all, it was your money, all of it. All neat and pretty."

"You can't prove any of that."

"We have your fingerprints on the gun," Suarez said to Durant. "Melnik's, too, but funny thing, Roberts's fingerprints aren't on the gun. It looks like he never touched the revolver. The fingerprints on the broken glass are yours, too, which puts you at Roberts's pool, and your fingerprints are on the chair by Roberts's safe. We have eyewitnesses who saw you on the street outside Roberts's house that night. You are going down for three murders, Miss Durant. And I'm sure Detective Alfano wants to pin the murder of Kitty Hill on you, too."

"She was the only good thing in this whole fucked-up

town," Durant said. "I didn't kill Kitty. I loved her."

"Sure you did. We always kill the things we love," Alfano said as he caught the handcuffs Tuttle pitched to him.

27

Alfano, Tuttle, and Suarez stood on the dead grass outside Kitty Hill's apartment. They watched as Durant and Longacre were trundled into the back seat of an LA patrol car. Durant took one long look at Alfano before the door was slammed shut.

Suarez grinned and said, "You're good, Alfano. Most of that was bullshit." Tuttle agreed.

"Good bullshit is based on real shit, and this crime is plastered with it," Alfano said. "She didn't flinch, even at the part about Roselli and the mob. I've been hearing about money going to Los Angeles from Chicago, so the connection makes sense—and she didn't blink—interesting. That's a bone for you to gnaw on, Detective. When the coroner finishes processing the bodies and confirms the fingerprints on that glass you slipped in your pocket, you can charge her with the murders of Melnik, Roberts, and his boyfriend. She might get the rope for Roberts, but who knows? With a good attorney, she could even skate. It will make the Fatty Arbuckle trial in San Francisco look like a cheap circus."

"Are you going to ask for extradition for Durant? She's the one who obviously killed Kitty Hill," Tuttle said.

"She didn't kill Hill, and neither did Melnik or Roberts,"

Alfano said.

"What? It sure as hell sounded like you had one of them pegged for the killing," Suarez said.

"It's a matter of the gun," Alfano said to Suarez. "The ballistics report you sent to my sergeant is being processed. Sergeant McDunnah is a diligent man"—he looked at the LA detective—"you know him, Tuttle."

"Truly diligent, Detective. I've known the boyo since we were lads in Bridgeport. No finer man, no finer a diligent man—and God-fearing he is."

Alfano smiled. "I talked to him this morning," he said. "McDunnah tracked down the ballistics reports and confirmed that Katherine Mooney, aka Kitty Hill, was shot and killed with the same weapon that killed Hines Melnik."

"That proves it. Melnik brought it to California when they returned, right? Then he was shot by the same gun," Suarez said.

"There's a twist, Detective. It is also the same gun used in at least a dozen other gangland shootings in Chicago and nearby suburbs. As you well know, a Colt Police Positive .32 revolver is an executioner's weapon; there's more blood on that gun than on the hands of Lady Macbeth."

"Are you saying that gun was in Chicago for the last ten years—maybe longer?" Suarez said. "Maybe Melnik bought it from someone while he was there, or a gangster, one of his mob buddies, gave it to him."

"All probable, but Mac dug deeper and found the honeypot, such as it is. Ten years ago, Katherine Mooney's husband and her brother were gunned down after they left a bar in Bridgeport. She was with them; they were celebrating, as Kitty had found out that she was pregnant. Life was good for a trio of two-bit gangsters, hustlers, rumrunners, and dance hall entertainers. The story takes a sad turn when they crossed Capone, and he had them eliminated. Kitty was also hit; she lost the baby. When she was well enough, she slipped out of Chicago and came here. Whether she knew Melnik before she arrived here in California, or meeting him was a fluke, or an accident, or a bit of luck, I don't know. But she built a life here, more like a California criminal enterprise. She returned to Chicago for two purposes: the film promotion, and to meet a gang contact with Melnik. Someone in Chicago recognized her, and they knew she knew who they were: the killer of her brother and husband. He finished that ten-year-old contract in that room of the Palmer House."

"Damn. That's quite a story," Suarez said.

"Sadly, a Chicago story. That's why I got out with my family," Tuttle said. "Too much temptation and evil in that town."

"Be careful, Gil, LA is getting its own reputation," Suarez said. He asked when Alfano was leaving.

"The hotel clerk checked the trains for me; there's one around seven tomorrow night. I want to stop by Sierra Films in the morning. They owe me for a few days' work. I need to cash in the airline ticket. I am *not* flying back."

"I'd do that in a second. What a way to travel," Suarez said. "Flying up there with the angels, seeing the whole countryside under you. It must be something."

"All I can see is crashing into the ground, a ball of fire, me in a thousand pieces," Tuttle added.

"I'm leaning toward Tuttle on this one, Suarez," Alfano said. "Besides, after the last five days, I need a vacation. I can use a couple days on a train for myself."

After a dinner of martinis, spaghetti, veal piccata, cannoli, and wonderful California wines, Tuttle offered to drive Alfano back to his hotel.

"You got anything this good in Chicago?" Suarez said.

"Don't start, Suarez," Tuttle said.

"There's a few places. When you get to Chicago, I'll take

you," Alfano said.

"A deal."

They said goodbye to Suarez at the curb in front of Perino's restaurant on Wilshire.

The day had been hot, and now warm air blew through the open windows of Tuttle's plain-wrap as they drove down Santa Monica Boulevard for what Alfano hoped was the last time. The inside of Kitty's apartment had been stifling, almost oppressive. He was glad to be out of there. Capturing Longacre was a bonus, though he wasn't sure what her part in all this was—babysitter, tired actress, ex-hooker, maybe a hybrid. Suarez would figure it out. Since Durant was arrested in LA, Tuttle had agreed to turn the two of them over to Beverly Hills. Alfano was sure that Tuttle did not want the headache or the possible exposure.

Alfano and Tuttle said their goodbyes standing out in front of the Georgian. The sun was a finger's width above the horizon.

"I could put you in a lot of trouble, Gil," Alfano said. "You know that. But what you do here has nothing to do with me."

"What are you talking about, boyo?" Tuttle said.

"Your part in all this, your connections to Chicago and the Outfit."

"The hell you say."

"You are the filler, the glue, the gum stuck on the bottom of my shoe," Alfano continued. "Sure, Melnik and Hill met with the money man in Chicago. That's why Spats Lanigan was in the meeting with the mayor, Melnik, Durant, and Roberts. Lanigan is Frank Nitti's houseboy, the one with an ear to goings-on in city hall. They needed someone out here to be on the receiving end of the cash when it went west. Sure, it was Melnik this trip, but not every time. And Lanigan's from your street, Tuttle. You two knew each other from Bridgeport. When McDunnah heard that Lanigan was at the meeting, he told me about you. Mac said, 'If Lanigan's in the meeting and you are going to LA, be careful, because as sure as there is a heaven, Gil Tuttle's got his finger in the pie.' I know he gave you a call. What I don't know is why the fuck you sapped me when I got here."

The answer took a long time.

"It's always that fucken Mick, even when we was kids," Tuttle said at last.

"That's not helpful. What the hell did Mac do that got me whacked on the head?"

"He was dating m'sister, Celeste, back in the day. That's long before Moira. They split up, I blamed him for taking advantage of her, so's I was pissed. Then out of the blue he calls and wants a favor. I got mad all over again. You were here, and Mac wasn't . . . I'm sorry; it was stupid."

"Damn, you fucking Irish carry a grudge longer than Italians. And yes, it was stupid. Any other day, if I weren't so tired, I might have shot you dead. Jesus Christ, Tuttle."

"I said I'm sorry."

"Right now, sorry is not enough. I just want to get out of this fucking town. Tuttle, you do what you do, I don't fucking care. Just keep it away from Mac and me. Got it?"

A wry smile came over Tuttle's face.

Alfano slugged him with his left hand, knocking the Irishman to the sidewalk. Tuttle rolled over to his side and gingerly propped himself on an elbow. "I deserved that. I'm such a fuck."

"Yes, you are." Alfano shook his hand, trying to remove the sting.

"Smart guy, using your left."

"Smart guys don't sap friends. And one more thing, if Maxime Durant has an accident, falls down a flight of stairs, walks in front of a truck, or in any way dies, I am holding you responsible. And I will make sure the wrath of God comes down on you."

Tuttle paused. It was one of those pregnant pauses, one that was looking for the father that had skipped town. "I don't know about all that, Detective. I never seen her before all this shit."

Alfano lit a cigarette and watched Tuttle drive up the street half a block and turn onto Santa Monica Boulevard.

"Hi, sailor, need some company?" a sweet voice said from behind him. Alfano slowly turned and faced Gloria.

"Company would be nice. It's been a very traumatic and wicked day," he answered.

"I've heard. There's a lot of rumors at the studio—even made the evening newspapers. Dead actors, connections to the pornography business, an actress arrested for murder; yes, a wicked day. I've seen Detective Suarez's name all over the story."

"I'd expect nothing less—and you can probably believe the rumors."

"Your name wasn't mentioned, not even a remark or comment about a Chicago detective or anything. Like it was a one-man operation, and the famous Dick Tracy from Chicago was left out."

"He and Tuttle can fight it out for the medals. Me, I'm going home."

"I figured that. That's why I'm here, to say goodbye. David will pick us up tomorrow and take you to the airport."

"I'm taking the Santa Fe Limited."

"Then the La Grande train station it is. I've never been to Chicago. Care for some company?"

"I'd love some, but not this trip. I intend to get twelve hours of sleep paired with twelve hours of nothing but the bar car. I'll be back at my desk on Friday morning. Honestly, I can't wait."

"By my watch, you have about eighteen hours with nothing

to do. Any ideas?"

"I'm guessing you do."

"Detective Anthony Alfano, you have no idea how good I am at killing eighteen hours."

28

Friday morning, after his train pulled out of the Kansas City station, Alfano comfortably watched the fall foliage of Missouri race by from his compartment, a compartment he'd only left to eat and drink or pick up drinks. In six hours, he would be walking through Dearborn station. He'd been gone exactly ten days, though it felt like a month—no, more like a lifetime. He honestly believed now that California could do that to you, to anyone. It was enticing, magical, beguiling, perverse, even obscene. Yet, it drew you in, with a promising and magnetic pull; he fought every come-hither and come-back-to-me thought that rolled through his head. And Gloria Downs was one of the hardest to forget. Everything about her was right; everything about them was wrong.

He was now certain who the killer of Katherine Mooney was. Her murder was less than three weeks old; if he hadn't gone to California, the case would never have been solved, of that he was certain. Maybe the ballistics on the bullets removed from Kitty's body would have done the job, but he was certain that they would not have looked at the past Chicago killings, made the right connections, put it all together, and wrapped it with a bow. Maybe that was something about California he could live with.

Surfing, Gloria called it, "riding the waves." Someday they would write songs about this strange recreation, she said. A bunch of guys floating on the sea, killing time, being away from their girlfriends, wives, maybe their kids. All a waste to Alfano's way of thinking. His shoulders still itched from the slight sunburn he got that day on the beach. The memory of Gloria slathering baby oil over his back; he could live with that thought through the coming winter.

Four people were dead due to greed, money, and sex—so California, so Hollywood. Sure, some neighborhoods were like those in Chicago, but mostly not. He was still pissed he hadn't gone back to the Apex to hear the Ellington band. There was still jazz in Chicago, still time before the fair closed at the end of October. He wondered how Deacon was doing. Ten days gone, ten days that felt like two years; he scratched his itching shoulders against the hard wood paneling of his compartment.

On the way to the train station, he and Gloria had picked up sandwiches at Bay Cities Deli, where he wished Tony DiTomasi well. They hadn't met up to talk about the old days. The sandwiches DiTomasi made lasted Alfano until Peach Springs, Arizona.

Gloria had told him about a new book by Erle Stanley Gardner, an author a friend of hers recommended. He picked up a copy at the La Grande station newsstand; it now lay dog-eared on the narrow bed in his sleeping compartment. He liked the writing and the character, Perry Mason. Mason wasn't like the wimpish lawyers Alfano knew in Chicago; the man was hard-core, uncompromising. Alfano had known of the writer Gardner from the pulp magazines his apartment landing neighbor, Alice Kowalski, would pass on. She left copies of the *Black Mask*, *Argosy*, and *True Detective Mysteries* for him outside his door. The Perry Mason story was good, the writing better; he'd look for another book—if there was another.

"Ten minutes to Chicago, ten minutes," a loud voice brayed

from the corridor. "Ten minutes!"

Alfano collected his few belongings and stuffed them in his grip, the book on top. He slipped on his suitcoat and set his fedora. The interior of the Dearborn station was packed. It didn't take a detective to see that many in the crowd were members of the American Legion. The American Legionnaires were the latest convention in town, and with the fair, another small windfall for the city.

After he walked out the front door of the station onto Polk Street, he stood in the chill fall air—it was a godsend. He breathed deeply; the aromas from the restaurant next to the train station plucked the strings of his stomach. The *Tribune* picked up at the newsstand, set tight under his arm, declared in two-inch-high letters the conviction of Chicago ex-detective sergeant Harry Lang for the failed shooting of Capone's capo, Frank Nitti. The shooting had been in the news since last December. For some unknown reason, Sergeant Lang had thought it necessary to walk into Nitti's office and shoot him. He failed to kill the gangster, only wounded him. There were some, possibly many, in the Chicago Police Department who believed that the February assassination attempt on Franklin Roosevelt, in Miami, wasn't directed at the president-elect, but at Chicago's mayor, Anton Cermak, who was traveling with him. They also believed that it was Cermak who had ordered Nitti's shooting. Alfano had his own thoughts about the whole Nitti misadventure. The one thing he was privately sure of, if he'd been the guy to go into Nitti's office, he would have been the only one to come out.

He walked up Dearborn Street, stretching his stiff legs. At Berghoff's restaurant he ordered a bag of food; while he waited for his order, he had a beer. With no coaxing, the bartender, an old friend, tucked a bottle of Canadian Club next to the schnitzel and potato salad. Alfano splurged and took a taxi home.

At the landing outside his apartment, he heard the radio from Teddy and Alice Kowalski's apartment. He would have to talk to Alice sometime, but tonight was not the night. She collected his mail while he was gone; he'd retrieve it the next day. She would also want to know everything about Los Angeles and California. For Alice Kowalski, the idea of LA was as exotic as visiting the Taj Mahal in India. She had been trying for years in every conceivable way to entice Alfano into her boudoir, a place that Alfano knew would not be the right place to land. She was lonely; Teddy worked at the steel mill on the far southside, and his schedule was erratic. Why they hadn't moved nearer to the plant, he never learned. She had family locally. He'd assumed that was the reason.

He quietly unlocked his door and stepped into his apartment. It was unbelievably comfortable; the heat of summer, the stifling air, the smells drifting up from the alley—gone. He turned on WMAQ. The news was on; it was all about the Lang trial and conviction. He felt sorry for Lang. The son of a bitch made one mistake: he missed. Alfano poured himself two fingers of the Canadian Club, lit a cigarette, and sat down. Sitting alone on the threadbare couch, at that moment, Los Angeles looked a whole lot better than the life he had in Chicago—everything from the past two weeks rolled over him like that surf at the beach. He rose and fell with the swells of his life, alone, waiting for the next big wave to lift him up and propel him forward. "Go to Hollywood, Tony," the mayor said. It had been a trip to the moon and back.

Alfano said, "Good morning, Sergeant," from his desk in the back of the detective's room.

Sergeant McDunnah stood in the middle of the room looking more shocked than surprised.

"What the hell are you doing here, Detective? I wasn't expecting you 'til Monday. You've more earned days off than

Methuselah. So's I'm thinking Monday."

"I missed you, too, Sergeant. I've traveled maybe four thousand miles, I've been up in the air, solved the murders of four people, had some outstanding food, walked in the Pacific Ocean, saw something called surfing, and discovered that the enticing temptress that is California is just a sham—a hooker with great makeup."

Sergeant McDunnah stood there looking at Alfano and shook his head. "That is the biggest pile of bullshit I have ever heard you sputter. Gil sent me an airmail letter. I got it yesterday; he told me everything. You are a fucking hero in Los Angeles, a real hero. The Beverly Hills Police want to pin a medal on you."

"Now that is bullshit. They are glad I'm gone. All I got was a sunburn, and I'm peeling."

"Always modest. I like that about you. Someday, when the glow of your success dims, you need to tell me all about it."

"I will, someday. Anything more about Kitty Hill?"

"It has been revelation after revelation; the key was the ballistics on the bullets from that Colt Police Positive. From there it all tumbles down through at least a dozen assassinations and executions, maybe more. The crime lab is still looking. They are now like dogs on a hunt. Once they've got the scent, they go down deep."

"Good, and the gun itself?"

"There's a better than even chance it was stolen after the shooting of a Chicago police officer in '22."

Alfano let out a low whistle. "That long ago. Wow."

McDunnah nodded. "A Corporal Dugan, patrolman, was responding to a brawl in an alley at a closed bar on South Wabash. Two men were shot and killed; Dugan may have been caught in the crossfire."

"It wasn't Mooney and O'Neal?"

"No, they were killed about a year later. But the same gun

was used to kill them."

"I remember that corporal getting gunned down. I was a sergeant then. When we arrived, there were three dead; Dugan was one of them. The others had connections to Capone."

"Right, and someone took Dugan's revolver. We now know that it's been a killer for the last eleven years."

"And has retired to sunny California. Hot damn."

"Who's been doing this?" McDunnah asked. "Capone and Nitti are done. One's in a Georgia prison, and Frank Nitti has more press following him than a bitch in heat. The rumor is the man has gone paranoid, hides in his office, guards at the door. You think this killer is still active?"

"I've a good idea that he is, and tomorrow we are going to make an arrest for the killing of Kitty Hill. You willing to work a little Sunday overtime, Sergeant?"

"Moira is teaching church school tomorrow; all I was going to do was listen to football. The Bears are playing the Giants. You know, they haven't lost."

"I will try to get you back before the game."

"So, yes, damn straight."

"Good. Here is a list of things I want you to chase down today. And get an arrest warrant as well."

"Who's the lucky winner?"

Alfano handed the sergeant a sheet of paper and a smaller piece of paper. McDunnah looked at the list and the name.

"Well, I'll be damned."

29

The name Alfano had given to McDunnah was none other than the head doorman at the Palmer House, Henry Bucci. Alfano had known Bucci for about four years. Back then, Alfano believed that Bucci was trying his best to keep himself out of jail due to his history with Al Capone. It was in January 1929—two weeks before the St. Valentine's Day Massacre where seven men were gunned down at a warehouse in Lincoln Park—when Bucci turned over solid evidence that got a few of the local gangsters arrested and sent away. After the massacre, there was a housecleaning in the Chicago Police Department. There were rumors that cops had done the shooting, but four years later, no one had been arrested for the killings. Until the Kitty Hill murder, there'd been nothing concrete about the shooters or even the motive. When Capone was convicted for tax evasion, in October 1931, Alfano had believed that the city, with the help of US federal agents, was on the right path. Now, he was certain it had all been a stunt—not the killings but the city's follow-up. As a bonus for Bucci's evidence, Alfano had helped him get the doorman's job at the newly rebuilt Palmer House. Now, he was sure that he'd not done a good thing, and in fact he had been played like a cheap trumpet.

Early Sunday morning, Alfano met Sergeant McDunnah at a coffee shop on West Monroe Street, about eight blocks from the Palmer House Hotel. He parked the Packard out front.

"Are you sure about this?" McDunnah said. "How the hell did you, more than two thousand miles away, figure out who killed Katherine Mooney, sweet Kitty Hill?"

"Sweet she wasn't, that I found out. She is proof that a leopard won't change its spots," Alfano said. "Was I right about the ballistics?"

"Yes, spot on. I was stunned. No one's been arrested for the Valentine killings in the four and a half years since the shooting, and yet you find one of the murder weapons in California. That Colt Police Positive, stolen from the body of that murdered patrolman, was later used in the massacre. It's been confirmed by two laboratories that five bullets removed from two of the dead men in that garage match the striations on the bullets from the killing of that director in Los Angeles and those found in the chest of Kitty Hill. So, it's Henry Bucci?"

"Yes, I believe Bucci was freelance, a gun for hire."

"And what brought this all together? Divine inspiration?"

"Brilliant detective work and a framed photograph on a shelf behind Hines Melnik's desk," Alfano said. "It was of two boys, about fifteen years old or so. One was Melnik, the other was Henry Bucci, or that's what he's calling himself these days. Bucci was a friend of Melnik's. Maybe they grew up together in LA. Did you find his fingerprints?"

"Yes, and they match the unidentified print you brought back—the one they found on the inside of the gun's grip panel."

"I want Bucci in jail, and it's a lot of circumstantial evidence," Alfano said, sipping his coffee. "Even the fingerprint—that's another matter. Did someone claim Katherine Mooney's body?"

"Yes, but it was anonymous. The Evergreen Mortuary

called the coroner, claiming the body. Since there were no objections, they picked it up. I called them; the burial is Tuesday at ten o'clock at Mount Olivet."

"I'm thinking there's a connection to Katherine Mooney through her dead brother and husband," Alfano said. "Bucci knew them—hell, maybe he was sweet on Mooney. Did anyone else call the funeral home?"

"The funeral home collected the body at the morgue; it was transported and prepared. The woman at the funeral home I spoke with asked someone in the office if there was any other information, while I waited. She said that two one-hundred-dollar bills had been mailed to them, with typed instructions, that led to claiming the body. It was more than enough for the funeral. Katherine Mooney would be buried next to her brother and husband; they are also in Olivet," McDunnah said as he crunched on a ribbon of bacon. "Simple service, a priest to say a few words, that's about it. How we going to take Bucci?"

"Head-on; he's not expecting us," Alfano said. "Why should he? It's been almost three weeks since she was killed, and he hasn't even been questioned. He probably thinks he's safe. I want you to go in from the hotel's State Street side, then head to the Monroe Street entry. He usually works there. I'll park in front and engage him. You be ready in case he bolts inside."

"That works," McDunnah agreed.

"I want no guns. There's people around, even on a Sunday morning. Let's keep this nice and quiet."

Ten minutes later, McDunnah walked out the East Monroe Street entry of the Palmer House. Alfano was leaning against the Packard smoking a cigarette.

"What happened?" McDunnah asked.

Alfano signaled to a tall black man in a uniform standing near the door; the man nodded and walked over to the pair.

"Sergeant McDunnah," Alfano said. "This is Mr. Albert Duke. He is the doorman here at the Palmer House."

"Mr. Duke," McDunnah said.

"Mr. Duke, please tell Sergeant McDunnah what you just told me."

"This Tuesday last, I was just getting off my night shift when the hotel manager walks up and asks if I could do a double. Now I was truly beat. American Legionnaires have been coming in all week for their convention. It had been a long night, and I wanted nothing better than to go home and crash. I asked the manager why. 'Where's Bucci?' I's ask. Bucci called in and quit, he says. Just like that, no warning, nothing. Sergeant McDunnah, Henry Bucci hasn't been here since Monday. Well, I did his shift, and the manager found a temporary replacement for my night slot. He knows I always wanted the day; he gave it to me."

"Have you had any contact with Bucci since he took off?" Alfano asked.

"No. I never warmed to the guy. He made me a little nervous. We overlapped a lot during the past four years—that was cool, no big deal. Even swapped a few shifts—again, no big deal. But he was as friendly. Always good to the guests, never socialized with us."

"I want you to think back to the night that the woman was found dead in the twenty-fourth-floor suite," Alfano said.

"The woman that was murdered?" Duke asked.

"Yes, that night. Were you working that night?"

"No, sir, it was my wife Imelda's birthday. I was home that night." Duke smiled. "I switched with Bucci. He worked that night and part of the next morning. I came in during the afternoon and put in eighteen, then he came back the next morning. Weren't unusual; we'd done it lots of times before. I like this day shift now . . . and so does Imelda."

"The manager, did he know about your switch?"

"I don't know, Detective. He lets us work out our schedules. As long as there's someone at the doors, it's jake with him."

"You don't know why Bucci quit? Did he say anything?"

"Not a clue. I thought he liked it here. We can make good money; the tips make it all work. And for a guy like me, that's a Godsend . . . and Imelda likes it, too."

"A guy like you?" McDunnah said.

"A colored man, Sergeant. It's damn hard to get a good-paying job anywhere, and that's the Lord's truth. Especially these tough days. With the fair and conventions coming, I'll do anything to keep this job. So why'd Henry quit? I just don't know."

"Mr. Duke, if you hear from Bucci, or anything about him, give me or Sergeant McDunnah a call." Alfano handed him a card. "All the information is here."

"Thanks. Is Henry in a lot of trouble?"

"Not sure, Albert. We just want to ask him a few questions about that night. You've been a big help. By the way, if he does stop by or you see him, don't let him know we are looking. It wouldn't be . . . jake."

Duke smiled. "Anything I can do to help."

Five minutes later, as Alfano drove along Michigan Avenue back to the Racine Street station, Sergeant McDunnah voiced the question to which they both knew the answer: "Do you think somebody tipped him off?"

"Yes. Somebody called him from California; had to have. And there's only one man who knew enough about what was happening here in Chicago to call Bucci and clue him in."

"Gil Tuttle."

"Bingo."

30

Alfano cooled his heels in the sparsely decorated office on the fifth floor of the office building at 221 N. La-Salle Street. He added his cigarette butt to the nearly filled ashtray on the small table. He was keeping company with two men who stood in the room with him: one at the office door and the other at the door that led to an inner office. There was a third man sitting in a chair outside; he had a clear view of everyone who came and went. The gunzel at the inner door had done a body search that barely stopped short of being a cavity search, though to no avail as Alfano had arrived un-armed. He knew they all carried guns. Why there wasn't one more gangster with a tommy gun sitting in the corner, he didn't know. Or maybe there was; he still didn't want to know.

The rest of the fifth floor was empty. After the freshly convicted Harry Lang tried to assassinate Frank Nitti, most of the tenants on the floor had moved out.

"Mr. Nitti will be with you shortly," the woman at the desk said. "You should have made an appointment."

"Thank you, it's a spur-of-the-moment thing," Alfano an-swered.

"What thing?" she answered. "What spur?"

The gunzel at the front door laughed. Alfano shot him a

sour look.

The box on the desk buzzed. "Tell Detective Alfano that he can come in," said a voice.

Gunzel two, at the inner office door, seized the door's round brass handle with the delicate hands of a boxer, twisted it like he was breaking the neck of a chicken, and opened it. Alfano turned sideways and stepped past him. The man's breath smelled of garlic and spaghetti mixed with cigars.

Frank Nitti sat at a large mahogany desk. A green glass brass lamp sat on the right side of the desk, a wire tray full of papers sat to the left, and a large semiautomatic pistol, that Alfano recognized as similar to the one he normally carried in his shoulder holster, rested in the center of the desk. It was a particularly strange paperweight. He regarded its owner. Nitti had a round head, a pronounced, flattened nose, curious small eyes, and a cleft chin. His black hair was perfectly in place and parted on his right. For a man now forty-seven years old, it was slightly greying at the temples.

Alfano had joined the Chicago police force in 1913. Nitti arrived in Chicago with his wife five years later and set up his liquor smuggling operation in the Italian neighborhood near Taylor Street soon after the start of Prohibition. The two, cop and gangster, grew up together, professionally speaking. Soon after arriving, Nitti joined with his cousin Al Capone, and for fifteen years they were the gangster face of the city of Chicago.

Nitti pointed to the chair directly across from him. Alfano sat.

"Detective Anthony Alfano, what has it been, six years?"

"Good memory, Frank. Six years next January. I stood outside the ship in Cicero when they rousted the joint. This whole time, I've wondered why you weren't charged with running the joint. Then again, I did watch you slide into the comfortable back seat of the Cicero captain's police cruiser. How nothing sticks to you still amazes me. And now, after last December's little incident, you are apparently invincible. Astonishing. How you feeling? You look good. You must be celebrating Lang's conviction."

Nitti glared at him. "Look, Alfano, what the fuck are you doing here all nice and pretty? Does Mayor Kelly have something special planned for me, like his predecessor?"

Nitti's fingers gravitated to the gun on the desk.

"No. In fact, the mayor doesn't know I'm here. This is my gig, as we say on South State Street."

"The hell you say. Look, you are a straight shooter," Nitti said. "Lord knows and the rumor goes if anyone knocked you down, their world would go black. You're as clean as the backside of a baby. I know Al tried; you were his one regret."

"Frank, he was bad for the city, very bad. You, the jury is still out."

Nitti furrowed his brow. "And you are here why?"

"Exactly three weeks ago, a woman was shot dead in the Palmer House; eleven days ago, a man was shot dead in Beverly Hills, California."

"So what? People get shot dead every day."

"They were both killed with the same gun, a gun that was also used during the past ten years by one of your enforcers to, as one might say, keep certain people in line. The gun is connected to at least a dozen murders, probably more."

"It must be a very busy gun. What the fuck does that have to do with me?" Nitti ran his manicured fingertips over the pistol on the desk.

"Its last two victims ran your Hollywood operation. They were your laundry—dirty money in and clean money out."

Nitti's eyes seemed to try to lean forward; for a moment, Alfano thought they actually moved. The cleft in his chin deepened. "So why you telling me this, Alfano? Hollywood, that's in California, too, right?"

"Yeah, Hollywood, California—and, on top of that, a

quarter of a million bucks is missing. It's not actually missing; the Beverly Hills Police have it. Nonetheless, it is missing from you. Gone. Poof."

Nitti's tensed fingers began to wrap around the handle of the gun. "That's a lot of laundry," he said softly. "Shit, somebody's going to be pissed."

"Yeah, I was thinking the same thing," Alfano said. "And it's all because of the killing at the Palmer House. You must have read **about it**—Kitty Hill, onetime chanteuse here in Chicago, connected to the O'Banions gang ten years ago, was shot down in her room. That happened the day after she and Hines Melnik had a business meeting with you. And then, ten days ago, Melnik was found dead in his fancy home in Beverly Hills, right as he was supposed to start production on your movie."

Nitti sat there and cogitated. "I don't know anything about all this shit," he said irritably. "What movie?"

"I'm sure that Handsome Johnny and Gil Tuttle have filled you in about the goings-on in Hollywood. Two more dead, and your baglady has been arrested and charged with murder. She's probably spilling her guts about now, and a quarter of a million has been recovered. Hell, there may be even more. And it isn't just the legit films; all those sweet little deals with the stag film industry are now ass over applecart. If I were you, I would be seriously pissed."

"As I said, I don't have any idea about any of this. Sure, I know John Roselli. He sends me flowers for my birthday, good kid. This guy Tuttle you mentioned, never heard of him. I assume he's some dumb Mick who thinks he's bigger than he is. And I had nothing to do with that gun."

"Every time I look at the guy's rap sheet—"

"What guy?"

"The Palmer House shooter, Kitty Hill's killer, that guy. I keep seeing your name . . . he's connected to the Outfit, been seen with Alfonse Capone. He was born in Naples, grew up in

Los Angeles. For all I know, he could be another cousin. But this guy stands out. Why? Because I know him. He used me; I got him a legit job. Then he pissed on me. I want it off."

"He snookered you! I need to write that down. Who the hell is this guy that you got such a hard-on for?"

"Henry Bucci."

Nitti's fingers were entirely wrapped around the grip of the pistol. His knuckles suddenly whitened. "I don't know a Henry Bucci."

"Sure you do, Frank. You may have known him as Enrico Bucciola. He's about forty, big man, wide shoulders, dark hair, wears it combed back, black eyes, smells like Old Spice."

"That shit, Jesus. So, maybe I know about the guy. It's a small town, really. I meet a lot of guys; buried a bunch, too. I still send flowers to a few of their mothers. What do you want me to do?"

"Give me Bucci."

Nitti released the grip, slid his hand away. As he talked, he pointed his finger at Alfano. "Turn over a goomba to you— why the fuck would I do that? What's in it for me?"

"A longer life."

The hand went back to the gun. "You fucking threatening me, Alfano? That asshole Lang, I hope he goes to jail, and they give him a nice, friendly fucking roommate, that's what I'm hoping. Cermak sent a *sciatto* to do a man's work and see what it got him. So, Antonio, you threatening me?"

Alfano smiled and slowly raised his hands about chest high. "Frank, don't get me wrong. I was just wishing you a long and peaceful life. Moments like that can change a man, I know."

Nitti released the gun and rolled his chair backward away from the desk. His eyes never left Alfano. "*Una vita lunga e tranquilla, si?*"

"Yeah, something like that. Most wish for a long life; for many, that wish is cut short."

Nitti shrugged. "I'll ask around about Bucciola, maybe somebody knows him. I ain't promising you anything. If I find him, I'll tell him you are looking for him."

"Gee, thanks." Alfano stood and headed to the door. "Stay safe, Frank. It's a tough city out there."

"Fuck you, Detective."

Alfano's next stop was Mayor Edward Kelly's office, which was only three blocks away. He parked the Packard in the designated police stall in front. The mayor had wanted an update about his trip to Hollywood. It had been a long two weeks since Alfano saw him last.

The streets around city hall were packed with Legionnaire conventioneers. Alfano had been warned by a general note posted on the bulletin board in the station that tomorrow was all hands on deck; there was a big parade planned down Michigan Avenue to Soldier Field. Just what he needed. He had other plans. He cooled his heels again in a spacious outer office; at least this time there weren't three guys ready to shoot him if he made a sudden and threatening move. Here in the mayor's office, they'd just strip you of everything you held dear and leave you out there to twist in the wind.

It was the same woman at the mayor's desk.

"Good morning, Miss Sarah Jean Alcott. Everything copacetic?" he asked.

"Don't go using vile words around me, Detective," Sarah Jean said.

"It's a good word," Alfano answered.

"It's a Negro word. I'll thank you for not using it in my presence."

"I will take care, Miss Alcott. I certainly don't want to get you all in a sweet lather."

"I know that one, too—you are a very dishonorable and rude man, sir."

"He is most certainly that, Miss Alcott. Why don't you come in, Tony—you have had a very busy couple of weeks."

It was the first time in maybe a dozen visits that the mayor came to the door of his office and personally welcomed him in. Maybe that was the way they did it in Joliet; the warden came to get you just before they threw the switch. Alfano patted his chest lightly, half thinking he might need his gun to protect himself—nothing. His gun was still in his desk back at the station.

He walked past Miss Sarah Jean Alcott, tapped her desk with his fingers, then slid past the mayor and into his office. His back and neck felt tense.

"I knew those three were no good the moment they walked into my office, Tony. No damn good, those Hollywood types. Trouble," Mayor Edward Kelly said. "Sit there, your usual spot."

Alfano looked around. The only other man in the room was Kelly's fixer, Patrick Nash—no Spats Lanigan this time. The mayor went to stand leaning back against his desk, his usual spot.

"Thanks for keeping the city of Chicago out of the papers when all that ugliness and brutality happened in Los Angeles," Nash said. "It is a Godless land; I'll tell you that."

"It is that," Alfano said. "But the weather's nice, and the food's good, too."

"There's more to life than sunshine and oranges," Kelly added.

Alfano thought for a moment. He'd not had one orange while he'd been away. "What can I do for you, Mayor?"

"Well, I originally wanted to say thank you and learn what went on in Los Angeles. A Detective Dominic Suarez called Friday and thanked me for your help in solving the murder of that director and actor. To think that actress was the killer. Well, I just don't understand it all."

"I will thank Detective Suarez for thinking of me."

"Yeah, make sure you do," Nash said. "He seems like a good cop for a guy with a Mexican name—he didn't have an accent or anything."

Alfano cringed. Nash was one clueless guy.

Nash took a few steps toward Alfano and stopped about three feet away. "What we want to know is what the hell were you doing at Frank Nitti's office not just an hour ago? That man is a cancer in this city. He and his people must be put down like dogs."

"I understand, Mr. Nash. You mean, like what Mayor Cermak tried to do, and since Cermak couldn't take a piss without you, Mr. Nash, holding his dick, I've personally concluded there were others involved. Lang said so, but nobody paid him any attention. Poor guy, I hope he makes it through the winter."

"That's insubordination. I'll have you fired and thrown in the street, Detective," Nash steamed.

"Patty, just hold on—no reason to get all in a dither," Kelly said. "Let the detective explain."

Alfano wanted nothing more than to spit in Nash's eye and walk out the door. Besides, Nash talking about putting Nitti down was like two rival street gangs fighting for the sidewalks of Chicago. Maybe it was the Irish-Italian angle, maybe it was the power angle, but in either case it certainly included the money angle.

Alfano dialed his temper back and began. "Frank Nitti and his Outfit are funding film productions in Los Angeles, and most of that money is coming from their illegal operations here in Chicago. That money is then washed through the production and distribution. Then, when it's nice and clean, it flows back to the syndicate, all neatly folded and sanitized. Melnik and his people were involved. However, it seems there was some internal squabbling about the money, and it is lots of money—and people died. One of them was a woman named Katherine Mooney. She was from your old neighborhood, Mayor, Bridgeport. She was the unfortunate victim I saw that morning at the Palmer House. That was just an hour before I met with Melnik and his cohorts here in your office. Kitty Hill worked for Hines Melnik and had connections to the O'Banions and Nitti. In fact, she and Melnik met with Nitti the day before they met with you.

"The police have been watching Nitti's office since the shooting last winter. I read the report about two unidentified people going into Nitti's building. It makes my skin crawl a little to think about them coming here the very next day."

"Detective, be nice," Mayor Kelly said.

Nash was holding a lit cigar. Alfano decided to take a chance and light a cigarette. No lightning bolt struck from above. He took a long drag and continued his story.

"It turns out that Katherine Mooney's murder—by the way, her alias for the last ten years was Kitty Hill—had nothing to do at all with the film production in Hollywood. It had to do with two Irish hoodlums and their sidewalk executions eleven years ago. She was involved with those gangsters, saw and knew the killer, and survived."

"Jesus, Mary, and Joseph," Kelly said. "You know the killer of this woman?"

"Yeah, I know him. I know him personally. And to get him out of his hole, I had to have his boss give him a push."

31

Detective Anthony Alfano stood alone at the foot of Katherine Mooney's grave. The white painted casket rested on two planks that straddled the hole. A priest from the Bridgeport parish, St. Mary of Perpetual Help, stood opposite Alfano reading from the Bible. An altar boy stood next to him holding an aspergillum to consecrate the coffin with holy water. A single massive bouquet of flowers, a mixture of white lilies and carnations, adorned the lid. To Alfano's right, one woman, a paid mourner he assumed, stood between Alfano and the priest. She sniffled at the appropriate moments, earning her per diem, as the priest read the service. At least the day was fair, Alfano thought, looking around at the clear October sky. High above, a V-shaped flight of geese were heading south—Alfano thought of the pelicans at Malibu.

"I didn't expect to see you here, Alfano," Henry Bucci said from behind him. "Thanks for coming. We hate to be buried alone."

Alfano was startled, even though he'd known the man would be there.

"And you're not a surprise either, Henry," Alfano said, not moving. "It was good of you to take care of Katherine. I am pleased that someone did."

"She deserved this. This wasn't all her fault."

"We each make our own story; no one else can."

Alfano watched the priest take the aspergillum and flick it over the casket and flowers. God's rain fell on both the casket and the blossoms. The mourner sniffled again and said "Amen" just a little too loudly. The priest, altar boy, and mourner all, as if signaled, turned and walked away from the grave. Fifty feet away, two men with shovels stood smoking cigarettes.

Alfano also turned and began to walk away.

"Follow me, Henry."

Henry Bucci did.

"You loved her, didn't you, Henry? That's a hard thing to get over, I know. It's a hard thing to find and a hard thing to hold onto. It's just hard."

"Star-crossed lovers, I guess," Bucci said as he walked next to Alfano.

"In the end, Shakespeare's lovers both take their own lives. What happened in your case?"

"I recognized Katherine when she got out of the limousine with those actor folks. I was shocked, you can imagine. So many years had passed since that day. She jumped in front of O'Neal; the bullet nicked her and killed him—wasn't supposed to be that way."

"Never is, is it? A contract, right?"

"I'm good, Detective, damn good. If it weren't for her showing up here in Chicago, you would never have caught me. But I'm a piece of shit. I made money, blew it all. Four years ago, you were there to help. I needed some cover and you provided it. Sorry."

"I guess I'm the chump. You played me. But that story is a bit false about seeing Kitty at the hotel, right? It was Nitti who told you about Kitty, that she was at the meeting with him."

"You are good. Mr. Capone said to leave Antonio Alfano alone, don't touch him. I never understood that. A cop's a cop, debris in the road. But what Mr. Capone says, I follow."

They had walked a hundred feet through the tombstones. The sugar maples and the hawthorns were turning color. More geese flew overhead.

"You and Hines Melnik, you go back a few years," Alfano said.

"Yeah, we came over on the SS *Manhattan* together from someplace in France. I can't remember the name of the city. We met onboard; we were maybe ten. I had my sad tale, he had his. A Jew from Poland meets a Dago from Naples. When his family moved to Los Angeles, I followed. We were both about eighteen then. He loved photography. I loved fast women and money. In time, he stayed. I made a mistake; I had to leave. I've been here over twenty years, through the war, Prohibition, and this Depression. Kept a low profile to avoid the draft. Simple, really. Do you mind?"

Alfano lit Bucci's cigarette and one for himself.

"We had dealings with the O'Banions then—that was about twelve years ago. I think that's when you and I first met, a roust somewhere. We were bringing hooch, good stuff, prices were high. That's when I met Katherine. She broke my heart. She told me to drop dead a few times; I persisted. I knew that nothing was going to come of it, but she took my fucking heart. What was I to do?"

"I understand. Honest to God, I do. You should have walked away."

"Well, that day it was all a blur. I fulfilled my contract. I believed she was dead from my bullet. Damn near ate that Colt that night. Then someone told me she was alive—but gone. She took off; I had no idea where to start. Then it got big here in Chicago—you remember, good times. A man with my skills was needed, but I burned through money as fast as I made it."

Alfano didn't say anything. He let Bucci talk. They kept walking.

"Then, a few weeks ago, she gets out of that limousine, damn. It was like I was knocked to the ground. Melnik gives me a hug and a handshake like it was old times. He knew I was in Chicago, but it had been years since we'd seen each other. And Katherine was with him. I was in a fucking fog. I drove the two of them to a restaurant where they met with Frank, then I took them back to the hotel. Melnik and his actors were going up to the premier of that movie. I came back to the hotel and switched for the night shift."

"You could have left her alone, not bothered to go see her."

Bucci gripped Alfano's forearm. "I couldn't. I had to see her."

"Stupid thing to do," Alfano said.

"Yeah, I know, but I'm not the brightest guy when it comes to these things."

"The gun?"

"I always carry it, in a back holster. You never know in this town. I went up to see her. All I wanted was a couple of minutes, honest, that's all. I called her Katherine; she said her name was Kitty Hill. She told me to get out, go away. I pushed my way in. She pushed back, took a swing, clocked me one good. I knocked her down; she kicked me in the knee. I buckled. I pulled my gun. She was screaming at me. She threw a bottle at me. I fired. Twice. I didn't mean it, but I went nuts. She slammed her hands against her chest, blood everywhere, then collapsed. The gun was . . . gone. I dropped it, I guess. I had to get out. I ran, slammed the door behind me. The elevator was just opening, so I went down the back stairs. Ten minutes later, I was back at the entry."

"You are one of the most stupid men I've ever known."

"I know that, Tony. Good God in heaven, I know that. And now I have to do what Mr. Nitti says I must do."

"You really don't—you can walk away."

"I can't walk away from all this. I can't walk away from her. I loved her. And that love will kill me." Bucci shoved Alfano away, knocking him to the ground. Kitty's star-crossed lover pulled a revolver from inside his coat, and as his arm rose, half his head exploded.

Alfano sat alone at a small table near the stage at D's Café Delite. The same blind kid and his sister from Jackson, Mississippi, had just finished their second set. The last song, "Dream a Little Dream of Me," hung in the air along with the thick smoke of a hundred cigarettes. Deacon Smith stood at the door welcoming folks and turning back the riffraff.

It had been a week since the sharpshooter next to Sergeant McDunnah had taken out Henry Bucci at Mt. Olivet Catholic Cemetery. Bucci had known what was coming. It had been all on his terms. Alfano tried to dredge up a tear for any of them; none came.

McDunnah was able to confirm that during the past eleven years, fourteen killings could be tied to the gun that was vacationing in California. Due to Bucci's skill, all were bad guys, not one innocent bystander. The mayor was pleased. Again his guy Alfano had solved crimes, tied up the loose ends, helped to make good the mayor's promise to clean up the city. Alfano poured another glass of Canadian Club and grimly saluted himself in the back mirror of the bar.

Detective Suarez had called him to say that Maxime Durant had been formally charged by the DA for the premeditated murders of Hines Melnik, Adam Roberts, and Wells Barker; theft of money; and public indecency. Suarez laughed at the last charge; half of Hollywood could be indicted on that charge. He thought Tuttle had enough grease to slide on any charges that might be brought, assuming any were brought. He had a lot of friends in Los Angeles city hall.

"One must have friends, Alfano," Suarez said. "No matter

who or where they are. Do you want the gun when this is all over?"

"No need. Let it stay in Tinseltown. It would be like a kid from Chicago making it big in California."

"The DA asked if I thought having you testify in the Durant trial was a good idea. I told him no. He mentioned something about a character witness for Durant." Alfano laughed at that.

"Try and keep me out it, if you could," Alfano said. "I don't want to come back to California."

"It's turning into the crime of the century."

"Suarez, there's a lot of century left. Don't cut it too short."

The *Los Angeles Times* had reported that Durant asked Clarence Darrow to be her attorney, Suarez told Alfano. Darrow politely declined, though he did admit it would have been the most glamorous of his victories. He recommended Jerry Geisler—"Shit, with him, she'll walk, and the city will buy her new shoes. We are a screwed-up world here, Tony, a screwed-up world."

Gloria Downs called just to say hello. She was seeing David, it might turn into something, she had a chance at a studio job at MGM, and she was going after it. She said that the few days she spent with Alfano had been the best days of her life. He told her to have a long life; things were bound to get better. He asked her to say hello to Tony at Bay Cities Deli.

The newly elected president, Franklin D. Roosevelt, had toured the Century of Progress World's Fair the day before Bucci was shot. And it had just been announced that the fair would reopen in May 1934, for another summer. McDunnah told Alfano that he might retire early if this same crap went on for another year.

"You doing okay, Detective?" Deacon Smith said as he pulled up a chair. "Where you been? You got some color to your face."

"Deacon, I've been to the mountain and looked over the top."

"And what did you see?"

"The future, Deacon. California, the future."

"And did you like it?"

"No."

The End

Reviews Please

Today authors rely heavily on the reviews posted by our readers. As an independent self-publisher this is even more important than traditionally published books. If you have enjoyed this book, please take a few minutes and post a review on Goodreads and Amazon.

About the Author

Gregory C. Randall

Mr. Randall is Michigan born, Chicago raised and Californian by choice. He makes his home in Northern California.

Mr. Randall is the author of fiction and non-fiction works available through the usual outlets and the Windsor Hill Publishing website.

For more on future Tony Alfano thrillers and information on the Sharon O'Mara Chronicles and planned sequels, please visit and connect with Greg online:

http://www.gregorycrandall.info

Read his blog:

http://www.writing4death.blogspot.com

Other books by Mr. Randall available both in print and as ebooks:

Fiction
The Cherry Pickers

The Alex Polonia Thrillers
Venice Black
Saigon Red
Sty. Petersburg White

The Tony Alfano Thrillers
Chicago Swing
Chicago Jazz
Chicago Fix
Chicago Boogie Woogie

The Sharon O'Mara Chronicles
Land Swap For Death
Containers For Death
Toulouse For Death
12th Man For Death
Diamonds For Death
Limerick For Death

Non-fiction
America's Original GI Town, Park Forest, Illinois

These books can be purchased as an ebook at Amazon.com.

I hope you enjoyed this story!